# PROTECTING HIS MISTRESS

## A KINDRED TALES NOVEL

## EVANGELINE ANDERSON

# Evangeline Anderson

BRIDES *of the* KINDRED   KINDRED TALES   KINDRED *Birthright*   ALIEN *Mate* INDEX

CyBRG Files   COUGAR-VILLE   BORN TO DARKNESS

www.evangelineanderson.com

# AUTHOR'S NOTE

In my previous Kindred Tales book, *Dark and Light*, I promised you the story of Imani and the Nightwalker Kindred. But once I started writing that book, *Unleashed by the Defender*, I only got three chapters into it before I realized there was another book—a kind of prequel—which had to be written first. That was this book, *Protecting His Mistress*. I promise that Imani's story is coming—in fact, I'm writing it now. In the meantime, please enjoy *Protecting His Mistress*.

Hugs and Happy Reading,
Evangeline
July 2020

# ONE

"Are you certain you're up for this assignment, Commander Karn?"

Commander Sylvan, head of the Kindred High Council and Karn's Commanding Officer, raised his eyebrows inquiringly. "Knowing your stellar record in the Elite Espionage Corps, I wouldn't ask, but it's not every male who can stand to be treated the way they treat males where you're going."

Karn inclined his head, indicating he knew what Sylvan was talking about.

"So I understand," he rumbled, running a hand through his thick, brownish-gold hair. He was a Hybrid—half Beast and half Blood Kindred—and he had the mismatched eyes to prove it. His left eye was sky blue and the right was blazing gold. But it was his status as a half-breed that allowed him not only to excel in the Elite Corps, but also to take the difficult and dangerous mission his commanding officer was offering him now.

As a Hybrid, Karn knew his chances of bonding to any females and starting a family were almost nil—which honestly didn't bother him. He had always known it, so he didn't allow himself to long for a mate as most Kindred did. Instead, he threw himself into his work. And the fact that he had no expectations or hopes for the future made him a formidable agent—ready to try anything.

Even posing as a bodyslave on the notorious Yonnie Six.

"I can handle it," he told Commander Sylvan with certainty. "You know I don't shy away from difficult or dangerous missions, Commander."

"Yes, I know. And I'm grateful you're willing to take this one on." Commander Sylvan looked pleased. "Very well, let me give you the details." He settled behind his desk and indicated a chair across from him for Karn. "Please, have a seat."

Karn settled his muscular bulk in the chair gingerly. As a Hybrid, he was also slightly larger than most Kindred warriors— over seven feet tall. No doubt it was one of the reasons Commander Sylvan had chosen him for this assignment. It was well known the Mistresses of Yonnie Six liked to have the biggest, most muscular, terrifying-looking bodyslaves they could get. It was a status symbol for them.

Well, Karn could stand to be a status symbol for a little while. After all, this wasn't a permanent assignment. He was up for anything.

Or so he thought at the time.

"All right," Commander Sylvan said. "Well, lately we've had reports of more and more Kindred warriors of all kinds from all areas of the galaxy being kidnapped by the Yonnites and taken as bodyslaves. I'm afraid our race has come into 'fashion' and we're now the preferred males for such service."

Karn winced.

"Ouch. That's a hell of a thing to be singled out for."

"It's becoming a real problem," Sylvan said seriously. "And the difficulty is finding exactly *where* each warrior has been taken. Once they get sucked into the Yonnite system, they can be traded and bought and sold so many times, it can be almost impossible to locate them."

"But I'm guessing you found a solution to that particular problem?" Karn raised one eyebrow.

"We think we have, yes." Sylvan nodded. "There has been a shake-up in the Sacred Seven—the ruling body of Yonnie Six. Reports of corruption resulted in a complete rearrangement and replacement of several members. And one of the new members is Mistress Mirabella. She's new to the power structure and she's been given the job of Archivist for the Sacred Seven. And, as Archivist, she ought to have a listing of all registered bodyslaves, their places of origin, their sale records, and their current locations."

Karn gave a long, low whistle.

"Whoever could get into her records could find every single one of the warriors who've been taken."

"Exactly." Sylvan nodded. "And that's where you come in."

"I'll be happy to infiltrate her household and get into those records," Karn assured him. "But how can you be certain she'll buy me?"

"We have an in at the private auction house where Lady Mirabella has bought her last six bodyslaves," Sylvan said. "A Lady Tikka—a lower tier Mistress with huge gambling debts. Creditors are breathing down her neck, which is the only reason she's willing to work with us. For the right price, she's willing to make certain you end up as Mistress Mirabella's newest bodyslave. And word on the street is that she's about to buy a new one since she got tired of her oldest one and sent him to the Diluthian Mines."

Karn frowned.

"Seven Hells, that's a death sentence!"

Diluthian was a toxic mineral which released deadly fumes when it was unearthed. It was useful in the refining process of Dream Gas —a product Yonnie Six was famous for. But workers that went to the mines, didn't last long.

"Yes, I know," Sylvan said blandly. "That's another reason I want you to be sure you want this assignment. It could turn deadly if you're not able to please Mistress Mirabella sufficiently."

Karn shrugged and grinned.

"I have yet to meet the female I can't please, Commander." As a Hybrid, he didn't have to worry about bonding anyone to him. So he'd had his fair share of amorous encounters, though he took care never to become emotionally involved with any of them.

"So I hear," Commander Sylvan said dryly. "It's yet *another* reason why I thought of you when this assignment came up."

"I'll do it," Karn said without hesitation. "I know there are risks but hell, there always are." That was part of the excitement of working in the Espionage Corps—you never knew what was coming next.

Sylvan smiled.

"You'll be doing your kinsmen a great favor, Commander. I know there are many in bondage right now, who need to be discovered and rescued."

"We'll find them, Commander Sylvan," Karn vowed. Both males rose and Sylvan offered his arm for a warrior's clasp. "We'll find every last one and bring them home," Karn said as he took the offered arm.

"I pray the Goddess will bless your mission," Sylvan said formally. "And I thank you for taking this risk."

Karn smiled. "Happy to do it, Commander."

Of course, at the time he had no idea he would be risking much more than his life—he would be risking his heart.

But by the time he found that out, it was too late…

# TWO

"Just stand still on the pedestal and try to look menacing," Mistress Tikka snarled under her breath. "Mistress Mirabella likes big, scary bodyslaves. They enhance her status."

"I can do that." Karn pasted a glare on his face and tensed, making his muscles bulge. He *did* wish he didn't have to be displayed naked—it really wasn't his preference to stand around with his shaft hanging out. But apparently those were the rules of the private auction house, since the minute Lady Tikka had met him, the first words out of her mouth had been an order to strip.

Not that she had much else to say to him, Karn thought, eyeing the sour look on her narrow face. She had bright green hair which went badly with her sallow complexion and seemed to hate her role, working for the Kindred. And no wonder, since all Yonnites considered males to be inferior. But apparently her huge gambling debts were more pressing than her hatred of men. So though she clearly despised what she was doing, at least she was doing a fairly professional job of it.

He was trying to be professional too—though posing naked wasn't his usual line of work, he thought dryly. Well, *mostly* naked.

He *was* wearing a thick black pain collar around his neck, as did almost all bodyslaves on Yonnie Six. It was a fake, though—thoughtfully provided by Commander Sylvan. It looked extremely real and even had a remote that went with it. Karn just had to remember to 'writhe in agony' when the pain button on the remote was pressed, which shouldn't be a problem.

The fake collar, of course, was absolutely vital to his getting out of this assignment in one piece. If he had been wearing a real pain collar, he would have been as trapped here as the other Kindred warriors which had been captured and enslaved.

As he stood there looking menacing, several of the Mistresses shopping for bodyslaves passed by the pedestal where he was standing. They all stopped to admire his physique and ask how much. But Mistress Tikka just shook her head.

"Sorry—he's already spoken for."

This happened three or four times and Karn was just beginning to wonder if Lady Mirabella was even there when the thin Mistress beside him hissed,

"Get ready—here she comes!"

Looking down the rows of displayed males, all naked and wearing pain collars like the fake one he had on, he saw a tall, thin, middle-aged woman coming around the corner. She had brassy gold hair the color and texture of the Christmas tinsel Karn had seen on decorated trees down on Earth, a long nose, and thin lips which she pursed in apparent disapproval of almost everything she saw.

Beside the forbidding-looking Mistress and walking a half step behind her was a much younger girl who appeared to be barely in her twenties. She was both shorter and plumper than Mistress Mirabella with softly rounded curves Karn found immensely appealing. Her honey-blonde hair hung in lose ringlets around her oval face and her big brown eyes were wide as she looked from side to side at the massive naked males on display.

"Come along, Lilliana," Mistress Mirabella snapped at her. "Don't shilly-shally so! I know you've never been to a bodyslave market before but there's no excuse to lag behind."

"I…I've just never seen so many males. And…and all without their clothes." The girl's voice was soft and uncertain. "I never knew what they looked like with no clothes on before!"

"Honestly!" Mistress Mirabella blew out a breath impatiently. "I knew I should have picked a more liberal place to have you raised until I was ready to make you my heir. But the Sisters of Chastity and Honor came so highly recommended." She frowned at the girl who must be her daughter—though they looked nothing alike to Karn. "*Do* stop staring at their shafts! It's not like they have any use to us—a bodyslave's shaft is only useful for display purposes. And we don't use that part of them for anything else!"

"But…but they're so *big*," Lilli murmured and Karn saw—with some discomfort—that her big brown eyes were now fixed on *him*. She was staring right between his legs.

"Yes, well. That's to be expected with this kind of slave. Kindred, is he?" Mistress Mirabella said to Lady Tikka as they came to a stop before Karn's pedestal.

"Indeed he is, Lady Mirabella." Mistress Tikka raised her chin. "And a prime specimen as you can tell. Are you looking for a protector or simply a big, frightening showpiece male to increase your status?"

Karn snarled menacingly to show that he was well able to fulfill either function. The expression showed off his fangs to best advantage, which were his heritage from the Blood Kindred side of his family.

"Both," Mistress Mirabella said shortly. "But not for me—for my daughter. She's only just come of age and this will be her first bodyslave. As such, he will have to be both protective and attentive as she's *very* inexperienced."

Karn quickly wiped off the menacing snarl he'd pasted on his face. If he was going to make the sale it was clear he would have to appeal to the girl, who was looking up at him with a mixture of fear and uncertainty on her lovely face.

"The Kindred can do that," Mistress Tikka said quickly. On top of her fee, she had been promised that she could keep whatever credit Karn's sale made her, so she was motivated to 'move the merchandise' as it were.

"But...he has *fangs,* Mother!" the girl protested faintly. "I don't know what to think about that—what if he ties to bite me?"

"Don't be ridiculous, Lilli! He has a pain collar—see?" Lady Mirabella pointed at the fake black collar Karn wore around his neck. "He *can't* bite you as long as you know how to handle him. Show her," she demanded, looking at Mistress Tikka. "Give him a good zap."

"Of course." Lady Tikka pointed the remote at Karn and made a big display of pressing the pain button.

Right on cue, Karn gasped and fell to his knees, grasping at the collar. Then, because he enjoyed being dramatic, he toppled off the platform and lay gasping and writhing at the feet of the three women.

"Oh, no! Stop—*Stop!*" Lady Mirabella's daughter, Lilli, came rushing over to bend down by Karn's side. "Stop it!" she cried again, looking up at Mistress Tikka. "Can't you see you're *hurting* him?"

"As you wish." Mistress Tikka pointed the remote again and pressed the button.

Karn went limp at once and lay panting, like a male who had just run a desperate race. His long hair was in his face but he made no move to brush it away from his eyes. It was annoying, but much better to look like he was so exhausted from dealing with the terrible pain that he couldn't even move, he thought.

Then, to his surprise, he felt a soft hand lifting the long strands away from his face. Rolling his eyes upward, he saw Lilliana—Lilli—bending over him.

"Are you all right?" she whispered, looking into his eyes as she cupped his cheek. "You poor thing! I'm so *sorry* they did that to you. It was dreadful—I would never treat you so. I promise."

Karn felt a sudden, unfamiliar pressure in his heart as those big, brown eyes looked down into his. It was like she had cupped the beating muscle in her soft little hand and given it a gentle squeeze. Gods, she was lovely!

"Lilliana, you mustn't treat a bodyslave too gently," Lady Mirabella was scolding behind her. "You can't let pity get in the way of discipline."

"Yes, Mother," Lilli murmured, but her eyes were still locked with Karn's.

He got to his knees and took both her hands in his.

"Little Mistress," he murmured and bent to press a kiss to each of her soft, sweet little palms.

"Oh…" Lilli's brown eyes got even wider. "What…what is your name?" she asked.

"I am Karn," Karn told her. "And I will serve you, body and soul, if only you will make me yours."

"That's enough of that!" Lady Mirabella snapped. "Get him back up onto the display pedestal, Tikka—I want to inspect him."

"Of course. Get up!" Mistress Tikka pointed the remote at him menacingly. "Don't make me shock you again, Kindred."

Karn climbed back onto the display pedestal at once, though he would rather have stayed down on the ground and talked more to the lovely little Lilli. Still, he would have plenty of time to talk to her if he could pull off this sale. Which was the important thing, he reminded himself—not the fact that he felt strangely drawn to the curvy female.

"Now look, Lilli," her mother instructed when Karn was back in position. "You must examine a male from every angle when choosing a bodyslave. Remember, this choice will reflect on you and me and our entire house!"

"Yes, Mother," Lilli murmured, looking up at Karn.

He caught her eyes again and winked gravely, making her giggle. When Mistress Mirabella turned to give her a reproving look, she hid her smile with her hand and turned it into a cough.

"Yes, yes…very nice. Excellent lines. Very good form." Lady Mirabella circled the pedestal, nodding as she took in Karn from all angles. He thought that he had never felt so much like a piece of meat in his life, but the fact that Lilli was looking up at him with wide-eyed wonder instead of the jaded eyes of a long-time bodyslave owner made a difference.

He had been prepared to endure being "owned" as part of this assignment. Now he thought he might actually enjoy it—or at least, enjoy being close to Lilli. If, that was, he could get her mother to buy him.

"I like what I see," Mistress Mirabella announced at last, after she had circled him three times. "But I want to know about his temperament. How long has he been a bodyslave? It's well known that Kindred make excellent bodyslaves *if* they're captured young enough."

"Oh, he was captured as a child and raised to it," Mistress Tikka said quickly. "So he's very docile—unless, of course, your daughter was threatened in which case he can be very protective," she added.

"I see. That's good—very good." Mistress Mirabella nodded, as though this ticked another box on her invisible bodyslave checklist. "He's a fine specimen," she added. "There's just one more thing—I need to see his shaft erect. For display purposes only, of course."

This was something Karn had been dreading. He didn't mind being put on display—even naked. But he disliked the idea of a female he didn't know or care for handling his shaft. Still, there was nothing to do but grit his teeth and bear it.

Clenching his fists behind his back, he widened his stance and waited as Mistress Mirabella took a firm grasp of his shaft. Her hand was cold as ice and bony as a skeleton's claw.

His shaft absolutely refused to respond to it.

Doggedly, Mistress Mirabella kept trying. But no matter how much she rubbed and tugged, Karn's shaft stayed stubbornly limp.

*Damn it!* Karn clenched his teeth and willed himself to get hard. He had never had this problem before. But then again, he'd never been handled by a female he didn't want. This was definitely a complication he hadn't expected.

"What's *wrong* with him?" Mistress Mirabella demanded at last, dropping his shaft and wiping her hands on a lace handkerchief fastidiously. "Are you trying to sell me a defective bodyslave, Tikka? I won't have a male in my household that can't get hard—what would my friends say if they saw such a thing?"

"Mother, can…could I try?" Lilli asked while Mistress Tikka sputtered out an explanation about how this usually wasn't a problem. "I think maybe…maybe he might react for me?"

"An inexperienced girl like yourself? Why, you've never touched a shaft in your life!" Mistress Mirabella gave a snort, as though this was a stupid idea.

"Please?" Lilli begged. "I think I can do it."

Mistress Mirabella shrugged.

"Well, he *is* supposed to be your bodyslave—*if* we buy him," she remarked. "So I suppose you ought to learn how to care for him. Go on, Lilli—give him a try. But mind you, if he won't rise for your touch, we'll have to find another. We can't have a male we can't display when we go out."

"Yes, Mother," Lilli murmured, but her eyes were on Karn's again. "Can I?" she asked him, reaching one small hand towards his shaft.

"Don't be ridiculous, you don't *ask* a bodyslave if you can touch him, Lilliana—you just *touch* him!" Mistress Mirabella exclaimed.

But Lilli's small hand hovered in place and didn't move until Karn gave her a slight nod.

Slowly, tentatively, she stroked her fingers lightly down his length. It was a soft, ticklish touch, but Karn felt it like flames licking over his skin.

At once, blood began to rush to his shaft and he felt himself begin to harden. He had a moment of relief—when Mistress Mirabella had been yanking on him, he'd wondered for a moment if his equipment was broken. The relief was followed by a burst of pure lust as Lilli's soft little hand came back to stroke him again, more fully this time.

"Oh," she whispered. "He's so *big.*"

"A very good length and girth." Mistress Mirabella admitted grudgingly. "Another Kindred trait, of course."

"What's *that*, though?" Lilli asked.

Looking down, Karn saw she was pointing at his mating fist—the thick swelling that went all around the base of his shaft. It was from his Beast Kindred side, as the fangs were from the Blood Kindred part of his family.

"My mating fist, Little Mistress," he said, answering her question since Mistress Tikka clearly had no idea. "It proclaims the Beast Kindred part of my heritage as my fangs proclaim the Blood Kindred part."

Lady Mirabella frowned.

"It's most unsightly! And you never told me he was a half-breed, Tikka."

"No, it's not!" Lilli objected, frowning at her mother. "It's *part* of him, Mother. And I don't care if he's a half-breed—I want him!"

"Those eyes, though…" Mistress Mirabella shook her head. "One blue and one gold? So *strange…*"

"I *like* his eyes," Lilli insisted. "I think they're beautiful."

"Well…he's going to be *your* responsibility," her mother warned. "You'll have to bathe him and train him and see that he's fed. And if your friends laugh at his unusual physique, it will be too late to take him back."

"I don't care what any of them think." Lilli frowned. "They're not really my friends—they're just the daughters of *your* friends, Mother. I never met any of them before last week when you brought me home from the convent."

"Well…" Mistress Mirabella sighed. "Just as you please, I suppose," she said. She looked at Mistress Tikka. "How much? We'll take him."

# THREE

L illi wished she could ride in the back of the ship with her new bodyslave but her mother had said that was "inappropriate" so she had to be content to sit in the front and just catch glimpses of him in the rear-viewer.

Every time the big Kindred caught her watching him, he looked right back at her with an unwavering gaze. Lilli tried to hold his eyes with her own, but she found she couldn't meet the intensity of his gaze for long and had to look away.

Deep down, she knew this wasn't proper. A bodyslave wasn't supposed to look a Mistress in the face. A well-trained one would look down at the ground when addressing a superior female and never, ever look her in the eyes. But Lilli found she liked the boldness of his stare and the way he dared to look at her right in the face. It was like a secret between them—a naughty little mystery that only she could solve.

When her Mother—who normally only visited her at the convent where she had been raised once a month—had come and told Lilli it was time for her to come home to Yonnie Six, she had been worried.

And when Lady Mirabella *further* informed her daughter that she would also be getting her first bodyslave, she was *terrified*.

But she didn't feel terrified now, she thought, catching the big Kindred's mismatched eyes in the rear-viewer once more and then looking quickly away. She felt…intrigued. Interested…curious. Excited, even. Though why she should feel all these positive emotions when she had just purchased the most enormous male she'd ever seen, Lilli didn't know.

Shouldn't she be frightened of him? Oh, certainly he had a pain collar on. She stroked the small, finger-sized remote carefully, being very certain not to press the big red pain button at its center. The pain collar should keep her safe. Only somehow, she had the strong feeling she didn't *need* to be kept safe from the big Kindred. As huge and as scary-looking as he could be when he was snarling or posing, as he had on the platform, he didn't seem like he would hurt her.

*You think that now, Lilli,* whispered a little voice in her head. *But what will you think when you have him alone and it's just the two of you. You know what Mother said—**you're** to be responsible for him. And you know she expects you to jump right in and not be shy or "shilly-shally" as she calls it when you drag your feet. You'll have to at least pretend you know what you're doing—especially when Mother's friends and their daughters come over.*

Which unfortunately, was going to be tonight—which was one reason Mother had been in such a hurry to buy her a bodyslave.

*"We'll be hosting some of the most important women in all of Opulex,"* she'd lectured when Lilli had protested that she didn't need a bodyslave just yet and would rather not have one. *"You must be on your best behavior and you must have a bodyslave. What will our guests think if you don't?"*

Mother herself had five bodyslaves—she'd had six but then she had sent poor Ragnor to work the mines, just because he'd been unable to make his shaft hard before a dinner party one night. Lilli had cried when she'd heard that. Ragnor had always been sweet to her when her mother made her monthly visits to the convent. He used to play dolls with her, even though he was a huge, hulking male, almost —but not quite—as big as her new Kindred.

*I don't think I've ever seen anyone as big as him—as big as Karn,* Lilli thought, glancing at him in the rear-viewer again. This time he winked at her and she found herself blushing as she hastily looked away. Then she berated herself—this would never do—she must not be seen blushing around her own bodyslave. Her mother would be scandalized, especially if it happened out in public or when they had company.

"…are you going to wear tonight?" Lady Mirabella's strident voice disrupted Lilli's thoughts.

"What?" She looked up at her mother quickly, putting her hands to her cheeks instinctively to hide the blush. Her face felt hot under her hands and she hoped her mother wouldn't notice.

"Honestly, Lilliana—where are you tonight? I've already asked you twice—what are you going to wear at our little reception tonight?" Lady Mirabella repeated impatiently. "I think your new gauzy green outfit would look lovely."

Lilli bit her lip. The "green outfit" was sheer up top and showed her nipples. Of course, dressing to accentuate your sexual assets was a Yonnite tradition and she knew she ought to get used to it. But back at the convent, she'd never worn anything see-through or low-cut or remotely suggestive. She wondered if she would ever get used to dressing as she had to for life in Yonnite society.

She had little choice, of course. Now that Mother was a member of the Sacred Seven, there were an endless number of balls and soirees and receptions where she had to be dressed up. So as uncomfortable as it made her feel, she still had to wear the outfits she was given.

"I guess…guess the green will be all right," she said tentatively.

Mistress Mirabella snorted impatiently.

"All right? *All right?* Lilli, you've got to look *better* than all right! This dinner is to honor *you*—your coming of age and formally becoming my heir. Several other members of the Sacred Seven will be there—as will your friends—their daughters."

Lilli thought again about pointing out how those girls were *not* her friends. All of them had been raised in Opulex, instead of being sent off to a convent to be raised. They were used to the opulent Yonnite lifestyle which included a devotion to fashion and a constant desire to one-up all your friends and enemies.

The meaning in such a life eluded Lilli, who had been raised to view simplicity, frugality, and modesty as the greatest good by the Sisters of Chastity and Honor.

She honestly didn't understand wanting to always be better than everyone else—to have the biggest buildings, the most credit, the most expensive clothes, the most ostentatious jewels, and the most impressive bodyslave. What was the point of all that, anyway? Material things didn't make you happy—having inner peace did.

But of course, she couldn't say such things to her mother. Lady Mirabella would be shocked and horrified to hear such thoughts. She had been born into opulent wealth and had amassed still more of it as she grew older. Influence and power ran in her blood and she would be very upset if she thought they didn't run in Lilli's blood as well.

*In fact, she might well disown me,* Lilli thought grimly. *After all, she didn't care enough to raise me herself. She always said she was too busy to have a child underfoot and that's why she paid the Sisters to raise me instead.*

She would have to do a credible job of acting like her mother's daughter tonight at the banquet, she told herself. Her mother wasn't one to suffer fools gladly and she would be unmerciful if Lilli embarrassed her.

*I'll do my best,* Lilli thought. *Having such a big, impressive bodyslave should help.*

She caught the Kindred's eyes once more and held them for as long as she could before dropping her own. How could he stare at her so steadily like that? And why did it make her heart pound when he did?

Lilli didn't have any answers. She only knew that her new bodyslave was something different—something special. She hoped he would help her make a good showing tonight.

But first, of course, she would have to get him ready.

# FOUR

"Give him a good washing," Lady Mirabella directed sternly when she and Lilli and the big Kindred slave were all standing in the entryway to Lilli's rooms. "Scrub him from top to bottom, Lilliana. You must get the stink of that market off him before our little soiree tonight."

Actually, Lilli didn't think the big Kindred stunk at all. To her, he smelled good—a warm, spicy, masculine scent that seemed to awaken her senses and make her want to get closer to him. But she couldn't say that to her Mother—Lady Mirabella expected her to wash her new bodyslave and so wash him she must. But there was *one* question on her mind.

"Must…must I wash him *everywhere,* Mother?" she asked, her eyes flicking down to his massive shaft. It was no longer hard, as it had been after she touched it at the slave market. But it was still immensely long and thick and rather intimidating, Lilli thought.

"You mean his shaft?" Lady Mirabella snorted. "Why should *that* bother you? You seemed eager enough to handle it back at the market."

Lilli felt her cheeks get hot.

"I…I was just curious, that's all," she said in a low voice. "But I never thought…I mean…couldn't he wash that part himself?"

"Look, Lilliana…" Her mother gave Lilli a stern frown. "Until you have a new bodyslave trained to your liking, you *must* handle him often. He has to get used to your hands on his body—he must submit to your touch without any kind of hesitation or flinching. Did you see the way he twitched away from me when I touched his shaft?"

Actually, Lilli hadn't noticed that. She'd been too busy feeling sorry for the big Kindred, who'd had a stony look on his face, as though he didn't really enjoy being stimulated. Of course for her, it had been a different story—he had come alive at once under her touch.

Which was kind of what she was afraid of. What if he got hard again, when she washed him? Would that be proper? And what if he spilled his seed?

She didn't know much about that—but she'd seen it in the porno vid one of her friends at the convent had smuggled in after a visit home. The Sisters had found the vid of course, and confiscated it. Then all visits home had been cancelled for a whole six months as punishment for everyone who had watched it.

Most of the girls had been devastated but not Lilli, since she never got to go home anyway. In fact, she hadn't seen home—her mother's home on the outskirts of Opulex, which was located at the very top of the huge building her mother owned—until a week before, when her mother had come to get her.

"…so you *must* do a thorough job. Do you understand?" Lady Mirabella demanded.

Lilli's thoughts had been wandering but now she snapped back to attention.

"Yes, Mother," she said quickly, though she wasn't exactly sure what she'd just agreed to do.

"Good. Now, look here."

Her mother took the pain collar remote and pressed some of the buttons—though not the big red pain button, Lilli was relieved to note.

"There," Mistress Mirabella said at last, handing it back. "That will make certain he can't touch himself and he can't touch *you*. Later you can set it so that your slave can massage you and do other things for you, but until he's trained, it's best to keep it at a non-contact setting. Only you can touch him and he won't be able to lay a finger on either his own equipment or you without getting a nasty jolt."

"All right." Lilli nodded and took back the remote. She supposed it was a good safety feature to have. It would keep a rebellious bodyslave in line and keep a Mistress who wasn't quite sure of him safe.

"Now take care of him and get the both of you ready," her mother ordered. "You only have a little over an hour before guests will begin arriving. Oh, and *don't* forget to oil his shaft and put a stay-hard strap on him. I want that impressive endowment of his on display tonight —Lady Paddlepants will be *so* jealous!" She smirked, clearly anticipating the jealousy and discomfort of one of her best friends.

Lilli felt her mouth go dry. She'd never oiled a slave's shaft before —or fitted one with a stay-hard strap. For that matter, she'd never touched a naked male and washed him all over. How was she going to manage all this?

But her mother was already turning away to get ready in her own rooms on the other end of the vast penthouse suite.

It looked like Lilli was on her own.

# FIVE

arn was beginning to feel sorry for the little female. She could hardly meet his eyes and she looked scared to death when her mother had ordered her to bathe him. And when she'd further ordered that Lilli must oil his shaft and put him into some kind of contraption to keep him hard at the party they were having that night, his new little Mistress had looked so terrified his heart melted in sympathy.

*Too bad I can't offer to wash myself,* Karn thought, as she led him through the elaborate suite of rooms which were clearly hers. But of course if he did that, he would be admitting that the remote was as fake as the collar he wore.

They went through a sitting room with rose-gold velvet plush Synthian furniture and then through a bedroom dominated by an elaborately carved white four-poster bed made of rare *gnoss* ivory. Finally they entered a cavernous bathing chamber made of expensive *hurtha* marble. The marble was a deep blue, shot through with swirls of silver, white, and gold. The effect was that of the galaxy laid out on the walls, Karn thought. A space-scape in the confines of a fresher.

"Fucking gorgeous," he murmured, looking around. All the

fixtures on the shower and the huge tub were pure gold and the bath-mats were woven of *tengu* grass which lived off the water that was dripped on it and sprouted tiny flowers when it was stepped on with wet feet.

"Oh, do you like my bathing chamber?" Lilli asked shyly. "It's so much different from the bathroom I used to share with the other girls at the convent."

Karn frowned.

"You lived in a convent?" He'd heard Lady Mirabella saying something along that line, but he wasn't sure he'd understood her correctly.

Lilli nodded her head.

"Oh, yes. Mother had me raised there after she gave birth. In fact, she had me brought right from the birthing and conception center to the convent. She said she didn't have time for children."

"That seems kind of harsh," Karn remarked. His own mother had been warm and loving and he felt sorry for the girl for not having had that.

"Oh, no." Lilli shook her head quickly, her golden ringlets rippling fetchingly. "She visited me once a month, you know, which was more than some of the other girls got to see their parents. She's just always been so busy with her business, you see."

Then she blushed, her cheeks going rosy and looked down at her hands.

"Hey, what's wrong?" Karn started to lift her chin so she would meet his eyes but remembered at the last minute he wasn't supposed to be able to touch her. Damn.

Instead, he leaned down to get their faces on the same level.

"What is it, little Mistress?" he asked gently.

"Oh, it's just that…I shouldn't be talking private business to you." She sounded ashamed, as though she had broken some very important rule. Her big brown eyes darted up to meet his and then darted away again. "A Mistress shouldn't talk to her bodyslave at all, except to give him orders and commands. And she ought to require his silence unless he's answering a direct question."

"Well, that sounds like a boring relationship," Karn said frankly. "I thought you wanted a bodyslave you could *talk* to."

"What?" Her eyes flew up to his again and this time she didn't look away. "What would give you that idea?"

"Well, you bought a *Kindred*," Karn pointed out. "We like to talk to a female and listen to her talk back. It's part of the way we get to know our Mistress—to understand her wants and needs."

"You…you do?" Lilli looked at him uncertainly.

"Sure, we do," Karn rumbled, giving her a charming smile. "Because the better I know you, little Mistress, the better I can protect and guard you. So you see, it's for your own safety that I want to talk to you."

"Well…" Lilli nibbled her lush bottom lip. "When you put it that way…I guess it makes sense."

"Sure it does," Karn agreed, smiling. "Of course, we'll only talk this way when it's just you and me," he added quickly. "I don't think your mother would approve if she knew you were talking to your bodyslave."

"No, she certainly wouldn't," Lilli agreed fervently. "She never talks to hers except to order them all around." She gave Karn a tentative smile. "But I like the idea of only talking when we're alone. It's like…our little secret."

"Yes, exactly." Karn nodded. And if she was willing to share one secret with him, hopefully she'd be willing to share more. Like the secret of how to get into her mother's files—wherever they were. He would have to try and get out and prowl around tonight to see if he could find them.

But for now they had to get ready for the fancy dinner party her mother apparently had planned so she could show off her new bodyslave—which was him.

# SIX

L illi liked the way her new bodyslave talked to her. Karn seemed warm and sympathetic and she liked the idea of the two of them getting to know each other better. Still, as nice as he seemed, she was afraid things were about to get awkward.

"I...I'm afraid I'm supposed to wash you now," she said, biting her lip as she looked up at him. "I hope you don't mind?"

"I don't," Karn said simply, smiling at her.

There was something so disarming in that charming, lopsided grin of his, Lilli thought as she looked up at him. It showed his right fang and the corners of his eyes crinkled, so that she could see the smile in his eyes as well as his mouth.

"Well...good," she said briskly, trying to act more like a Mistress and less like a scared little girl. "Then let's get started."

"As you wish, Little Mistress," Karn rumbled, nodding his head submissively. "But..."

"But what?" Lilli asked, frowning.

"Well, *I'm* all ready to get wet." He nodded down at his massive, muscular, nude body. "But are you coming in the shower with me? If you are, I'm afraid you'll ruin your gown."

"Oh…" Lilli looked down at herself with a frown. The Kindred had a point. She was wearing a fetching dusty-rose gown which she didn't want to ruin.

Well, *she* thought it was fetching, anyway. Her mother had sniffed and called it "dowdy" because it didn't show enough skin. But that was the exact reason Lilli liked it and she didn't want to get water-marks on the delicate Dresdian silk it was made of.

"I…I guess I should get undressed too," she said and blushed helplessly.

She had never gone naked in front of anyone before—not even the other girls at the convent—because nudity was strictly prohibited. But she knew what her mother would say if she refused to wash her new bodyslave just because she was ashamed of him seeing her naked.

She would first point out that it didn't matter what the bodyslave saw because they weren't really people and didn't count. And then she would get angry with Lilli and call her "prudish" which was apparently one of the worst things you could be in Yonnite Society.

"Hey, little Mistress?" Karn's deep voice cut through her inner turmoil and she looked up to see a concerned expression on his face.

"Yes, Karn? What is it?" she asked, trying to keep her voice steady.

"If you'd rather not take off your clothes around me, I under-stand," he told her. "That must be hard for you, if you were raised in a convent."

Lilli was surprised at how perceptive the big Kindred was. He had picked right up on the source of her distress and was sympathetic to it instead of making fun of her.

"That's very kind of you," she said, lifting her chin. "But a Mistress must not be shy around her bodyslave."

He frowned.

"Why? Because we're just furniture? Because our opinions don't count?"

Lilli bit her lip. The fact that he'd just said almost exactly what she'd imagined her mother saying was awful. Maybe her new bodyslave was *too* perceptive.

"That's what *most* Yonnites would say," she answered carefully. "And I know it's what my mother would say."

"Well, what do *you* say, little Mistress?" He raised an eyebrow, his mismatched eyes fixed on her intently.

"I...I don't know," Lilli admitted. "I've only been here for a week. I'm not really used to Yonnite society and customs yet."

"Of course you're not." His voice softened. "Forgive me, little Mistress. I didn't mean to distress you."

"You didn't." Lilli lifted her chin. "But we can't stand here talking all night. I have to get you ready for the banquet."

And resolutely, she began to strip.

# SEVEN

Karn eyed her as she took off her pretty pink gown and began slipping out of her undergarments. Gods, she was as lovely naked as he'd imagined! Her breasts were large and ripe, her nipples were pink and puffy, and her full hips curved down to well-shaped legs. Between her thighs, her soft little pussy had a mound of delicate, light blonde curls which did nothing to hide the plump outer lips of her sex.

Just looking at her was enough to make his shaft rise again. For a moment, Karn tried to stop it by thinking of mathematical formulas but then he reasoned that there was no point. Lilli was going to have to see him erect—see him and touch him as well—so she might as well get used to it.

It was a strange culture, he couldn't help thinking, that ordered a young, virginal girl to take a large, naked male and bathe and handle him intimately. But then again, there were many aspects of Yonnite culture he found strange—not the least of which was their propensity to take males as slaves.

"Oh!" Lilli's eyes widened when she finished getting undressed and turned to him. Her gaze was fixed on his shaft, which by now was hard and throbbing. "Why…" She looked at Karn uncertainly. "Why is it, uh, hard again? I haven't touched you or anything."

"My shaft got hard in response to seeing your lovely body, little Mistress," Karn told her frankly. "Forgive me if it's, uh, impertinent but I can't help my body's natural reactions to yours."

"Your body reacted to mine?" Her eyebrows shot up. "But…is that proper?"

"Probably not." Karn grinned at her. "But it *is* natural. At least with my people. Maybe it's not with yours."

"I don't think any of my mother's bodyslaves react to her the way you're, uh, reacting to me," she murmured, still eyeing his shaft.

Remembering Lady Mirabella's cold, bony claw yanking his equipment, Karn could see why not. There was absolutely nothing about the Yonnite Mistress to make a male hard as far as he could tell. But of course, he couldn't say that to her daughter.

"Probably her bodyslaves are better trained than I am," he said, bowing his head humbly. "I guess you'll have to teach me not to react to your body when you bathe me, little Mistress."

"I…I don't know how to do that," she confessed softly. "I've never trained a bodyslave before."

"Well, maybe we can learn together," Karn suggested. "But for now, aren't you supposed to be bathing me?"

"Oh…oh, yes!" She glanced at the chronometer on the wall. "We must hurry—the banquet is coming up fast. Come on."

She took a remote off a peg beside the huge, opulent shower stall and pointed it.

"Now let me see—I'm still getting used to this myself," she murmured. "How hot do you like your water?" she asked, looking up at Karn.

He was charmed by her innocent question. How many Mistresses of Yonnie Six would care about their bodyslave's preferences? He was guessing the number was close to zero and yet Lilli really seemed to take an interest in his well-being.

"I'm sure whatever is comfortable for you will be fine for me, little

Mistress," he rumbled softly. "But thank you for asking after my comfort."

She bit her lip.

"I suppose I shouldn't do that. Mother would be angry with me if she heard."

"We don't have to tell her," Karn suggested. "It'll be our secret."

"All right." She smiled at him and did something to the remote so that the door slid open and the ceiling of the shower stall began raining steaming, scented water. "Um—that's how I like it. Should we get in?"

"Of course, little Mistress." Karn made a gesture with one hand. "After you."

"All right."

And Lilli stepped into the shower.

# EIGHT

The big Kindred came into the shower stall with her and the automatic door slid shut behind them. He came to stand beside Lilli in the steaming rain and loomed over her.

Suddenly, she was reminded all over again of how very *huge* and muscular he was. Though the shower stall was big, he seemed to take up most of it with his broad shoulders and long legs.

At that moment, Lilli remembered she had left the remote to his pain collar on her pile of folded clothes outside the stall. And Karn was blocking the exit.

She looked up at him, frozen for a moment with fear. Would he try something on her? Something like what she'd seen in that porn vid her friend had smuggled into the convent? Would he try to kiss her? To touch her?

"What's wrong, little Mistress?" he rumbled, frowning. "You seem distressed."

"I...do I?" Lilli's voice came out sounding high and frightened. She cleared her throat and tried again. "I mean, of course I'm not distressed. I'm fine."

"Yes, you are. You're thinking that you left the remote to my collar outside the shower," Karn remarked, once more showing that amazing Kindred intuition of his.

"Oh, well...yes." There didn't seem to be any point in denying it —he could apparently see right through her. "Yes, I *was* thinking that," Lilli admitted. "Though it shouldn't matter since Mother set it to shock you if you tried to touch me or yourself. And I'm *pretty* sure it will work," she added, wishing she didn't still sound so frightened.

"Even if my pain collar was completely nonfunctional, you still would have nothing to fear from me," Karn assured her softly.

"What?" Lilli frowned. "But...why? How?"

"Because I'm Kindred," he said simply. "We don't hurt females. Ever."

"Really?" Lilli looked up at him, wanting to believe but still not quite able to.

"Really," Karn assured her. To her surprise, he knelt suddenly in front of her. He was so tall, they were still almost face to face but he did have to look up a *little* to meet her eyes. "Look at me, Lilli," he murmured. "I swear by the Goddess, the Mother of All Life, that I will never lift a hand against you or harm you in any way. For as long as we are together I will live only to serve you and give you pleasure. Do you understand?"

Lilli leaned forward and found she was cupping his face in her hands.

"You really mean that?" she whispered.

The water raining down around them made his long hair fall in a smooth waterfall down his back and his thick lashes were matted and bristly with it, making his mismatched eyes look like jewels. He was, she suddenly thought, one of the most beautiful people she had ever seen, though one didn't usually think of males as beautiful.

"I mean it," Karn murmured, still looking at her with that intense gaze of his.

He nuzzled his cheek against her hand and Lilli felt the rough drag of his stubble against her palm and fingers. It was a pleasant feeling, she decided, and so was being this close to the big Kindred, especially when both of them were naked. Why, he was so close he could have bent his head and sucked one of her nipples into his mouth, which was something she'd seen on the porn vid.

The idea made Lilli feel hot and cold all over and she tried to push the mental image away. What was it about the big Kindred that brought such illicit thoughts to the surface of her mind?

"All right," she whispered. "I believe you, Karn. You can…can get up now. I'd better wash you before it gets any later."

"As my lady wishes," he murmured and rose smoothly to tower over her again.

Lilli tried to ignore how physically intimidating she found him and reached for the sponge glove which fit over her right hand. It began secreting bubbles and lightly scented foam at once and she reached up and began to rub his broad chest.

Karn moved obligingly, bending down so she could wash his shoulders and back and holding out his arms so she could soap his massive biceps. Goddess, he was just so big *all over,* Lilli couldn't help thinking. But the part that was *really* big was the one she'd been putting off until last.

Finally there was nothing left to wash but the Kindred's massive shaft. Biting her lip, she looked up into his eyes as the soapy glove hovered over his equipment.

Karn nodded slightly.

"Go on, little Mistress. I don't mind your hands on me."

"Thank you," Lilli whispered. She didn't care what her mother said, she didn't like to touch him so intimately without his permission. Taking a deep breath, she wrapped her sponge-gloved hand around his shaft and began to stroke slowly up and down.

A low groan broke from his lips as she soaped him. Lilli froze at once, her hand in mid-stroke.

"Did I hurt you?" she exclaimed. "Was I too hard?"

"No, little Mistress." His mismatched eyes were half-lidded as he looked down at her. "You didn't hurt me—the opposite. Feels damn good to have your soft little hand on me—even with the sponge glove between us."

"Oh, it…it does?" Lilli bit her lip. "How good does it feel? I mean, are you going to…to spill your seed?"

He raised his eyebrows.

"Do you *want* me to spill my seed, little Mistress?"

"I…I don't know." Lilli felt like she was blushing all over her body at once. "I…the girls at the convent…one of them brought in a vid—a porno vid—and lots of us watched it before…before the Sisters confiscated it."

"So I take it there was a jerk-off scene in this vid you saw?" he rumbled.

Lilli frowned.

"Jerk…off?"

"Where someone strokes a male's shaft until he shoots his seed," he explained, still giving her that half-lidded look. "The way you're stroking mine now."

"I…I'm cleaning you," Lilli protested.

"Mmm-hmm." He nodded. "Keep cleaning then if you really do want to see my seed. I won't be able to hold back if you keep stroking."

Lilli bit her lip. Should she do this? Her mother had said nothing about it—but she *had* said the big Kindred would have to get used to Lilli's touch. Still, maybe she had better not. Though she kind of wanted to…

"Lilliana, aren't you ready yet?" Lady Mirabella's voice calling from the com box in the corner of the room made her gasp and jerk her hand away from the big Kindred's shaft. "Hurry up! The banquet is in less than an hour!" her mother shouted through the com system.

"Almost ready, Mother," she called back loudly.

"Very well, then. Hurry! I've left the shaft oil and stay-hard band out on your dresser. Oh, and a pair of nipple drops—wear them with the green outfit we talked about—they're all the rage right now."

Lilli heard the com box click off and breathed a sigh of relief.

Karn had gone as tense as she had when her mother was shouting. Now he relaxed somewhat and gave her that lopsided grin of his.

"Looks like it'll have to be later on if you want me to spill my seed for you, little Mistress," he rumbled.

"Yes, I…I guess so." Lilli nodded. "I, uh, think you're clean enough now. Maybe we'd better get out of the shower."

"As my lady wishes," he murmured and looked pointedly down at his shaft. "But you'll have to stop soaping me in that case."

"Oh!" Lilli realized that her hand had crept back to his thick shaft, which was still just as long and hard as ever, and she was slowly stroking him up and down. What was wrong with her? She jerked her hand away. "I…I didn't mean to," she blurted.

"Doesn't matter." Karn shrugged, his broad shoulders rolling with the motion. "You'll have to touch me again in a minute when you oil me up."

Lilli supposed he was right. But she was still embarrassed about how much she *wanted* to touch him. It didn't seem right to want that —he was, after all, only a bodyslave—only a male and thus inferior, at least according to Yonnite society. She *shouldn't* feel so attracted to his body or be flattered that he was attracted to hers.

But she would have to think about her confusing feelings later. Right now the banquet was coming up.

"Well, let's get out of the shower," she said briskly, putting down the soap glove. "Come on—step out onto the mat and you'll be dried by the blowers," she told Karn.

"Yes, little Mistress," he rumbled and did as she asked.

# NINE

The blowers were two nozzles mounted in the ceiling above the entrance to the shower that rotated and shot jets of hot air at him as soon as Karn stepped out of the shower. They felt good and dried him off in no time but damn if his shaft wasn't still throbbing from the touch of his new Mistress's hand!

Karn tried to ignore it as he stepped aside so Lilli could come out of the shower and be dried as well. But he couldn't help looking at her softly curved, naked body, and wishing he could touch her as intimately as she had just touched him. She was full-figured—what the Twin Kindred called an "Elite"—and she looked like a goddess as the warm jets of air made her long hair float around her face like a golden crown.

At last, when they were both dry, Lilli went to get dressed. The garment she picked out of her walk-in closet—which was the size of Karn's entire suite back on the Mother Ship—was much different from the one she'd taken off. It consisted of a see-through green top which clearly showed her full breasts and a long black skirt which split up the middle to show a pair of matching green lace panties.

Karn had to wear a pair of tight black leather trousers with no crotch, which clearly showed his shaft and balls. He bit back a curse when he saw the trousers, but he wasn't surprised. It seemed that Lady Mirabella liked to show off her slaves—he would just have to get used to having his shaft on display.

While he was getting into the leather slave trousers, Lilli sat under a hair-styler which fashioned her honey blonde hair into a rather fussy up-do that Karn didn't like nearly as well as her natural ringlets. Then she put on some lip gloss and a bit of eye paint—much less makeup than he'd seen other Yonnite Mistresses wear—and looked at herself anxiously in the bathroom mirror.

"There, I think we're all ready. Come on, Karn," she said, nodding at him.

"Uh, little Mistress? Aren't you forgetting something?" he asked and nodded down at his still hard shaft. "Aren't you supposed to, uh, oil me?"

Normally he wouldn't have reminded her of such a thing but he wanted to feel her soft little hands on him again—this time without the soap glove in the way. Also, he didn't want her to get into trouble.

"Oh, you're right! Mother said she left the shaft oil for me on my dresser. Just a minute!"

She ran out of the bathing chamber and returned in a moment with a handful of items.

"Here we are—come over to the counter, please," she said, setting everything down on the wide marble counter beside the sink.

There was a small bottle of bright red oil, a short black leather strap with a silver buckle, and two tiny gold rings with large pear-cut diamond drops hanging from them.

Karn came to stand beside her and waited patiently while she decided what to do.

"All right, let's see. This is the shaft oil, I guess…" Lilli picked up the small red bottle. "But should I pour it directly on his shaft or pour it on my hands and rub it in?" she muttered, examining the back of the bottle, as though looking for instructions.

"You have to rub it in, Little Mistress," Karn told her. "It works best that way—if you want me to be nice and hard for display, anyway."

Though he doubted he would get soft any time in the future as long as she was wearing that naughty little see-through outfit where he could clearly see her plump nipples and lacy panties.

"Oh of course—thank you, Karn." She smiled at him gratefully and squeezed a generous squirt of the bright red oil into one palm. She rubbed her hands together and then, tentatively, took him in hand.

Karn leaned back against the marble counter and gripped the sides of it with both hands. He had to bite back a groan of pleasure as she began to smooth the slippery red oil up and down his cock. It turned the skin of his shaft an angry bright red which looked kind of ridiculous, but he didn't even care because her soft little hands felt so good.

"Oh my," Lilli remarked, her eyes growing wide as she stroked him. "I...I think you're getting even bigger, Karn! And harder too."

"That's because your soft hands feel so good on me, Little Mistress," He growled softly. "Don't forget to oil my mating fist too—and my balls. But be careful with those—they're sensitive."

"They are?" Lilli poured more oil into her palm and carefully cupped his heavy sac, gently massaging the oil in.

"Gods!" Karn threw back his head, both hands gripping the marble countertop behind him so hard he felt like he might crack the stone. This was torture—sheer, sweet, sexual torture—and he never wanted it to end.

"I'm not hurting you, am I?" Lilli looked up at him anxiously. "Or are you getting ready to spill your seed?" She eyed the drop of precum which had formed like a pearl on the tip of his cock. "I...I think I see some ready to come out right now."

"No, Mistress—that's just precum," Karn told her.

"Pre...come? What's that?" She frowned.

"It's what comes before the seed. It gets a female ready to take a male's shaft deep in her pussy." Karn had to fight to keep his voice from dipping down into a lustful growl as he imagined pressing the flaring crown of his own cock between his little Mistress's plump pink pussy lips.

"Oh, but we don't do that!" Lilli exclaimed. "I mean, on Yonnie Six, anyway. Females *never* allow males to penetrate them."

"Well, that's not the way it is in most cultures," Karn pointed out. "In *my* culture, the male penetrates the female deeply and thrusts his shaft all the way into her soft little pussy before he spills his seed. That's how they make a child together," he added, thinking that she might be so ignorant she didn't even know the facts of life.

Lilli frowned as she finished stroking the oil on his shaft and straightened up.

"I'm well aware of the conception methods on other planets, Karn. It's just that here on Yonnie Six, we all go to *conception centers* instead." She shivered, a haunted look coming over her face. "I used to hear stories about the centers back at the convent from girls whose older sisters had gone. It sounded *awful.*"

"Really? Why? How do they do it?" Karn was genuinely interested.

"From what I've heard, they strap you down in this chair with two parts to it. The top part holds you in place and the bottom splits open to spread your legs." Lilli's eyes went wide. "And then they use this big metal phallus—as big as yours—" She gestured down to his shaft. "To put the baby-making goop inside you."

"Do they at least use some lube?" Karn asked. "You know, to get the girl ready first?"

"You mean like your, uh, precum?" She eyed the droplet on the head of his cock again.

"Uh-huh. Only my precum has chemicals in it that help a female open and stretch to take my entire shaft and mating fist without pain," Karn told her. "Do they use something like that at the conception centers?"

Lilli shook her head.

"I don't think so. From what I've heard, it sounds like they just, uh, shove it in."

"Doesn't sound too fucking pleasant," Karn growled.

"Oh, it's not!" Lilli assured him. "And it's cold too. My friend said her sister felt like it was an *icicle* sliding inside her. They press all the way to the end of your channel and then fill you up with the goop. Then they press a kind of plug that blocks the entrance to your, er, sex and keeps it from leaking out until they're sure you're pregnant with a daughter."

"Daughters only, hmm?" Karn rumbled. "With my race, we have almost all sons."

"Oh, it would be a terrible disgrace to get pregnant with a son," Lilli said candidly. "I've heard it happening every once in a great while but generally the sperm sorter they use at the conception center is so good it almost never happens."

"Well, thank the Goddess for small mercies," Karn said dryly. "Wouldn't want to have a son in your belly, I guess."

"I don't want *any* baby in my belly—not for a long time, at least," Lilli said honestly. "I'm just not ready to care for one all by myself and I don't want to have a child and give it to someone else to raise for me."

"The way your own mother did?" he asked.

Lilli bit her lip.

"You have to understand—she was very busy with her business at the time. And she *did* come and see me once a month."

Which, according to the Yonnite calendar, equaled to roughly one visit every fifty to sixty days—they had long months on Yonnie Six. Which wasn't nearly often enough to see your own child, in Karn's opinion. He felt sorry for his new Mistress all over again, but he also sensed she didn't want to talk about her mother's neglect right now.

"Hadn't you better put that uh, harness thing on my shaft?" he asked, tactfully changing the subject.

"Oh—the stay-hard band. Yes, of course!"

Lilli picked it up off the counter and knelt in front of him to put the harness on his cock. "Let's see now," she murmured. "These things can be so tricky…"

Her position with her face so close to his cock made Karn throb even more. He tried to hold still for the ticklish business of her fitting the black leather strap around the base of his shaft. At first she wasn't sure if it should go above his mating fist or below it. But the mating fist was too big for it, so that answered that question. Then she had to work out how to fit the bottom part of it around his balls which was fucking uncomfortable and made his sac look even bigger than it was.

But finally the entire black leather contraption was on and buckled in place so that his shaft stuck out like a big red exclamation point, Karn thought dryly. He felt faintly ridiculous but he supposed every male at the banquet tonight would look the same, so there was no point worrying about it. He wasn't here for a fashion show, after all, but to get the names of the kidnapped and enslaved Kindred warriors.

And also to spend some time with his enchanting new Mistress.

# TEN

"Lilliana—aren't you ready uet?" Lady Mirabella's sharp voice came again from the com box just as Lilli had finished getting Karn all ready to go. "The guests are starting to arrive!"

"I'm ready. Er…almost!" Lilli looked down at herself. "That is, I have my bodyslave all ready to go and I'm dressed, but I still don't have the nipple drops on," she called, looking down at her bare nipples, which showed clearly through the front of her top.

"Well then *put* them on! We can't greet our guests half dressed," her mother scolded. "Now *hurry!* I expect you out here in five minutes!" The com box clicked off.

Lilli reached quickly for the diamond nipple drops but her fingers were still slippery with the shaft oil and the little things slipped right through her fingers.

"Oh!" she exclaimed and bent to pick them up. She got them in one hand and started to raise her top…but remembered just in time that she would get oil all over it if she touched it.

Laying the drops carefully on the counter, she went to the sink and began scrubbing her hands. But the slippery shaft oil wouldn't come off completely, no matter how much she scrubbed. Still, she got enough off that she could touch the edge of her top without marking it and raised it quickly to bare her breasts. Watching herself in the mirror, she attempted to put the little gold ring around her right nipple…only to have it squirt like a slippery seed out of her fingers again and fly through the air, headed right for the drain of the sink.

"Oh, n—" Lilli started but Karn caught the nipple drop in one hand, showing amazingly fast reflexes, she thought, for such a huge male.

"Mistress," he said, holding it up to show her it was safe. "Why don't you let me help you put these on?"

"Oh, but…you can't touch me right now—can you?" Lilli would have liked his help very much, but she didn't want him to be shocked by his pain collar.

"I think if you just press the pause button on my collar's remote I'll be able to touch you," he said. "Why don't you try it? You're never going to get these little things on by yourself, I'm afraid."

Lilli was sure he was right. She'd never worn nipple drops before and she didn't particularly want to start now. Still, what her mother said was law so she had no choice.

"All right," she said. Picking up the remote, she pressed the little "pause" symbol on it and looked anxiously at Karn. "Now can you touch me?"

"Yes." He nodded and gave her that charming, lopsided grin which only showed one fang. "But I need to get you where I can reach you first. Here, little Mistress."

And reaching out, he took her by the waist and lifted her up to sit on the high marble countertop beside the sink.

"Oh!" Lilli gasped. She was a bit flustered at being picked up and moved around so easily, as she hadn't been since she was a child. She certainly hadn't been the thinnest girl at the convent but the big Kindred lifted her as though she weighed no more than a doll.

But there would be time to marvel at his strength later. For now, they were going to be late to the banquet if she didn't hurry up and get the stupid nipple drops on.

"All right now, little Mistress," Karn rumbled. "Lift your top again so I can get to you."

Blushing, Lilli did as he said, lifting her thin green top out of the way so that her bodyslave could get to her bare breasts and nipples.

"Mmm, so fucking gorgeous," he rumbled, eyeing her breasts appreciatively as he opened one of the little gold rings.

"Oh, do you think so, really?" Lilli asked, blushing again. "Because big breasts aren't in fashion at the moment—at least that's what the daughters of my mother's friends have told me."

"Not the fashion?" Karn's eyebrows shot up. "When they're so full and ripe and beautiful? How can that be, little Mistress?"

"It's just the way things are this season." She sighed. "Everyone here has had body-mods to make their breasts tiny and flat so the nipple drops are better displayed."

"Body-mods?" He frowned.

"Oh, body modifications," Lilli clarified. "They're used to make your breasts bigger or smaller—to make you thinner—that kind of thing." She sighed. "Mother wants me to have a body-mod too—to make me more slender and with smaller breasts—but I don't want one."

"Don't let her make you." Karn cupped her right breast gently in his big hand and looked Lilli seriously in the eyes. "You're *beautiful*, Lilli, just the way you are. Don't let anyone tell you different or make you change."

"Well...thank you." Her voice came out sounding rather breathless, she thought. Maybe because the big Kindred was brushing the ripe bud of her nipple gently with his thumb, circling it round and round which sent strange, pleasurable sensations throughout her entire body. "What...what are you doing?" she asked, nodding down to where he was touching her.

"Just getting your nipple hard enough so I can put the ring on it," Karn murmured. "I'm not hurting you, am I?"

"No." Lilli shook her head. "In fact it feels…feels good," she admitted. "It makes me think of…" She trailed off. "Never mind."

"Makes you think of what?" Karn urged. He tugged lightly at her ripening bud, making Lilli gasp. "Remember, little Mistress, I *want* to know your thoughts," he reminded her.

"Well, it…it makes me think of that porn vid I saw at the convent again," Lilli confessed, feeling her cheeks get hot.

"Why?" His mismatched eyes were half-lidded as he spoke. "Did the male play with the female's nipples in the vid?"

"They…he…he sucked them," Lilli said, feeling naughty and hot all over as she spoke. "Sucked them deep in his mouth while she moaned and…and begged him to suck some more."

"Mmmm…" Karn gave her a lazy smile. "Well, sucking your nipples *would* be one way of making them hard enough to put the nipple drops on."

"Oh, I…I never meant you had to…that I expected you to—" Lilli began.

"But what if I *want* to, Mistress?" Karn growled softly. Ducking his head, he captured her left nipple between his lips and sucked it deep into his hot, wet mouth.

"*Ohhh*," Lilli moaned as he traced her sensitive bud with the tip of his tongue. He lapped gently at first and then sucked hard, sending sparks of pleasure straight from her sensitive tips to the place between her thighs. At the same time, he kept tugging gently at her other nipple, continuing the pleasurable sensations there as well.

Lilli found she was writhing on the countertop and thrusting out her chest, giving him better access to her bare breasts. She couldn't help it—it was like someone else had control of her body and was making her react to the big Kindred's touch.

"Oh…oh, Karn," she gasped. "I…I'm not sure we ought…ought to be doing this."

Finally he released her tight bud with a last, sucking kiss.

"But Mistress," he said reasonably, as he fastened the diamond nipple-drop to the stem of her peak. "I'm only doing what I have to in order to get you ready. Isn't that what a bodyslave does? Helps his Mistress?"

"I…I suppose so." Lilli watched helplessly as he sucked the other nipple as well. Once more she found she was thrusting out her chest and also, her hands had somehow found their way to his head and her fingers were carding through his thick hair. "Oh, *Karn,*" she moaned as he nipped her very lightly and then lapped at the sensitive tip as though to soothe the small ache he had caused. "That feels so… so *good.*"

He released this nipple as well, with another soft kiss.

"That's as it should be, little Mistress," he murmured as he began fastening the second nipple drop in place. "A bodyslave must give his Mistress pleasure, right?"

"I…I guess so." Lilli felt rather dazed. She was throbbing all over in places she'd never throbbed before and her nipples felt so *sensitive* now, especially with the heavy diamond drops hanging from them. They were dark red from being sucked too—a fact she hoped her green top would hide. What would everyone say if they knew she'd been letting her bodyslave suck her nipples in private?

Of course, it was a time-honored tradition to allow a bodyslave to suck one's nipples in *public.* Many Mistresses put two different powders on their nipples—one red hot and the other icy cold. They forced their bodyslaves to suck the powders off as a form of punishment—Lilli had seen it done. But she didn't think it was proper to do it in private and without the punishment powders.

Still, Karn *had* done it and there was no taking it back now. She just wished it hadn't made her feel so very wet and hot between her legs, especially when they were about to go out in view of all her Mother's friends and their daughters.

There was no help for it now, though—Lilli told herself she would think about it later. For now she just had to get through the banquet tonight without any major problems.

"Well," she said shakily. "I…I guess we'd better get going. The banquet's about to begin."

"Indeed it is, little Mistress." Karn nodded at her. "And I'll be by your side every step of the way."

"Come on then," Lilli told him and led the way—on rather wobbly legs—out of her rooms.

# ELEVEN

Lilli's apartment was located in an out of the way wing of the huge mansion Lady Mirabella had built for herself at the top of her tallest building. She was obscenely wealthy—Karn had learned that from his research on her before he came to Yonnie Six. Her holdings were mainly in Dream Gas mining, so her estate was located outside the boundaries of Opulex, the capital city and the hub of all Yonnite high society.

He had been brought in through the service entrance when he had first arrived, but now Karn got a sense of how huge and richly furnished Lilli's mother's home actually was.

Looking over the banister of the upstairs foyer, he could see down to the opulent entryway with its pure white marble flooring, shot through with streaks of gold, silver, and platinum. Tall golden vases from the Vastar Dynasty of Porgum Five were filled with rare Thousand Year blossoms from Y'lll Prime.

The flowers were extremely rare and expensive and were named for the fact that they only bloomed once every thousand solar years and then only for a day. After that, they went dormant for another whole millennium. They were in full bloom at the moment, their vast blossoms as big as a male's head, the petals—each bigger than his hand—a red so dark it was almost black shot through with vivid crimson.

It was an entry fit for a monarch but the Yonnite Mistresses milling around in it didn't look impressed. There were seven of them, Karn saw, including Lady Mirabella herself. Three of the guests were middle-aged women, about their hostess's age and four of them were younger, around Lilli's age. All of them had bodyslaves in tow—one for each Mistress—and the combined amount was quite a large party —though they were still dwarfed by the sheer size of the marble entryway.

"I see you had some Thousand Year blossoms imported," one of the middle aged women remarked to Lady Mirabella in an off-hand way. "They're nice, though nothing to what I had in my own parlor just the other week. Rare *blue* Thousand Years, don't you know. You can hardly get them for love or money, but when I heard of them I simply *had* to have some."

"Oh?" Lady Mirabella's smile looked rather strained. "Do tell, Lady Tempertant. Did you get them for a special occasion?"

"Oh, no." The other woman—who had bright purple hair teased out into a kind of halo around her head—shrugged. "I just wanted some, that's all."

"I see." Lady Mirabella looked up at that point and caught sight of her daughter coming down the vast, curving staircase with Karn at her heels. "Lilliana, do hurry up," she called sharply. "Everyone is here now and we must go in to dinner before the *mooshmush* gets cold!"

"Coming, Mother!" Lilli trotted more quickly down the stairs and Karn followed her at a respectful distance. At least he wasn't the only one with his shaft hanging out, he saw, as he eyed the other bodyslaves. Each and every one of them had an oiled, erect shaft sticking out of his crotchless trousers and all of them also wore pain collars.

*Poor bastards,* Karn thought. *They're stuck here with no way to escape.* Thank the Goddess he had on a fake collar and a plan to get out of here when he had the information he had come for. Though at the moment, he was in no hurry to complete his mission—his sweet little virgin Mistress was far too intriguing for him to want to leave any time soon.

"Now then, Lilliana," Mistress Mirabella said when they finally reached the bottom of the grand staircase. "I know you've met some of the Mistresses here, but you haven't been *formally* introduced. And since we have four of the Sacred Seven here tonight, I think now is a good time for formal introductions. Lady Tempertant, you already know. And her daughter, Priss."

She nodded to the woman with a halo of bright purple hair and a girl with sharp, pretty features and wide blue eyes. She looked very little like her mother because while Lady Tempertant was short and somewhat blocky, despite obvious body-mods. Her daughter was tall and thin with blue hair which was styled into a startling sunburst all around the crown of her head.

In fact, all of her was thin including her eyebrows—which had been plucked into two skinny, elegant lines and her lips which looked like a ribbon of scarlet under her narrow nose. The only thing about her that *wasn't* skinny, Karn thought, was a slightly rounded bump in her lower abdomen. This was clearly visible since she was dressed in true Yonnite style with a skirt which hung low on her hips and split in the middle to show her panties.

"And here's Lady Paddlepants and her daughter Yulla," Lady Mirabella continued.

A thin woman with a patrician nose and a permanently sour expression on her face nodded briefly to Lilli. Her daughter was a dull-looking creature with watery gray eyes and an upper lip which didn't quite meet the lower one. This resulted in her top teeth showing at all times, which made her look very much like the Earth animal called a rabbit, Karn thought. They both nodded at Lilli, who nodded back politely.

Yulla, too, had a softly rounded abdomen. Karn frowned—was it some kind of body-mod? But why would females who were so self-conscious about their weight modify themselves to look less than sleek and perfect? He had no idea but it seemed very strange.

"And finally, meet Lady Bodypom and her twin daughters, Beelie and Bodie," Lady Mirabella finished, nodding at the last of the party.

Lady Bodypom had a tower of bright pink hair and a self-important look on her sallow face. Her daughters both had silver-tipped, black hair and wide purple eyes which they turned on Lilli in unison. They, too, had slightly rounded abdomens which stuck out above their long, silver, split skirts.

"Hello, it's very nice to meet all of you," Lilli said, trying to smile, though Karn could see what the effort cost her. He hadn't known her long, but he thought his new Mistress was something of an introvert, which meant that this kind of social gathering was going to be difficult for her.

"Well…" Lady Mirabella clapped her hands. "Shall we go in to dinner? I have us in the smaller dining room, since we're just an intimate little party," she added, and smiled at her guests.

There was a general murmur of agreement and the entire party followed their hostess through the grand entryway, down a long marble hallway, and finally into a vast banquet hall.

*So this is the **smaller** dining room?* Karn thought, looking around in awe. The hall could have comfortably seated two hundred or more, so their party of nine Mistresses and their accompanying bodyslaves was dwarfed by the echoing chamber. He wondered if Lady Mirabella really did have a larger banquet hall somewhere in this immense palace or if she was just showing off for the other Mistresses.

They all trooped to the center of the room where two separate tables had been set up under two huge glittering gold and diamond chandeliers. Here, as everywhere in the mansion, Lady Mirabella's vast wealth was on display.

All of the plates and eating utensils were solid platinum. The crystal goblets were actually diamond, Karn realized, after one of the girls knocked one over with a swish of her dress and it chipped the marble floor rather than shattering.

The wine in the solid gold serving ewers had the faintest scent of Elysium spice which meant it had to be a vintage from the bubble grape fields of Zinzu Tertia. The planet was renowned for wines that cost so much a single sip would buy an entire home on most other worlds.

Lady Mirabella seemed eager to please—trying too hard, Karn thought—to impress her important guests. He knew she had only recently been appointed to the Sacred Seven and that she was at a social disadvantage because she lived outside Opulex rather than inside the city itself. But was this obscene display of wealth really necessary?

"Now, I have two separate tables so the grownups can talk business while the youngsters socialize," she said, fluttering around the tables to show everyone their seats—even though there were already gold and silver engraved name cards at every seat. "You girls enjoy yourselves," she told the daughters of her friends. "And Lilli, be a gracious hostess," she added sharply to her own daughter. "You must sit at the head of the table and make certain everyone has enough to drink and that conversation flows smoothly."

Karn saw Lilli's face go pale but she nodded obediently and tried to smile.

"Yes, Mother. Um, shall we all sit down?" she said, speaking to Priss and Yulla and the twins, Beelie and Bodie.

"I suppose if we *must.*" Priss, the tall thin girl with sharp features and big blue eyes threw herself into a chair at the head of the table—which happened to be the place where Lilli's name card was positioned.

Lilli cleared her throat uncomfortably.

"Um, Priss? I think you're in my seat," she said. "Not that I care about that kind of thing but Mother gets so upset—"

"She'll get over it." Picking up the gold and silver engraved name card with Lilli's name on it, Priss tossed it to her left. "You can sit *there,* Lilliana—I'm not moving," she announced.

Lilli looked like she wanted to say something but wasn't sure what she could do to change the situation without sounding rude.

It was Priss who was being fucking rude, Karn thought, a low growl rising in his throat. But there was nothing he could do about it. He—like the other bodyslaves standing around the table—was only there to serve his Mistress. If someone attacked her with direct force, he could intervene. But he couldn't do a damn thing about the rich bitch girls at the table being snarky.

Lilli took the seat Priss had indicated as graciously as she could while Yulla and Beelie and Bodi settled at their places as well.

"Well?" Priss swiveled her head around to look at her bodyslave— a male with a fierce ruff of *tangor* fur encircling his neck, just below the collar. "I'm thirsty! Why are you not pouring my wine, H'rare?"

Casually, she picked up the remote to his pain collar—which she wore dangling on a diamond chain around her neck—and pointed it at her bodyslave. She gave it a quick press and the hapless H'rare stiffened suddenly as though someone had shocked him.

The next moment his body relaxed and he quickly took an ewer of the expensive wine and poured it into his Mistress's diamond goblet where it fizzed and popped as large bubbles rose from the bottom of the glass to the top.

"That's better." Priss picked up the goblet and brought it to her nose. She took a long sniff and then narrowed her eyes at her bodyslave.

"H'rare, is this wine *alcoholic?*"

"I…I'm sure I don't know, my Lady," H'rare said uncertainly. "I simply poured it because you said you were thirsty."

"Actually, it *does* have alcohol in it," Lilli volunteered. "It's bubble wine from Zinzu Tertia. Mother says it's the best."

"Did you hear that, H'rare?" Priss asked, still speaking to her bodyslave and ignoring Lilli. "It *is* alcoholic. Come here."

"Yes, Mistress?" H'rare bent down, a wince on his face as though he was anticipating another shock from his pain collar.

But instead of using her remote, Priss threw the full glass of dark purple wine right in his face. The bodyslave stiffened but didn't move as the fizzing purple liquid ran down his cheeks.

"H'rare," Priss said to him. "You *know* I'm expecting right now. What do you think drinking a big glass of bubble wine would do to my quick-grow?" She held the empty wine glass up in one hand and patted her swelling lower abdomen with the other.

"I…I don't know, my Lady," H'rare muttered miserably. "I'm not…I don't know such things."

"Which is the *only* reason I'm *not* having you sent to the Diluthian mines!" Priss snapped. She pressed the remote again and watched with a smile curving the corners of her thin lips as her bodyslave stiffened in pain. This time she did not let up immediately but watched with that same nasty smirk as H'rare writhed in front of her.

Karn felt sorry for the poor bastard—clearly his young Mistress was a burgeoning sadist. But when he looked at his own Mistress, he saw that Lilli was upset by the display.

"Oh, please—you're hurting him!" she exclaimed, putting out a hand to Priss. "Please, don't!"

The other girl shot her a disdainful look.

"You can't be too easy on your bodyslaves, Lilliana, or they'll walk all over you," she snapped. "However, since we *are* at the dinner table…"

She let up on the remote and H'rare—who had been frozen in a rictus of pain—sank to his knees panting.

"Clean up this mess," Priss barked at him. "And bring me something *non*-alcoholic to drink."

"Yes, Mistress." H'rare nodded quickly. "At once."

"Wait." Priss glared up at him. "Aren't you forgetting something, H'rare?"

Her bodyslave swallowed and Karn saw a look of pure hatred flash in his eyes. But it was gone so quickly no one else noticed it.

"Thank you for correcting me, Mistress," he said mechanically. "Truly, I am most grateful."

"Of course you are." Priss snapped her fingers at him. "Now go. And if you don't know the way in this ridiculously huge barn of a house, I'm sure one of the other bodyslaves who works here can guide you." She looked at Lilli. "Lilliana, have your bodyslave take my H'rare to the kitchens to get me something more appropriate to drink."

"Oh, well actually, Karn hasn't been with me very long," Lilli said, glancing back at him. "So he doesn't know where the kitchens are either."

"That's all right, little Mistress," Karn told her. "I'm sure I can find my way. Come on." He nodded at the other bodyslave, who nodded back, and the two of them set off for the far corner of the long banquet hall where there was a swinging double door. That seemed the most logical place to find the kitchens and even if it wasn't, this was a golden opportunity for Karn to explore.

He only hoped Lilli would be all right with the awful Priss while he was gone.

# TWELVE

"So, that's a nice new bodyslave you have, Lilliana—though he's a bit too quick to speak to his betters if you ask me." Priss remarked, toying with the food on her plate.

The servants had come and served everyone but the skinny girl had hardly touched a thing as far as Lilli could see. She wished Karn was back behind her chair. His solid presence made her feel grounded, but he and Priss's bodyslave were still gone to the distant kitchens to clean up and get the picky Mistress something new to drink.

In fact, none of the girls was drinking the bubble wine, though her mother had said it was extremely expensive and sure to be a hit. Lilli had ordered one of the serving girls to bring a bottle of sparkling *goochi* juice to the table instead and they were all sipping that, though it only cost a fraction of the other exotic vintage.

"Yes, Karn is a Kindred," Lilli said, trying to be gracious though she was disliking Priss more and more every minute they sat at the same table together. She especially didn't like the way the other girl had treated her bodyslave.

"A Kindred, is it? No *wonder* he has such a big shaft." Priss popped a single *sedju* seed between her teeth and crunched noisily. "Most impressive, I must say. Maybe I'll tell my mother to buy him from your mother for me."

"Oh, but you can't do that!" Lilli exclaimed. "Karn is *mine.* He's my very first bodyslave—Mother bought him for me specially."

"Karn is *mine,"* Priss sing-songed in a baby voice. "Honestly, I can't believe you're only just *now* getting your first bodyslave. I've had five already, counting H'rare."

"Five?" Lilli looked at her in surprise. "But, well…where are they?"

Priss shrugged. "They're all so *troublesome.* Every single one had to be sent to the Diluthian mines because they couldn't behave correctly. Mother complains that I go through them too quickly but she always buys me another when I tell her to."

Lilli was aware that the girls in her circle—the ultra-rich of Yonnie Six—didn't even bother to recycle their expensive bodyslaves by selling them on the second-hand slave market. Instead, they treated the males they bought to serve them as disposable and threw them away, much the way one might throw away a tissue after using it.

But just because she was part of this social class didn't mean she had to like it. She hadn't been raised in the convent to treat people like dirt or throw them away. In fact, they had been taught that all lives were sacred—even the lives of males.

"I don't think it's right to send a bodyslave to the Diluthian mines just because he doesn't please you," she said, lifting her chin. "Do you know how long the life expectancy is there? Barely a week before the gasses do permanent damage to a male's lungs."

"What do I care about his lungs?" Priss demanded, frowning. "It's his *shaft* and his service I'm worried about! H'rare has a good enough shaft for display—though it's nothing like that monster your bodyslave has—and he's *generally* good at service, so I'll probably keep him for a while. At least until my quick-grow comes out." She stroked her abdomen again, making Lilli frown.

"Your, er, 'quick-grow'?" she asked. "What do you mean by that?"

"My daughter of course—my heir." Priss rubbed her belly some more. "It's all the fashion now to go to the conception center and get having your heir out of the way while you're young. That way you don't have to bother with it when you get older and you're too busy with business to have a baby. Why, Mother *insisted* I have it done now that they have the quick-grow shots that make the whole business so much faster."

"My mother had me do it too," Yulla volunteered timidly. "It doesn't take long—you're only pregnant for about three months."

"Do they use some kind of quick-growing sperm, then?" Lilli asked.

"Goodness, no!" Beelie, one of the twins spoke up.

"The sperm is whatever kind you choose," Bodie continued.

"It's the shots they give you beforehand that makes the baby grow quickly," Beelie said.

"We only got impregnated the other day and look how far along we are already," Bodie added as both twins rubbed their swelling abdomens.

"And we chose sperm from the same male—so our daughters can be sisters and not just cousins," Beelie said.

"Isn't that just perfect?" Bodie asked.

"But…but what will you do with the babies when they come?" Lilli asked. "Are you going to raise them yourselves?"

"Certainly not," Priss sneered. "We'll send them off somewhere or have a nannybot raise them. They have some very advanced AI tech now—some nannybots even produce milk calibrated to your heir's nutritional needs. Why, you never even have to look in on them at all! Just give them to the nannybot the moment they pop out and don't bother with them until they come of age twenty years later."

She laughed and the other girls giggled along as well.

"My mother says that if there had been nannybots when I was little she would have used one," Yulla said.

"Our mother too," Bodie added.

"She says your mother, Lady Mirabella, was smarter that she was—never having the bother of raising you at all," Beelie added, speaking to Lilli.

"Well, I don't like the idea." Lilli shook her head. "I mean, I don't feel ready to have a baby now. But if I did, I'd want to raise her myself—not just send her off to a convent or shove her off on a nannybot."

"Well, it doesn't appear to be a problem since *you're* not pregnant," Priss sneered. "Honestly, Lilliana, when are you *ever* going to get with the times?"

"I don't care if it's in fashion to have a, uh, quick-grow baby," Lilli said, lifting her chin. "I don't want to do it—I'm not ready and I don't think you are either," she added, looking at Priss.

The other girl's eyes flashed.

"What do you know about me or anything at all, for that matter? You were raised in that backwards convent where they don't even let you dress right—let alone do anything else that's in fashion!" She made a sweet, simpering face at Lilli. "Actually, I feel *sorry* for you, Lilliana—honestly I do. You're just so hopelessly out of sync with the rest of society—you'll probably end up like old Mistress Hownow who actually raised a bodyslave as her heir because she always wanted a 'son.' Can you imagine?"

She laughed nastily and the other girls did too. Lilli said nothing because she had no idea what Priss was talking about. She wished heartily that Karn would come back so she didn't feel so alone. At least she could talk to the big Kindred. Having a nice conversation with the spoiled brats at this table was impossible—especially the awful Priss.

"So she raised him as her heir?" Yulla asked Priss, frowning in apparent confusion.

"Yes—she did! And *he* was a Kindred too, just like your new bodyslave," Priss turned to Lilli again. "You know, she wanted to leave him all her wealth and set him free? Luckily her niece, Lady Bittle-bum, put an end to *that* nonsense. She contested the will and sold the old lady's bodyslave at a 'troubled slave' auction because he wouldn't behave."

"Why didn't she just send him to the mines?" Beelie asked, frowning.

Priss sniffed.

"Probably because Mistress Bittlebum is such a penny-pincher she can't afford to toss a slave without trying to make a profit on him. Why, my mother says she doesn't even own her own building down-town! But you'll never guess what happened next, girls..." She leaned forward excitedly.

"What?" Bodie and Beelie and Yulla all asked together.

"Why he *killed* his new Mistress!" Priss whispered. "Yes, I know—isn't it *dreadful?*" She shook her head and looked at Lilli. "And *that's* why you have to constantly stay on top of your bodyslaves and never let them get the upper hand. Males are violent and unpredictable and if you give them an inch, they'll take a parsec!"

"That's what our mother always says too." Bodie and Beelie were both nodding.

Just at that moment and much to her relief, Karn reappeared at Lilli's side.

"Here you are, Mistress," he rumbled, setting a chilled golden cup with beads of condensation on the outside in front of her. "Frosted *li'ta* juice. I hope you enjoy it."

Lilli saw at once what he was doing because H'rare was sitting an identical cup in front of Priss. Clearly if she took a drink and approved the juice, Priss would have a more difficult time refusing it.

Quickly, she picked up the glass and took a sip.

"Mmm, delicious! Thank you, Karn," she said, smiling up at the big Kindred.

Priss frowned at her.

"You're *awfully* trusting, Lilliana. What if that was poisoned?" she demanded.

"Poisoned? Oh, Karn would never—" Lilli began.

"How do you know? You told me yourself you just got him," Priss waved a large, gaudy ring with a clear stone over the cup H'rare had put before her. The clear jewel beeped and turned green and she nodded and took a sip. "Very good, H'rare—you may get down and kiss my feet," she said to her bodyslave.

H'rare at once dropped to the floor and began kissing her bare toes which were exposed by her thin, strappy sandals.

"There—that's how you do it. Never trust anything your bodyslave gives you unless you poison-check it first," Priss lectured.

"My Mistress has no fear that I will harm her because I have given her my oath only to serve and pleasure her," Karn growled. "Also, I am a Kindred and we do not harm females."

"Oh my Goddess!" Priss put a hand to her bony chest and looked up at Karn as though she couldn't believe he had dared to open his mouth. "Lilliana, *do* something!" she demanded.

"Do what?" Lilli looked at her in confusion.

"Your bodyslave just spoke to me as though he was my *equal*," Priss exclaimed. "He looked me in the eyes and everything! You can't allow such behavior!"

"Karn was only explaining why I don't have to worry about him hurting me," Lilli said defensively. "Kindred are different from other bodyslaves. They never harm women."

"Right," Priss snorted. "Have you not been hearing a word I was saying? That bodyslave of Mistress Hownow's was a Kindred and that didn't stop him from ripping off his new Mistress's head, now did it?" She sniffed. "Anyway, at least he's in jail now. And scheduled for execution." She pointed a finger at Lilliana. "Mark my words—it starts with letting a bodyslave speak to you like an equal and ends with a bellyful of poison or some other horrible violence. You have to keep on top of them *all the time.*"

"I…I don't believe that," Lilli said, but now she wasn't quite sure what to think. Was Priss telling the truth? Was there really another Kindred bodyslave who had ripped off his Mistress's head?

*Surely not,* she thought. *Priss is just trying to frighten me because she's such an awful bully.*

Priss shrugged. "Look it up for yourself. Your mother is the Archivist for the Sacred Seven, isn't she? She ought to have all the information on file."

"I don't have to look it up to know you're lying. You're just jealous." Lilli frowned at the other girl. "Because I have a Kindred bodyslave and you don't."

"The Kindred bodyslaves *do* have the biggest shafts," Beelie remarked and Bodie nodded.

"Certainly he's the biggest we've ever seen. Well, except for that Trollox bodyslave Mother had for a while but he was *disgusting.*"

The twins shivered together as though remembering something truly horrific.

Priss frowned, her blue eyes narrowing.

"How dare you say the Kindred's shaft is bigger than my bodyslave's?"

"Well, because it *is,*" Yulla pointed out. She looked between H'rare and Karn, frowning in a confused way. "Isn't it? Didn't you admit that yourself?"

"That doesn't matter!" Priss snapped. "I don't care how big your bodyslave's shaft is," she added, glaring at Lilli. "Because I *know* my slave can beat him in a seed-shooting contest!"

"A what?" Lilli asked, frowning.

Bodie and Beelie giggled behind their hands.

"Oh my—she doesn't even know what a seed-shooting contest is!" Bodie whispered loudly to her twin.

"They must have kept her so *ignorant* in that convent!" Beelie whispered back.

"A seed-shooting contest is where you take your slave in hand and give him a manual release," Priss explained loftily. "Of course, my H'rare can shoot *more* seed *farther* than any other bodyslave in Opulex. But I wouldn't expect your Kindred to be able to compete at that level—seeing as how you all live out in the country here and you have such backwards ways."

"Karn can beat your slave at anything!" Lilli said hotly. She was tired of the other girl's posturing—tired of being bullied in her own home. "Anywhere, anytime," she added.

"Fine." Priss gave her a nasty smile. "Prove it."

# THIRTEEN

Well *this* was a fucking interesting turn of events, Karn thought dryly. Though he supposed he shouldn't be surprised. H'rare had warned him in the kitchens—once they found them—that his Mistress was a monster.

"A fucking cruel bitch," was how the other bodyslave had put it, his face a twisted mask of helpless rage. "But I can't do anything but obey her because she'll send me to the Diluthian mines otherwise."

"I'm sorry, Brother—you have a heavy burden to bear." Karn had clapped him on the shoulder.

"Your Mistress seems all right," H'rare said. "Or at least she's not a sadist."

"Lilli is something special," Karn admitted, as much to himself as to the other male. "But she was raised in a convent—not that snake's nest they call Opulex. It's made her kinder and less jaded than the other Mistresses, I think."

"You're lucky," H'rare had said with feeling. "I'd do anything to have a Mistress like that."

Karn had to admit that he *was* lucky—especially since he hadn't expected to have someone like Lilli for his Mistress. When he had accepted this mission, he'd gone with the idea that Lady Mirabella would be the one who bought him.

*The Goddess is looking out for me to send me to Lilli instead,* he'd thought. *She must approve of my mission.*

He had thought it again when he and the other bodyslave came back into the banquet hall and he'd heard Priss speaking about a jailed Kindred bodyslave. Then he'd heard that the poor bastard was scheduled for execution.

*Have to look into that,* he'd told himself. As soon as he knew where to look, anyway. The trip to the kitchen hadn't gotten him any closer to finding Lady Mirabella's private office, though he *did* have a better understanding of the layout of the vast mansion now.

He got an even better one now, as everyone at the dinner table got up and trooped out the golden double doors to stand on the broad marble balcony.

"Wherever are you girls going?" Lady Mirabella called as they left the table.

"Out for some air, Mistress Mirabella," Priss called helpfully before Lilli could say anything. "And to admire your view—I understand it's quite breathtaking."

"Oh, well—so it is." Lady Mirabella preened. "Thank you, Priss— do enjoy yourselves."

"Oh, we *will.*" Priss's blue eyes flashed as she glanced at Lilli.

Karn didn't like the way the other girl was glaring at his little Mistress one bit, but again, there was nothing he could do unless Priss offered Lilli some kind of physical harm. Until that happened, he had to keep his mouth shut and his hands to himself.

In the moonlight streaming down from above, the balcony was a vast, silvery gray platform. Far to the South, Karn could the lights of Opulex gleaming. A waist-high banister ran around the edge of the marble platform for safety, but he was going to be certain Lilli got nowhere near it. They were eighty stories up and a gust of wind might carry her away.

"So…how exactly does this contest work?" Lilli asked uncertainly as Bodie and Beelie closed the double doors to preserve their privacy.

"It's easy enough." Priss shrugged. "You just release your bodyslave's stay-hard band, take him in hand and stimulate him until he shoots his seed. Whoever's bodyslave shoots the farthest and the most wins."

"Oh, uh…I see."

Lilli looked up at Karn uncertainly and he could tell that she didn't want to touch him without permission. He caught her wide brown eyes and gave a brief nod, letting her know it was okay. He didn't love the idea of being in a jerk-off contest but if it was Lilli's soft little hand doing the jerking, he thought he could live with it.

"What's the matter?" Priss sneered, seeing Lilli's hesitation. "Haven't you ever manipulated a male to completion before?"

"Well…no." Lilli lifted her chin. "But I'm sure my Karn will win."

"I wouldn't be too sure about that. Here—I'll go first. Come at once, H'rare."

Her bodyslave came to her obediently and Priss unbuckled the stay-hard band from around his shaft. Then she positioned him so that he was standing about five feet from the banister at the edge of the balcony and stood beside him.

"Listen up, H'rare," she told him as she began to roughly jerk his shaft. "You'd better shoot a *lot* of seed and shoot it *far*. If you don't win this contest for me, you'll be in real trouble!"

"Yes…Mistress," H'rare panted. His legs were spread and he appeared to be doing his best to hold still as his Mistress jerked at his shaft. At last, with a loud grunt, he came. His seed shot a good three feet and landed with a *splat* on the marble balcony.

"There!" Priss straightened up and wiped her hands on a handkerchief daintily. "Beat *that*," she said to Lilli. "And remember if you don't, you forfeit your slave to *me.*"

"You never said anything about that!" Lilli exclaimed, her face turning pale. "I refuse to put Karn up as any kind of prize."

"But that's *always* the way it is with a seed-shooting contest," Beelie protested.

"Yes, the winner gets the loser's slave," Bodie agreed with her twin. "Priss took my bodyslave, Yorn that way."

"And then sent him to the mines," Beelie added, frowning. "Which really wasn't very nice."

Priss made a shooing gesture as though it was of no consequence.

"He was troublesome and didn't kiss my feet the right way. But the point is, Lilliana, you *can't* go against the rules of the seed-shooting contest. Why, if your Kindred beats my H'rare, you get to keep *my* bodyslave—it's only fair if it works the other way as well."

Lilli opened her mouth—clearly to refuse again—but Karn put a hand on her arm.

"It's all right, little Mistress," he murmured. "I can handle it."

She looked up at him, her big eyes huge.

"Are you sure, Karn? I don't…don't want to lose you."

"You won't," he assured her. He wasn't worried about the contest —he knew his own physical limits very well and he was certain he could outmatch Priss's bodyslave. Plus, this way maybe H'rare could get free of the sadistic Mistress. It might be his only chance to live, since she apparently regularly sent her bodyslaves to the Diluthian mines.

"All right." Lilli nodded at him. "I trust you, Karn."

"Then release my shaft and take me in your soft little hand, Mistress," Karn growled. "Let me win this contest for you."

# FOURTEEN

Lilli did as he said with shaking hands. She had only gotten the big Kindred bodyslave that day but already she felt extremely attached to him. She never would have agreed to the contest Priss had challenged her to if she'd known she might lose him.

*But he seems very confident,* she told herself, trying to calm her nerves. *Maybe he knows something I don't—maybe Kindred can shoot their seed especially far.*

She hoped so, anyway, because if Priss took Karn away from her and then sent him to the awful Diluthian mines, she didn't know what she'd do.

Karn stepped to a spot right beside H'rare, who was standing there with a limp shaft, now that he had spent his load. Priss was watching with a look of barely suppressed glee in her sharp blue eyes. Clearly she thought she had this contest in the bag.

*Well, we'll see about that!* Lilli thought and positioned herself to the side and a little behind Karn, so that she could reach around and grasp his shaft.

He was so thick at the base she couldn't get her fingers wrapped all the way around him but that didn't matter—she was still able to get a good hold on the warm, pulsing cock in her hand.

Lilli liked the way his skin felt—soft as petals but hot and hard at the same time. Thank goodness the shaft oil she'd used on him earlier made him slippery enough that she could slide her hand up and down without too much resistance.

She felt him stiffen as she began to stroke, his big, muscular body tensing against her much smaller one.

"Gods, little Mistress," he groaned as she slid her fingers up and down his thickness. "Your little hand on me feels so *good!*"

Priss pursed her thin lips.

"You shouldn't let your bodyslave talk to you that way, Lilliana!" she lectured.

But Lilli found she liked it—liked hearing the groans of pleasure from the big Kindred and knowing she had caused them. So she didn't answer the other girl—she just kept stroking.

"Come on, Karn," she murmured, for his ears alone. "Come for me—shoot your seed just for me."

Her words seemed to have a great effect on the big Kindred because he suddenly stood stock still and Lilli felt his shaft growing even bigger and harder in her hand. Then, with a low roar, he shot his seed.

Lilli watched it fly, looking like a silver stream, out into the moonlight. It soared past the puddle H'rare had left and over the balcony—a full six feet, she was certain—before falling to the ground far below.

"There!" She turned in triumph to Priss, whose lips were compressed into a nearly invisible line. "Karn won!"

"He did not!" Priss's eyes flashed dangerously. "He *lost* because we didn't get to see how much he shot. So by rights your bodyslave is now *mine.*"

"What? No! That's not right!" Lilli exclaimed, her hands clenching into fists at her side. "You said the winner was whoever shot further and Karn clearly did."

"It's not just distance, it's the *amount* of seed," Priss argued, glaring at her. "And since he shot over the side of the balcony and we can't see the amount, H'rare is clearly the winner! So you have to give your slave to *me.*"

"Never!" Lilli glared back at her. She might give way to the other girl to a certain point because she wasn't used to fighting with such an awful bully, but there *were* limits to what she would endure.

"You *have* to!" Priss snapped. "If you don't—"

"Mistress, let me suggest a rematch," Karn said, putting a hand on Lilli's shoulder to get her attention. "We can move further from the edge of the balcony so I'll be certain not to shoot off the edge."

"Yes—a rematch!" Lilli exclaimed, grasping at the idea.

"What? But we'll have to wait at least fifteen minutes for that," Priss said, frowning. "Everyone knows a male has to recover for a time before they can shoot their seed again."

"Not me," Karn said simply.

Lilli looked down and saw that he was right—his massive shaft was still as hard as it had been before he'd shot his seed for her.

Priss looked as well and her eyes widened in apparent surprise.

"But everyone knows the second load of seed is much *smaller* than the first," she protested, still trying to find a way out of the rematch.

"Then test my second load against H'rare's first," Karn suggested.

Lilli looked up at him fearfully. She didn't know much about males and the amount of seed they made, but she couldn't help being worried.

"Karn, do you really think it's wise?"

He looked at her, his mismatched eyes half-lidded in the moonlight.

"Little Mistress, trust me. I can win this contest for you—I can and and I will. I'll do anything to feel your soft hands on me again."

Lilli felt her heart flutter as she looked up into his strangely beautiful mismatched eyes.

"Well...all right," she murmured. "If...if you think you can do it."

"I know I can," he promised. "Trust me."

Lilli nodded and turned to Priss.

"Well? Will you accept the terms?"

"Your Kindred's second load of seed against my H'rare's first?" Priss asked, nodded at the blob of white her own bodyslave had released.

Lilli nodded. "Yes."

"All right." A cruel smile curved Priss's thin lips. "Why not? Just be prepared to hand your bodyslave over to me once he finishes."

"That's *not* going to happen," Lilli said, lifting her chin. "Come on, Karn—show them what you can do," she said.

"As my Mistress wishes," he growled. "Take me in your hand again and let me prove my worth."

# FIFTEEN

Gods, Lilli's soft little hand on him felt good! Karn willingly submitted to her slender fingers curling around his shaft again. He had no fears about losing the contest. All Kindred males were multi-orgasmic and he produced more seed than most. So when Lilli began to stroke him again, he pumped his hips and fucked into her delicate hand with confidence and pleasure.

He could feel her behind him, her full, plump breasts—bare except for the sheer top she wore, pressed against his back. The sensation made him remember sucking her ripe pink nipples into his mouth which made him even harder. Gods, if only he could lick her lower too! If only he could press his face between her legs and kiss and lick her ripe little pussy…

The thought of tasting her got him off almost as much as her soft little hand stroking him. With a low groan, Karn came for a second time—this time making sure his seed splattered on the marble floor of the balcony, not a foot from H'rare's offering.

He willed himself to keep it up, drawing out his orgasm with thoughts of kissing and licking Lilli's pussy as she continued to stroke him. Pumping into her hand, he imagined he was coming inside her, filling her up, making her his as he bonded the two of them together forever…

That was impossible, of course—only a fantasy. As a Hybrid, he couldn't bond a female to him. But just thinking of making Lilli his forever made him come over and over, the seed jetting out of the tip of his cock and forming a large, silvery puddle beside the small splatter of the other bodyslave's seed.

At last he finished coming, though his shaft still didn't go down.

He stood, panting a little beside Lilli. His little Mistress had stopped stroking him, though she still hadn't moved her hand from his shaft. She seemed to like the feel of him, Karn thought as she continued to cup him loosely.

"Wow," Yulla remarked, taking a step forward to look down at the puddle of seed. "That's amazing! I've *never* seen a male shoot that much!"

"Us, either!" Bodie and Beelie came up for a look as well.

"Well, I guess you finally lost, Priss," Bodie remarked.

"Which means that H'rare now belongs to Lilliana—right?" Beelie asked.

Priss's thin lips had narrowed down to an invisible line in her face and her blue eyes were flashing.

"Fine," she said at last, glaring at Lilli. "You win—*this* time. H'rare!" she bellowed at her bodyslave who came to stand beside her quickly.

"Yes, Mistress?" he asked uncertainly.

"Well, I'm not your Mistress anymore, am I you *idiot!*" Priss screamed in his face "Go on—get away from me!" She threw his stay-hard band at his face but H'rare ducked and it sailed over the balcony.

Quickly, he ran to stand behind Lilli and Karn.

"I'm tired of this," Priss abruptly announced. "I'm going inside."

She turned and flounced back through the golden double doors in a huff.

"We'd better go too!" Beelie and Bodi and Yulla and their bodyslaves all hurried in after her.

Lilli sagged in relief and then realized she was still touching Karn intimately.

She pulled her hand reluctantly away and looked up at him.

"You did it," she murmured, smiling. "You beat him."

"Couldn't have done it without you, little Mistress," he growled, smiling. "Come on, let's go back in before she gets up to any more mischief."

# SIXTEEN

Priss was in a *terrible* mood once they got back inside but there was clearly nothing she could do about it. H'rare wasn't hers anymore, so she couldn't take out her ire on her former bodyslave. She was reduced to slamming her cup on the table and clattering her utensils loudly against her platinum plate. She remained mute and refused to talk, which meant the other girls at the table were reluctant to speak as well, since she was clearly the leader of their little band.

Lilli carried on the conversation as well as she could, making small talk and asking questions but getting only monosyllabic answers from the others. She was immensely relieved when her mother and the other Mistresses rose from their table at last and began getting ready to go.

"Come, Priss," Mistress Tempertant called as they left the banquet hall and began gathering their things in the entryway. "It's a long way back to Opulex and I must get up early tomorrow for a meeting."

"Yes, Mother." Priss flounced over, her arms crossed over her nearly non-existent breasts, a scowl still on her face. "I'm ready," she announced. "Let's get out of here!"

"All right." Lady Tempertant frowned. "But where's your latest bodyslave? The one that cost me so much at the Flesh Bazaar?"

H'rare, of course, was nowhere in sight because Lilli had sent him away with Karn. She'd thought it was best if the two of them were out of the way for just this reason.

"I lost him," Priss said shortly.

"*Lost* him?" Lady Tempertant's eyebrows—which were as purple as her hair—lifted incredulously. "What—do you mean he's run away?"

"If so, I'm certain we can find him," Mistress Mirabella said quickly. "I'll have my catcher-bots deployed at once!"

"He didn't run away," Priss snapped. "Lilliana won him from me. She asked if we could do a seed-shooting contest with our bodyslaves as prizes."

This was such a bald-faced lie that Lilli found herself speechless for a moment. Unfortunately, her mother always had something to say.

"Lilliana!" she exclaimed, rounding on her. "How *dare* you suggest playing games of chance with your guests? Don't you know how rude it is to take away another Mistress's bodyslave?"

"I…but I…" Lilli began helplessly.

"Oh, I don't really mind," Priss cut in. "Besides, I felt sorry for Lilliana, so I let her win."

"You felt sorry for her?" Mistress Tempertant frowned at her daughter. "What are you talking about, young lady?"

"Well, I felt sorry for her because she's the only one of us girls who *isn't* expecting," Priss explained. A cruel smile curved her lips. "She was just saying how she so *wanted* to be in fashion and have her heir early, so she didn't have to worry about it later."

"I never—" Lilli began indignantly but once again she was cut off.

"Oh, poor dear! It truly is a shame she's so behind the times." Lady Tempertant clucked her tongue disapprovingly. "Tell me,

Mirabella, is there some *medical* reason she can't have a quick-grow heir like the other girls?"

"Oh no—certainly not!" Lilli's mother exclaimed. "It's just that she hasn't been here long—I only picked her up from the convent last week and brought her home. And I didn't realize—"

"That having an heir early was the fashion now? Ah, such a pity." Lady Tempertant shook her bushy purple head. "But that's what happens when you live *outside* of Opulex—fashions change so rapidly and it's easy to fall behind."

"Lilliana is *not* behind," Lady Mirabella said quickly. "Why, I have plans to take her to the conception center by the end of this week!"

"Then you'll want her to start taking the quick-grow shots *now,*" Lady Tempertant advised. "I'll tell you what—I have an extra quick-grow kit out in my hovercraft. I *was* going to give it to Lady Toodleoo for her daughter when I saw her next, but I can send my servant out for another one to give to her later."

"Oh, really?" Lady Mirabella clasped her hands between her breasts. "Thank you, my dear Mistress Tempertant! That's so kind of you!"

"Not at all…" Lady Tempertant waved a hand dismissively. "After all, you're part of the Sacred Seven now—we can't have you or your daughter looking less than fashionable, now can we?"

"The next time you see us, Lilli will be expecting her heir," Lady Mirabella promised, much to Lilli's horror.

"Excellent." Lady Tempertant nodded. "Let me send my bodyslave to get the kit—ah, here he is already. Excellent, Yorn!" she said to her bodyslave, who had broad shoulders and shaggy black hair. "He's so good at anticipating my needs," she told Lilli's mother. "I swear I haven't even *considered* sending him to the mines more than once or twice since I've had him."

She took the kit from her bodyslave's hands—it looked like a miniature black briefcase, Lilli thought numbly—and opened it. Inside were two long, silver syringes with wickedly sharp multi-needles. They were filled with a bright green formula that looked poisonous.

"Now, you'll want to give her one in the evening about a week before she goes to the conception center and one the night right before she goes," she instructed. "Of course, there are a *few* side effects."

"Side…side effects?" Lilli finally managed to get out through lips that felt as dry as dust.

"Oh my, yes! There's quite a strong ovulatory response. It made my Priss rather grumpy, don't you know?" Lady Tempertant giggled. "But of course that's necessary in order to get the womb ready for implantation by whatever sperm you pick. And it makes the process at the conception center *so* much easier."

"It does?" Lady Mirabella frowned.

"Well, you *know* how large those conception injectors are. Why they can't modify them to be a bit more manageable, I really don't know."

"You certainly have a point, there." Lilli's mother nodded sagely. "So how do the shots help?"

"Why, by the time the chemical cocktail in these finishes working on them, all the girls are just *dying* for the conception injection!" Lady Tempertant tapped the silver and glass syringes in the case meaningfully with one sharp fingernail. "Priss even insisted on going back *twice*—just to be certain the process had taken, of course," she added.

"Mother!" Priss glared at her. "That's *private.*"

"Sorry, my pet, but you can't deny it's true. The quick-grow formula is really *quite* strong," Mistress Tempertant remarked.

"Yes, it is." Priss's frown was abruptly replaced by a thin, crafty smile. "Mother, don't you think it would be better if you showed Mistress Mirabella how to give the injection? After all, didn't she say that Lilliana is scheduled at the conception center in a week? So wouldn't tonight be the best time to give her the first shot?"

"Well, you know, I do believe you're right, my dear." Lady

Tempertant turned to Lilli's mother. "Would you like me to show you?"

"Yes, indeed—please do!" Mistress Mirabella nodded eagerly.

"Very well. Now, it goes in the inner thigh…"

And Lady Tempertant plucked one of the syringes out of the box and came towards Lilli.

# SEVENTEEN

U p until that moment, Lilli had been held in a kind of trance—
frozen in place by the awful things being said. She kept
thinking to herself that the other women could talk all they wanted
but the minute everyone left she was going to tell her mother she
didn't feel ready to have a baby yet. Why, she had only just come of
age herself! She had no wish to suddenly get pregnant!

But now, with Lady Tempertant bearing down on her with that
awful syringe and its multi-needle spikes leaking bright green fluid,
she found it was too late.

"Stop!" She turned to her mother belatedly. "Mother, wait—can't
we talk about this?"

"What's there to talk about, Lilliana?" her mother snapped. "Mistress Tempertant has graciously offered to give you your first injection. Now hold still and take it!"

"But I don't *want* it!" Lilli protested wildly, still backing away. She
wished desperately that she hadn't sent Karn away. She was certain the
big Kindred would have had her back. But she was all alone, with no
one to help her. What was she going to do?"

"Is this a problem?" Lady Tempertant frowned. "Does your daughter not *wish* to be in style?"

"Oh, she's just scared of needles—that's all!" Lilli's mother said quickly. "H'urk—Tonlor—hold her!"

Two of her mother's hulking bodyslaves came quickly to grab Lilli by her arms. She struggled but there was no helping it—they were so much stronger than her and they obeyed her mother without question.

"Please!" she begged, feeling tears sting her eyes. Her throat felt thick and her heart was pounding. "Mother, *please*—I don't *want* this!"

"Hush, Lilliana and don't be a baby!" her mother scolded angrily. "It'll be over in a moment!"

Lilli choked back a sob—there was no help here. Above all things, her mother hated to be out of fashion. And since they lived outside of Opulex, falling behind the times and being thought of as a "country bumpkin" was her greatest fear.

Bending down, Lady Tempertant pressed the wickedly sharp end of the multi-needle to the inside of Lilli's thigh. Lilli gasped as she felt the bite of a thousand tiny pricks as the metal spikes sank into her flesh. The next moment she had a painful itching sensation as the burning liquid invaded her flesh.

"No!" she cried but it was more of a moan.

It was too late—the deed had been done and she'd been injected with the awful quick-grow hormone stuff. Who knew what would happen to her now?

"There—see? All done," Lady Tempertant straightened up briskly and put the first syringe back in the case. "And you only need one more on the night before you go to the conception center. Before you know it, you'll have a baby bump just like my Priss."

She smiled at her daughter who nodded and smiled back. Then she turned her smile on Lilli and it became a smug sneer.

"Enjoy getting impregnated, Lilliana," she purred. "I'm sure you'll find it very *entertaining*. Oh, and tell H'rare if I ever see him again, I'll have him castrated," she added in an off-hand way.

Then she and her mother and the rest of the Mistresses waved goodbye and left.

Lilli watched them go, feeling strange and somehow detached from her own body. The place where she had been injected was painfully tender but all she could think about was the fact that she wasn't ready to have a baby yet and she didn't know what she was going to do.

# EIGHTEEN

"Little Mistress, what's wrong?" Karn looked at his new Mistress with concern. She'd sent him and H'rare away as the banquet was ending and he'd placed the other bodyslave in the kitchens, which seemed like a safe place for him. He could help with the serving and hopefully escape Lady Mirabella's notice. Then Karn had gone back up to Lilli's suite to wait for her.

But when she came in, she seemed detached and distant. And... were those tear tracks on her pale cheeks? Karn needed to make sure.

"Mistress," he said again, since she hadn't answered him. "What's wrong?"

"I...I don't...I can't talk about it." Avoiding his eyes, she went to the bed and laid face down on it. "Please, Karn—just leave me alone. You can have the rest of the night off." Her voice was muffled in the bedclothes but she sounded very close to tears.

Karn knew he ought to go—this was the perfect opportunity to explore the rest of the vast mansion and find the information he was seeking. He especially wanted to see if he could locate the Kindred warrior who had been accused of murder and sentenced to execution.

But he couldn't leave just yet. Not when Lilli was so upset. He couldn't help himself—he *had* to know what was wrong.

"Come on now, little Mistress," he murmured, going to sit on the bed beside her. "It can't be as bad as all that, can it?"

"Yes, it can." Lilli's voice was barely a whisper, but he could hear the quiver in it.

"What happened?" Karn asked. "Did that Priss bitch say or do something else to you after you sent me away?"

Just the thought made him clench his hands into fists. That little sadist was a piece of work, all right! He didn't like the way she tried to win him away from Lilli, just to hurt her.

"You could say that." Lilli turned her head so that he could see at least the side of her face. She looked miserable, Karn thought, and his heart squeezed in his chest.

"What did she do?" he demanded. "I thought we got her pretty good with the seed-shooting contest. And you probably saved her bodyslave's life," he added. "If you hadn't won him, he'd be off to the Diluthian mines in a matter of days."

"I'm glad he's okay," Lilli whispered. "But, well, I'm *not.*"

"What happened?" Karn urged. He put a hand on her back, feeling her soft skin through the silky, see-through top she still wore. "Please tell me, little Mistress."

"I…she…" Lilli's face twisted in a way that showed she was trying not to cry. "She told my mother that I wanted…wanted to get impregnated—like the rest of the girls," she whispered. "You know I *don't* but she convinced my mother to give me the first quick-grow shot. And now Mother's on the viewscreen this minute making an appointment for me at the conception center for the end of the week!"

"What?" Karn frowned. "That's fucking awful, Lilli! Can't you tell her no? That you don't want to do it?"

Lilli shook her head.

"It's all the rage right now and Mother is *so afraid* of falling out of fashion. She'll do *anything* to keep up with the Mistresses who live in Opulex."

"Well, that doesn't give her the right to force you to have a baby!" Karn said indignantly.

"I tried to tell her I didn't want one—that I wasn't ready. But she wouldn't...wouldn't listen."

Lilli's words ended in a sob and she buried her face in her arms, her shoulders shaking with muted grief.

Karn sat there feeling helpless. His heart ached for Lilli. He wanted desperately to solve this problem for her, but it seemed to be beyond him. How could he, in his role as a lowly bodyslave, stop the evil Mistress Mirabella from forcing her daughter to have a baby before she felt ready? There was nothing he could do. Nothing that wouldn't end up with him being executed or sent to the Diluthian mines for insubordination, that was.

Nothing but try to comfort Lilli.

"Come here, little Mistress," he murmured, turning her over. Her face was red from crying as he pulled her into his lap and wrapped his arms around her.

"Karn..." She buried her face in his chest and sobbed miserably. "Karn, I'm not ready! I might not mind having a baby if I had someone to help me raise it. But I don't want to just have one and then shove it off on a nannybot or send it to a convent. I can't...I just *can't.*"

"You shouldn't have to," Karn said fiercely. He frowned thoughtfully. "But you know...who *says* you have to?"

"Who says?" Lilli looked up at him, her brown eyes still filled with tears. "Why, *Mother* says. And she'll be so angry she'll probably disinherit me if I don't show up at the conception center!"

Karn was thinking hard.

"Okay, she wants you to go to the center. But tell me this—does the conception process *always* work?"

"Well...no." Lilli sniffed. "I've heard of some Mistresses having to try two or three or even seven or eight times. And with some it never takes and they have to have their baby in an artificial womb—which is *very* unfashionable," she added.

"I'm sure it is," Karn said dryly. "But listen, why not go to the center and just *not* have the process done."

"What?" Lilli looked scandalized. "Are you serious?"

"Of course I am!" Karn told her. "Listen, why not let your Mother *think* you've had the impregnation procedure done and that it didn't take? Then you don't have to have a baby you're not ready for, and it won't be your fault."

Lilli's tear-streaked face brightened.

"You know, the process *is* fully automated. So it's not like there's an attendant who can tell on me for not having it done."

"Sounds like the way to go, then," Karn remarked.

"Oh, do you really think that would work? You think I could pull it off?"

Karn shrugged.

"Why not? Unless your mother comes in the center with you, I don't see how she could know you didn't really have the procedure done."

"She won't," Lilli said quickly. "She's already talking about sending me by myself—well, with you along, of course—because she's going to be busy that day."

"Well, there you go." Karn grinned at her. "Problem solved."

"You know…you could be right." A tentative smile came over her face as she looked up at him. "Karn, what would I do without you?"

"Get impregnated by some cold machine, I guess." He shook his head and grinned at her. "Luckily for you, I *am* here."

"I *am* lucky to have you." Lilli sighed and snuggled in his arms and looked up at him. "Tell me something—why do I feel so comfortable around you?" she asked and yawned. "Why do I feel like you're the piece of my life that I've been missing for years without even knowing it?"

"I don't know, little Mistress." Karn cuddled her close. "But I kind of feel the same way about you," he admitted—both to himself and to her.

What was happening to him? Was he going soft? He was on a mission here, he reminded himself. He had to find the Kindred warriors who had been taken by the Yonites as bodyslaves and get that information back to the Mother Ship.

And yet, he couldn't bring himself to stop holding Lilli. The very full day and the emotional release of her tears seemed to have tired her out. She cuddled against his chest like a sleepy kitten and sighed contentedly.

"You're falling asleep, little Mistress," Karn murmured. "Let's get you changed for bed. Where's your nightdress?"

"In the closet. One of the drawers on…" Lilli yawned. "On the right."

Karn laid her gently on the bed and went to find the garment in question. After searching through several drawers, he finally found a sheer, silky white gown as virginal and innocent as Lilli herself.

He also found a pair of long white sleep trousers made of the same silky material for himself. Were they the remnant of some former bodyslave who had been sent to the mines by Lilli's mother? The thought didn't bear thinking about. Karn grabbed them along with the nightdress—at least they had a crotch, which made them preferable to the black leather trousers he was wearing now.

Coming back to the bed, he helped Lilli undress—yawning all the time—and got her into the soft little nightdress. He took down her hair, letting it flow free over her shoulders, and removed the diamond nipple drops as well. Then he tucked her under the covers and—very gently because he couldn't help himself—placed a tender kiss on her forehead.

This seemed to wake Lilli up again because as he turned to go, she reached for him.

"Karn," she begged, putting a hand on his arm. "Don't go. Sleep with me tonight."

Karn frowned.

"Sleep with you? Is that proper, little Mistress?"

She shook her head, her honey blonde curls tumbled around her face.

"I don't care about that. I want you beside me—please?"

Karn couldn't deny her. Exchanging the uncomfortable bodyslave gear for the sleep trousers, he slipped under the covers with her.

Lilli turned to him at once and pillowed her head on his chest.

"Mmm, you're so warm, Karn," she murmured and yawned again before snuggling even closer to him.

Karn put an arm around her and relished the feel of her soft, curvy body pressed against his own. This was certainly not the way he'd expected to end his first night as a bodyslave on Yonnie Six, but he wasn't complaining.

Later, when she was completely asleep, he would get up and search for Mistress Mirabella's private study. But for now, he told himself, he would simply enjoy holding the curvy little female in his arms.

She felt so right there—it was a shame their relationship was only temporary.

The thought made his heart fist in his chest and he pushed it away. As long as he was here, he would live in the moment, he promised himself. He would get his mission accomplished, but he wouldn't think about the end or leaving Lilli. He would stay with her and care for her as long as he could…

It was the only thing he could do.

# NINETEEN

L illi woke up the next morning because her leg was tingling. The inside of her left thigh felt so strange and the tingling seemed to be moving…changing. What was wrong with her?

She shifted and felt an unfamiliar sensation—someone else was in the bed with her.

At first she thought she was back at the convent and one of the other girls had climbed in her bunk in the middle of the night to keep warm. The convent was built of centuries-old solid gray stone which seemed to hold in the cold and chill no matter what season or temperature it was outside.

But none of the other girls at the convent had been so big…or so muscular. And none of them had smelled so *good*. A warm, dark, masculine spice that seemed to awaken all her senses and make the tingling in her leg move up to the tips of her breasts and between her legs.

The tingling got stronger and Lilli shifted and squeezed her thighs together tightly, trying to ease the ache which was growing there. This action pressed her bottom against the person behind her and she felt a hard lump rubbing between her thighs.

*Mmm, feels good,* Lilli thought. Still half asleep, she parted her thighs a bit and tilted her hips backwards. This pressed the hard lump directly against her outer pussy lips, which felt even *better.*

With a little moan, Lilli widened her stance, opening her thighs and pressing back *hard*, so that the heated ridge of flesh parted her outer lips and rubbed her sensitive inner folds.

It wasn't exactly an ideal angle, but suddenly she felt so hot and needy between her legs, she couldn't seem to help herself. She moaned again and pressed harder, working herself against the hardness, getting closer and closer to the peak she so desperately needed to reach...

"Having fun, little Mistress?" a deep voice rumbled in her ear.

Lilli gasped and froze, uncertain of what was going on and who was behind her.

*Karn!* whispered a little voice in her head as she finally came fully awake. *Your new bodyslave—remember? You asked him to sleep with you and now you're rubbing against him like a she-slink in heat!*

Deeply embarrassed, Lilli pulled away and clamped her thighs closed. What was wrong with her? She had never done anything like this before. Then again, she'd never slept with a male in her bed before either. But having a male in her bed couldn't explain her wanton behavior, or the tingling neediness she felt in her nipples and pussy...

"Hey, Lilli?" the big Kindred rumbled. Taking her by the shoulder, he tugged gently until she turned to face him.

"I'm sorry." Lilli could feel how hot her cheeks were—it almost felt like she had a fever! "I...I didn't mean to," she said, unable to meet his eyes. "I was...I was only half awake and I didn't...didn't know what I was doing."

"It felt to me like you were rubbing your soft little pussy against my shaft," Karn murmured. He looked down at the white silk sleep trousers he was wearing and Lilli was mortified to see that there was a wet spot over the straining bulge of his morning erection.

"Oh my Goddess—did I do that?" She felt like she wanted to sink through the bed and then keep on going, through the building beneath them and on into the ground, straight to the center of the planet. Anything so she wouldn't have to see the embarrassing result of her morning desire. "I'm so sorry!" she told Karn. "I never meant to—I mean I don't...don't know why I would *do* such a thing."

"Maybe because you were feeling excited?" he suggested. He lifted her chin with one finger so that she had to meet his eyes. "Hey, Lilli —don't look so upset. I don't mind."

"You...you don't?" Lilli looked up at him, searching his gold and blue eyes to see if he was telling the truth.

"Hell, no." He gave her that charming, crooked grin of his and she felt herself melting a little.

"I...but I ruined your sleep trousers," she pointed out.

"No you didn't. And even if you had, I wouldn't care," Karn murmured. "I think it's damn sexy your little pussy got so hot and wet when you rubbed against me. Hell, if I hadn't had the trousers on, I might have slipped right in the way you were working yourself on my shaft."

Lilli looked at him with wide eyes.

"Then it's a really good thing you had them on! Mistresses are *never* supposed to let their bodyslaves penetrate them."

"Of course not," Karn agreed easily. "But they don't generally let their bodyslaves sleep with them, either—do they?"

Lilli bit her lip.

"I...I guess not. I was just so upset last night and you were so sweet about holding me and making me feel better. I...I didn't want you to leave."

"That's all right, little Mistress—I didn't want to leave either," he murmured and brushed a strand of hair out of her eyes. "You're beautiful in the morning—you know that?"

Lilli blushed again, but this time in pleasure.

"You really shouldn't say such things to me," she murmured.

"But shouldn't a bodyslave always tell his Mistress the truth?" Karn countered. "How can I lie when you look so fucking gorgeous?"

"Karn…" Reaching up, she cupped his cheek in one palm. She liked the rough scratch of his morning whiskers against her palm. "You're beautiful too," she whispered. "Or, well, handsome, I guess you'd say."

"Thank you." He turned his head and pressed a kiss to her palm.

"You know, when Mother said I had to get a bodyslave, I didn't expect to like him," Lilli admitted. "I've always been a little bit afraid of males—maybe because I was raised in an all-female convent. I liked one of my mother's bodyslaves who was kind to me, but she sent him to the mines years ago and I never really got to know any others." She sighed. "What I'm trying to say is, I never thought I'd feel this way about a male—especially my own bodyslave."

"And what way are you feeling, little Mistress?" His mismatched eyes were half-lidded as he asked the question.

"I…I don't know," Lilli confessed. "I just know that when I'm with you I feel safe and protected. And I like talking to you and being around you." She shook her head. "I don't have a word for all that, I don't think. I just know I want to be near you."

"Want to be near you too, baby," he murmured, stroking her hair again. "And it's okay not to have words for it—the feeling is enough, I think."

"I shouldn't let you call me baby or pet me like this," Lilli whispered, nuzzling against his hand. "And I shouldn't…shouldn't feel so strongly about a bodyslave. Especially when I only just met you yesterday."

"I know," Karn said simply. "But I don't see you kicking me out of your bed, Mistress."

"Maybe because I don't *want* to kick you out." Lilli gave him a flirtatious little smile, even though she knew she shouldn't flirt with her bodyslave. "But…" She paused, not sure how to continue.

"But what?" Karn asked and the look on his face said he was really interested and would wait all day if necessary to hear her thoughts.

"Well, it's just…something that Priss said last night that's kind of bothering me."

Karn snorted.

"Just *one* thing she said bothered you? I thought pretty much everything that came out of her mouth was fucking awful."

Lilli knew she shouldn't let him speak ill of another Mistress like that, but it just so happened that she agreed with him a hundred percent.

"She is *awful,*" she admitted. "But she said something about a Kindred bodyslave, uh, killing his Mistress."

"Oh yeah—I heard her talking about that." Karn's face was grim. "She was getting pretty graphic, wasn't she?"

"She said he…he ripped her head off," Lilli whispered. "But I thought you told me that the Kindred don't hurt women?"

"We don't." Karn's voice was firm. "We're biologically hardwired to protect and care for females. It's probably one reason we've become such a popular choice for bodyslaves among the Yonnite elite," he added ruefully.

"I'm sorry—I shouldn't have asked," Lilli said, looking down at her hands.

"Of course you should. You have a right to feel safe with me," Karn said, frowning. "It's my belief, though, that this Kindred bodyslave Priss was telling you about, was framed. I just don't see how any Kindred could kill a female so brutally—not even one who had enslaved him."

"Priss *did* say I ought to check my mother's records," Lilli said, brightening. "I wonder if she would have something about the case in her files?"

"Possibly," Karn rumbled, looking thoughtful. "Though you'd have to be certain not to do it when she was around. I could help you, little Mistress. We could investigate the case together."

"Oh, I like that!" Lilli exclaimed. "Like another secret—just between the two of us!"

"Exactly." Karn cleared his throat. "You, uh, know where your mother keeps her information from the Sacred Seven, do you?"

"Oh, yes. It's her private office in the far corner of the East Wing," Lilli said. "She showed it to me and gave me the combination to open the door the first day she brought me home. She's very proud of her place in the Sacred Seven," she added, frowning. "I think she hopes I'll follow in her footsteps."

"Do you want to?" Karn asked.

Lilli shook her head.

"Not really. Being in the Sacred Seven seems to mean attending lots and lots of parties and events and award ceremonies and banquets like the one last night." She made a face. "I *hate* that kind of thing. I'd much rather stay home and read a good book or watch a vid all snuggled up on the couch."

"You're an introvert," Karn said, giving her a smile. "I thought so. Being around a big group of people makes you feel nervous and drained."

"That's exactly how I feel!" Lilli looked up at him. "How can you already know me so well?"

Karn raised an eyebrow.

"Isn't it a bodyslave's job to know his Mistress's likes and dislikes?"

"Well, yes, I suppose. But I never knew of a bodyslave who took such an interest in his Mistress's thoughts and feelings before."

"Well, I'm interested in *yours*, little Mistress." Karn stroked her cheek. "*Very* interested. I want to prove to you that Kindred can be gentle."

"You...you do?" Lilli whispered. For some reason her heart had started pounding as she looked up into his mismatched eyes.

"We have to be," Karn rumbled. "After all, we're often so much larger than our mates. For instance, if you were my mate and I was going to make love to you, I'd be extremely careful because you're so much smaller...so delicate and sweet."

Lilli, who had always been on the plump side, had never been called "delicate" before. But she found she liked it—liked it a lot.

"What…what would you do if I was your mate?" she asked Karn. "I mean, how…how would you touch me?"

He stroked her cheek gently.

"Would you like me to show you, little Mistress? It might be easier for you to understand that way."

Lilli nodded her head even though she was pretty sure this was wrong.

"Yes," she whispered. "Yes, Karn—show me."

"Lie back against my arm, then."

He got her settled comfortably in the crook of one muscular arm so that Lilli was lying on her back and he was leaning over her.

"First of all," he murmured in her ear. "If you were my mate instead of my Mistress, I'd touch you very gently, all over."

Lilli shivered as his big, warm hand brushed lightly over her body, paying special attention to the ripe tips of her nipples, which were pressing up through the thin fabric of her nightdress, and the V between her legs. Involuntarily, she parted her thighs, giving the big Kindred easier access to her pussy, which was just barely covered by the bottom edge of her dress.

"Oh, Karn," she whispered. "That feels really *good.*"

"Of course it does, baby," he murmured, looking into her eyes as he brushed over her nipples again. "Feels good to me too, to bring you pleasure."

"You, uh, certainly are," Lilli admitted. "Though…" She bit her lip. "I'm not exactly sure you should be. Touching me like this, I mean."

"But I'm only touching you over your nightdress—just to show you how I would treat you if you were my mate," he pointed out. "I can stop if you want me to, though. I'll never do anything you don't want, Mistress."

"No, don't stop," Lilli begged softly. "I guess it's okay as long as I have my nightdress on. And…and you can call me Lilli or baby if you want to—just when we're alone, like this, I mean."

"Of course, baby," Karn rumbled. He cupped one of her breasts and leaned down to suck her nipple through the thin fabric.

"Ohhh…" Lilli moaned and arched up, thrusting her nipple more fully into his mouth. This wasn't so bad, she told herself. After all, he had sucked her nipples the night before when he was helping her apply the diamond nipple-drops. Surely it couldn't hurt to let him do it again.

But then his big hand moved down between her legs, to cup her pussy.

"Um…Karn?" she whispered breathlessly, shifting uncertainly under his hand. "I…I'm not sure about this."

He released her nipple with a sucking kiss and looked at her with half-lidded eyes.

"I'm just touching your soft little pussy to show you how I would treat you if you were my mate, baby," he murmured. "And of course, the nightdress is still between us. Though I can stop if you want."

He started to withdraw his hand but Lilli stopped him with a hand on his arm.

"No, wait!" she begged.

The need inside her was growing, the tingling that seemed to come from the place on her inner thigh where she had been injected the night before was growing stronger—more insistent.

"It's okay," she told Karn. "I mean, since we *do* have my night-dress between us."

"Yes, we do." His long fingers stroked over the sensitive outer lips of her pussy, tracing her slit with a light, teasing touch that made her feel hot and trembly all over. "Though of course," he added, "This thin little nightdress is so short that if you spread your thighs a little further it would pull up and only cover the *top* part of your soft little pussy. And I'm afraid that would leave the entrance to your pussy all open and bare."

"Oh…" Lilli bit her lip. "Would…would that still count as having the nightdress between us, do you think?"

Karn appeared to think about it for a moment.

"I think so, yes," he said at last, nodding. "After all, it would still be covering *part* of your pussy, which makes it more proper since you're my Mistress, not my mate."

"But I want to know what you'd do if I *was* your mate," Lilli whispered.

"Then maybe you'd better spread your thighs a little more, baby," Karn growled softly, looking down into her eyes. "Though I warn you, opening your thighs nice and wide might make your soft little pussy lips open too. And I can't promise that my fingers might not slip inside your hot little cunt."

His hot, dirty words made something low in her belly clench with need. Heart pounding and breath coming short, Lilli parted her thighs as wide as she could.

As Karn had said, the nightdress rose up with her gesture and her pussy lips—now swollen with need—parted as well, opening to show him her slippery inner folds.

She half expected the big Kindred to dive right in, but Karn surprised her by simply cupping her again.

"See there?" he murmured, nodding down to where he was touching her. "Your nightdress is still covering the top part of your soft little mound. So this is all right, don't you think, baby?"

Actually, Lilli thought it was *far* from all right and she couldn't believe she was acting this way. What would the Sisters of Chastity say if they could see her now?

But the tingling in her thigh, which had spread to the other sensitive parts of her body, was getting stronger. It helped her overcome her inhibitions and open to the big Kindred—it made her never want to stop.

"It...it's fine," she whispered, reaching up to stroke his bristly cheek again. "Now show me, Karn. Show me how you would touch me if you were my mate."

"I'd be very, very gentle," he murmured and she felt one long finger slide into her slippery folds and begin circling her clit. "Because you're a virgin, aren't you, baby?"

"Oh!" Lilli gasped and her hips bucked up at the gentle contact. "Oh, Goddess! Yes…yes, I am," she panted as Karn continued to pleasure her. "I mean I…I've never been penetrated before."

"And do you have a maiden barrier? Inside?" He illustrated by sliding that single finger into the opening of her pussy and pressing gently inward.

Lilli shook her head.

"N-no," she stuttered. "I know some females in other cultures or species do, but I don't."

"Good. Then there's nothing to stop me from doing *this*."

Karn slid his finger all the way inside her and she felt him press against the end of her channel.

"Oh!" Her hips bucked again. "That feels…different."

"Do you want me to stop?" His thumb had replaced his fingertip now and he was once again circling her aching clit. Lilli had the urge to press her legs together, to push him in deeper for some reason. She had to fight to keep her thighs spread wide instead.

"No," she whispered. "Oh, Karn, that feels so…so I don't even *know*. I…I feel like I'm climbing towards some kind of peak somehow."

"You're getting ready to come—to have an orgasm, baby," he murmured. "Have you ever had one before?"

Lilli shook her head doubtfully.

"I…I don't think so. I know an orgasm is what happens when males spend their seed. But I don't…I didn't know women could have them too."

"Oh, they most certainly *can*, little Mistress." Karn's eyes flashed. "It would be my very great pleasure to give you your first orgasm, if you'd let me."

"How…how will you do it?" Lilli gasped.

"Just like this," Karn assured her. "Slow, steady, gentle stroking all around your Goddess pearl should bring you over the edge before you know it."

"Yes," Lilli whispered, moving her hips again. "Oh Goddess, yes —I can see what you mean. Oh, Karn, I feel so *close*—"

"Lilliana, aren't you up yet?" her mother's voice interrupted her bliss—blasting from the com system box over her bed. "This is ridiculous! I've never known you to sleep in this late. Whatever are you still doing in your bedroom at this hour?"

# TWENTY

"I'm up!" Lilli jumped guiltily and looked at the box. Her heart was pounding as she sat up in bed and pulled the covers up to her chin, as though her mother could see her instead of just hearing her.

"Well get a shower and come down for breakfast," her mother instructed. "You can't stay all day in bed, sleeping your life away!"

"Yes, Mother," Lilli said quickly. "Are you waiting for me to eat?"

"Certainly not—I don't have time for that," Lady Mirabella snapped. "I have business to attend to. Oh—and while you're in the shower, be sure you shave. The Civics Award banquet is tonight and you'll need to wear formal panties along with your outfit."

"Formal panties?" Lilli asked doubtfully. She still wasn't sure about all the different forms of dress she was supposed to get used to. Back in the convent things had been so much *simpler*.

"Yes—they're very small and ornamental," her mother said. "I got you a whole drawer-full along with the rest of your wardrobe before I brought you home from the convent. Be certain they fit you correctly. Oh—and be sure that new bodyslave of yours knows how to kiss them."

"Kiss them?" Lilli asked blankly.

"Oh, I forgot this will be your first truly formal social event." Her mother sighed in a long-suffering way that sounded extremely loud through the com box. "When you're presented at a formal event, your bodyslave must kneel and kiss your panties. It shows your power over him and his respect for you. Be certain your bodyslave knows how to do it correctly. I do *not* wish to be embarrassed at a formal event!"

"Yes, Mother," Lilli said again. "We'll be ready. Um, when is the awards ceremony again?"

"I told you already—*tonight*," her mother snapped. "So be certain you're ready."

"Yes, M—" Lilli began but the com box clicked off before she could finish.

"Well, guess we'd better get moving," Karn remarked. Slowly, he withdrew his long finger from her pussy channel and sucked it into his mouth. "Delicious, little Mistress," he growled softly.

"Oh, you...you think so?" Lilli asked.

"Of course." Karn gave her half-lidded look. "Do you want to finish what we started before we go down to First Meal?"

Lilli was tempted to say yes. She wanted to ask him to touch her again—to give her the orgasm he had promised. Her pussy was throbbing with need and she felt terribly unfulfilled.

But a summons from her mother could *not* be ignored.

"Better not," she said reluctantly. "Let's grab a quick shower and then get downstairs. Even if Mother isn't eating breakfast with me, she'll still want to see that I've obeyed her."

Karn nodded. "As you wish, little Mistress." He raised an eyebrow. "Are we showering together again?"

Lilli bit her lip. She was fairly certain that she wasn't supposed to be taking regular showers with her bodyslave. But the idea of soaping him up again was too tempting to ignore.

"Yes," she said, lifting her chin and trying to look like she was in charge. "After all, you're my bodyslave so I must bathe you."

Karn gave her a lustful grin.

"You'll get no complaints from me, baby. Love the feel of your soft little hands on me."

"I like the feel of yours on me too," Lilli admitted, feeling her cheeks get hot. "You…you're so *good* at touching me in just the right way, Karn."

"Well, a bodyslave has to be good at giving his Mistress a massage," he pointed out. "Especially an *intimate* massage—to help release her tensions."

Lilli hadn't thought of it like that. Maybe it *was* all right to let him touch and stroke her. If only her mother hadn't interrupted, she would have happily let the big Kindred continue for hours.

"Well, maybe later you can, uh, massage me again," she said, smiling up at him.

"That would be my pleasure, little Mistress," Karn rumbled, getting out of bed. "Come on—let's get showered before your mother comes looking for you."

The thought of her mother bursting in on them in the shower got Lilli moving. Shedding her nightdress, she followed the big Kindred into the bathroom where he had already gotten the shower going.

They stepped in together and Lilli donned the sponge glove. She washed Karn as she had the day before, saving his long, hard shaft for last.

"Why are you always so hard around me?" she asked, looking up at him as she stroked up and down his cock.

"Told you already, Mistress—my body reacts to yours," he growled softly, looking down at her. "I can't help getting hard when I see your sweet, curvy little body or feel you pressed against me."

Lilli bit her lip. "I like your body too," she admitted. "I like how big and hard you are." To emphasize her point, she stroked from the thick base of his shaft, over his mating fist, and up to the flaring crown where a bead of precum was forming.

Karn threw back his head and growled in pleasure.

"Gods! Love the feeling of your soft little hand stroking me like that!" He gave her a lustful grin. "For a virgin, you've got quite a technique, little Mistress."

"I *like* to touch you," Lilli admitted recklessly. She was facing him, looking up into his eyes as she stroked his shaft. "I like to bring you pleasure the way you brought me pleasure."

"Well, if you're not careful, you're going to bring me too *much* pleasure and I'll wind up painting your belly with my seed," he growled hoarsely. "I mean it, Lilli—I'm really fucking close here. Exploring your soft little pussy and tasting your pussy honey earlier has me right on the edge."

Lilli licked her lips.

"Maybe I *want* to bring you too much pleasure," she said. "I…I really liked, uh, jerking you off last night." She looked up at him. "Did…did you mind me doing that?"

"I like it better this morning, when it's just the two of us," Karn growled.

"And do you mind me making you spend?" Lilli inquired.

Karn spread his hands.

"Mistress, if you want to bring me to completion and make me spill my seed, that's your prerogative. You own me, after all—body and soul."

The way he said it sent a shiver down Lilli's spine.

"You act like I own you because you want me to—not just because my mother bought you," she said.

"Maybe I *like* being owned by you," Karn murmured. "You're different from any other Mistress—any other female—I've ever met. I like your mixture of innocence and daring—the way you've never touched a male before but you're willing to take me in hand and make me spend for you."

"Oh…" Lilli whispered. She didn't know what to say to that. She only knew that the closer she got to the big Kindred, the closer she *wanted* to get.

She'd never dreamed that she would want to do the kinds of things she'd been doing with Karn ever since they'd met. She'd been encouraged to live a sexless existence at the convent and the blatant, aggressive sexual dominance of Yonnite society left her cold. Yet somehow, Karn had helped her find a middle ground—one where the two of them pleasured each other and didn't worry about who was in charge.

Karn leaned down, his face close to hers as she stroked him.

"Make me come, baby," he growled softly, looking into her eyes. "Your little hands on me feel so good—make me spend for you."

"Yes, Karn," she whispered breathlessly. Slipping off the sponge glove, she took his long shaft in her bare hand and began to stroke in a hot, quick rhythm. At the same time, she reached beneath his shaft with her other hand and cradled the heavy sac hanging there. She weighed his balls in her palm and then gently tickled them, using just the tips of her fingers.

"Gods, little Mistress—coming! Coming so *hard,*" Karn groaned and leaned over her, bracing his hands on either side of her head at the back wall of the shower.

His face was tight with pleasure and Lilli felt the massive shaft grow suddenly even harder and thicker in her hand. Then his cock spasmed in her fingers and the first spurt of his cream shot out.

It was followed by another and another and—because of their position—each one hit Lilli in her lower belly.

She watched, mesmerized, as his hot seed ran down to the soft curls of her mound. It was an erotic sight and with Karn looming over her and blocking the flow of water from the ceiling, there was nothing to wash it away. It dripped down through her curls and into the slit of her pussy and then Lilli noticed something strange.

From the moment she'd woken up, the tingling in her pussy—which had spread from the site where she'd been injected—had been nearly constant. It was an uncomfortable feeling—the same pins and needles sensation you got when you sat on your foot or slept wrong on your arm and the body part in question falls asleep.

This was an odd and distracting sensation to have in her pussy—especially in her sensitive clit. It had gotten better when Karn was rubbing and touching her, but the moment he stopped, it had returned.

Now, as Lilli watched the white cream drip down into her slit and find its way between her puffy pussy lips, she felt an easing of the strange sensation. It was almost as though the big Kindred's cream was a soothing balm which eased the tingling ache.

As he had the night before, Karn kept coming and coming and spurt after spurt of creamy white painted her belly, just as he had predicted. Experimentally, Lilli pushed his throbbing cock lower, pointing the head directly between her pussy lips, which she spread with trembling fingers.

As the first spurt of cream hit her throbbing clit, she felt a surge of relief. Goddess, it felt so much better than it had! Until she'd gotten a rest from the awful tingling, Lilli hadn't realized how bad it was. She felt like a person with a sunburn at last applying soothing cool-gel ointment.

But the moment Karn saw what she was doing, he attempted to pull back.

"Whoa, little Mistress," he growled, frowning. "What do you think you're doing?"

"Well, I…" Lilli felt her cheeks get hot. "I just…wanted to see what your cream felt like inside me," she confessed. "Why—shouldn't I?"

"Not unless you want a big belly," Karn growled. He sighed and shook his head. "You're damn lucky I'm a Hybrid Kindred, Mistress, and unable to impregnate you. Otherwise, you might be in real trouble."

"You can't?" Lilli asked, looking up at him. "I mean, why not?"

He shrugged, his broad shoulders beaded with water.

"It's just the way it is with Kindred—we can't get a female pregnant until we bond with her and Hybrids can almost never bond. So this is safe with me…" he nodded down to where the head of his shaft was nearly touching the pink pearl of her clit. "But don't ever try it with any other male."

"I wouldn't want to," Lilli said. "You're the only one I want to do this with, Karn." She looked up at him. "Can you…could you shoot again? I…I like the way your cream feels on the inside of me."

His voice dropped to a low growl.

"You mean the inside of your pussy, baby?"

"Uh-huh." She nodded and looked down to where she was still holding her pussy open with two fingers. "Can you do it, Karn? Can you, uh, cream me one more time?"

"Gods, you're so sexy," he growled. "And the sight of your soft little pussy all filled with my cream makes me so damn hot, baby…"

As he spoke, the shaft in her hand—which she was aiming directly at her open pussy—jerked once more and a healthy load of the big Kindred's seed landed right on her sensitive clit and then slid lower, finding its way into her inner pussy. Lilli knew because she could feel it. It eased the uncomfortable tingling and left a warm sensation of pure pleasure instead.

"Mmm…" she moaned. "Karn, that feels so *good.* Love to have your cream in me!"

"And you look damn sexy with your hot little cunt all coated in it," he acknowledged. "But it's getting late, little Mistress, and we still haven't shaved your mound yet."

"Oh, right." Lilli had gotten so wrapped up in making him spend his seed and the delicious feeling of it inside her that she hadn't even remembered that she was supposed to shave. "Uh…I've never shaved myself there, before," she confessed.

"Not to worry—I'll help. In fact, I'll do it for you," Karn offered. He picked up the wet laser-shaver from its shelf at the back of the shower stall and held it up. "If you trust me, Mistress?" he asked, raising his eyebrows.

"Of course I trust you," Lilli said. "If…if you don't mind doing it, that is," she added a big shyly.

Karn gave her a look that was half lazy lust and half amusement.

"Baby, I'm there for anything to do with your soft little pussy."

He grinned. "Besides, we need to get my seed off your mound—you can't go around sticky all day."

"Okay," Lilli said. "But..." She nibbled her bottom lip.

"Yes, baby?" Karn had already dropped to his knees before her and he looked up to meet her eyes. "What is it? Getting worried about me using the shaver?"

"No." Lilli shook her head. "It's just...can we leave the seed that's inside me? Inside my, uh, inner pussy, I mean?" She could feel her cheeks heating but she made herself go on. "I mean, I understand we need to wash it away from my outer mound but I want what you shot inside me to stay. It...makes me feel better. Makes me feel *good*."

Karn's mismatched eyes were half-lidded.

"Of course, baby. If you want to keep my cum in your pussy all day, that's up to you. It's just a damn good thing I'm a Hybrid."

"I'm glad you are too," Lilli admitted. It was good to remove the threat of pregnancy from this equation—especially since she really didn't feel ready to have a baby she would have to raise alone.

"All right then," Karn murmured. Gently, he pinched her outer pussy lips closed and flipped the on-switch on the shaver. At once, a short beam of red light—about three inches long and very finely colli-mated—shot out of one end. "Now hold still," he murmured. "We'll have you all nice and smooth in no time..."

# TWENTY-ONE

K arn couldn't believe how neatly and quickly everything was coming together. He hadn't even been in Mistress Mirabella's home for two days and already he was being handed the keys to his mission on a silver platter.

Of course, he admitted to himself uneasily, he *did* feel a little guilty about who was handing him those keys. He liked Lilli—liked her a hell of a lot—and he felt bad about deceiving her.

*But it's not like I'll be in her life for long,* he told himself. *I'll be gone almost before she knows it. And she'll forget me pretty quickly.*

But would she? Karn wondered as he stood behind her chair, watching her eat her First Meal. She'd asked him to sit and eat with her, but he hadn't thought it was a good idea. Not when her mother might walk in at any moment. Instead, he'd had H'rare slip him a protein bar which staved off hunger and kept him lean and alert.

He knew that he would never forget Lilli—who even now was wearing his seed inside her creamy little pussy. Creamy because he had shot inside her—well, inside her inner folds, anyway. Gods, the memory of her pointing the head of his cock at her spread pussy still had the power to make his shaft hard.

Luckily, he was wearing trousers with a crotch today, so his state of arousal wasn't quite so evident. Apparently as long as they were just staying in and not going to any banquets, it was all right for a bodyslave to be covered.

Karn was grateful for that. A male's shaft and balls got damn cold hanging out in the open, as they had been all day yesterday. And he also thought—

"Ah, Lilliana—there you are. *Finally* out of bed, I see." Mistress Mirabella's sharp, shrewish voice cut through the thoughts in his head as cleanly as a laser cutting through clay.

"Oh, hello Mother." Lilli looked up quickly and put down the piece of toasted *pengu* bread she'd been eating. "How are you this morning?"

"This morning?" Lady Mirabella sniffed. "Why it's nearly *afternoon* by now. Honestly, Lilli, what were you doing in bed so long today?"

Lilli's cheeks went red and she started to stutter out a reply. But Mistress Mirabella cut her off with a wave of her hand.

"I understand if you feel the need to self-pleasure. Lady Tempertant *did* tell me that the quick-grow hormones you were injected with would cause increased libido. Tell me, do you need any toys?"

"T-toys?" Lilli stuttered, her face scarlet.

"Oh, of *course* you do." Mistress Mirabella snapped her fingers. "Because those wretched Sisters of Chastity and Humility wouldn't allow you to have any. Well, I'll have a selection sent up to your rooms for later, when you have time."

"Um, thank you, Mother," Lilli said faintly. She looked mortified, poor thing, Karn thought. Clearly she still wasn't used to the blatant sexuality of the Yonnite culture. Though she appeared to have no problem opening up to *him*. He couldn't help remembering the way she'd spread her legs for him and moaned as he explored her pussy…

"…out all day today." Lady Mirabella's sharp voice cut through his thoughts again.

"Where will you go?" Lilli asked, looking up at her mother.

"Out on business. I won't require you to accompany me today, as I know you're still breaking in your new bodyslave," her mother said. She gave Karn a sharp look. "How he working out, by the way?"

"Oh, good!" Lilli said quickly. "Excellent, in fact. You were right, Mother—he was an excellent choice."

"Well…I *am* a good judge of bodyslaves, if I *do* say so myself." Lady Mirabella preened briefly before getting back to business. "Anyway, I'm glad you're pleased with him. Why don't you spend the rest of the day making certain he's ready to make a good showing at the awards ceremony tonight and I'll meet you back here by six to pick you up?"

"Where is the ceremony being held?" Lilli asked.

"Oh, the old Zangelo building—but only because it's been planned for months," Mistress Mirabella said. "Though after what happened there, I think people would have liked to move it if they could. Still, we'll be two floors down from the residence where it happened so there's no need to think about it if you don't want to."

"Where *what* happened?" Lilli asked, looking confused.

"Never mind." Lady Mirabella looked at the jeweled chronometer strapped to her wrist. "Oh, is that the time? I must run! I'll see you tonight at six, Lilliana. See that you're ready to go!" she ordered and strode quickly out of the breakfast nook where Lilli was dining.

"I wonder what that was all about?" Lilli murmured to Karn as her mother swept from the room. "What could have happened at the Zangelo building?"

"Dunno." Karn shrugged. He was more interested in getting into Mistress Mirabella's files and sending the list of Kindred bodyslaves straight to Commander Sylvan. It was possible he might even be done with his mission by tonight!

Not that he was ready to leave yet, he thought, looking at Lilli's lovely face. He ought to at least stay with her until the end of the week when she went to the conception center. His little Mistress needed him for moral support—especially when it came to going against her overbearing mother's orders.

*I'll see her through this difficult time,* he thought to himself. *It's the least I can do for her, after she's been so kind to me.*

He didn't admit, even to himself, that he was looking for any excuse not to leave her side. His heart, so long completely untouchable, was already beginning to become entangled in the soft, silky web of desire, longing, and love. But Karn refused to examine the feelings growing inside him for his little Mistress.

After all, he had a mission to complete and no time for anything else—or so he told himself.

# TWENTY-TWO

"This is Mother's secret study," Lilli explained, pressing in the code exactly as she'd been taught.

"I see." And he did—Karn kept a watchful eye on the combination, memorizing it as she punched it in. This was almost too easy, he thought. In all his years in the Kindred Elite Espionage Corps, he'd never just been handed the information he'd come looking for like this.

"Here we go." Lilli let them into a richly decorated room. The walls were lined with leather-bound tomes of Yonnite law and literature and the space was lit by the soft glows of many tall, purple *pulta* plants, whose blossoms had a glowing pink center.

"It's a good thing Mother is gone for the day," Lilli remarked, shutting the door behind them.

Karn arched an eyebrow.

"Because you don't think she'd like you being in here on your own?"

"Well, that and the fact that every time she brings me in here she tries to teach me all about her job with the Sacred Seven." Lilli sighed.

"Honestly, the paperwork part of it isn't so bad. But all the parties and public appearances you have to make are *awful*."

"Well, let's see if we can find what we came for and get out of here," Karn suggested. This was feeling almost *too* easy—he didn't trust it.

"Mother's communications and computing system is right here."

Lilli walked around to sit behind a massive crystal desktop which floated, seemingly with no support, about three feet off the richly carpeted floor. On it was placed a single computing unit with a liquid crystal screen. It had a manipu-cube rather that a keyboard, but that was fine with Karn—he was well versed in all kinds of tech.

"Let me see now…" Lilli seated herself in the cushioned leather office chair which immediately conformed to her shape and lifted her to the perfect height to work at the desk. "Mother showed me how to do this," she muttered, touching the cube hesitantly. "But I haven't got much experience—there was no communications tech at the convent…"

Karn watched impatiently as she began handling the manipu-cube. He normally would have given her as much time as she needed to do anything which was new and unfamiliar to her, but he really wanted to get in and out of this office. What if lady Mirabella came back unexpectedly?

"Mistress," he said, "Maybe if you let me have a try? In my last assignment, I was charged with using this kind of tech." Which was technically the truth.

"Oh, really?" Lilli got up at once and let him have the chair. "What Mistress were you with? Was she kind to you? Did you…like her?"

Karn shot her a glance as he seated himself behind the desk.

"I think what you're asking is if I liked her as much as I like *you*," he remarked as he began manipulating the cube with expert quickness.

"Well…" Lilli blushed prettily, looking down at her hands, as she often did when she was embarrassed. "I mean—"

"The answer is no." Karn grinned at her. "I've never had any Mistress I like as much as you, Lilli."

Which, again, was technically the truth, since he'd never had any Mistress at all before this mission.

"Really?" Her big brown eyes were bright as stars when she looked up at him and Karn couldn't help himself—he put an arm around her waist and pulled her down for a gentle kiss. She tasted of the *silki* fruit she'd been eating at First Meal—a sweet, fragrant delight.

Lilli froze for a moment and then kissed him back eagerly.

"Oh, Karn," she whispered, when he broke the kiss at last. "I'm pretty sure we shouldn't do that but it's *really* nice."

"I like it too, baby," he murmured, smiling at her. "But I guess we'd better get down to business," he added when the cube beeped at him softly, letting him know it had found what he was looking for.

The liquid crystal screen, which floated above the desk the same way the desktop floated above the carpet, suddenly filled with a list of names and locations.

"Oh…" Lilli leaned on his shoulder and stared at the screen with wide eyes. "What's that?"

"A listing of all the Kindred who are currently being kept as bodyslaves," Karn said grimly.

Surreptitiously, he pressed the fingernail of the ring finger on his left hand. The tiny spy device that had been grafted onto the nail buzzed quietly to life at once, sucking data from the computing unit and transferring it directly to the Mother Ship, hundreds of thousands of light years away.

*There—mission complete,* he thought. But was it? He thought not.

Quickly, he began manipulating the cube again.

"What are you looking for now?" Lilli asked.

"I'm searching the list for any known felons," Karn answered. "Or any convicted of crimes. I…*there*—there it is!"

He pointed at the liquid crystal screen where a single name was outlined in red. Quickly, he twisted the cube to highlight it and asked for more information.

"Oh, *my*," Lilli said faintly, reading the grizzly details over his shoulder. "This is *awful*, Karn."

"What he's accused of certainly *is* awful," Karn agreed grimly. "But I'm not convinced he actually did it. Look—it says the records are incomplete."

"Oh, and look where the crime happened," Lilli exclaimed. "The Zangelo Building!"

"*Fuck*," Karn swore softly to himself. "The very place we're going tonight."

It had to be more than coincidence, he thought. The Goddess must be facilitating this—she was still blessing his mission. She must mean for him to find out more about this Kindred bodyslave—a Nightwalker, by the information he was reading—and help free him.

"We can search for more clues when we get there," Lilli said excitedly. "Well, if we can get away from the awards ceremony, that is."

"I think we can manage somehow," Karn said. He did a brief search for any more information and came up with nothing. Anything further would hopefully be found at the Zangelo Building. "Come on, little Mistress," he said to Lilli. "Let's get out of here."

"And do what?" Lilli asked. "We still have hours before Mother comes to pick us up for the awards ceremony tonight."

"Well…" Karn gave her a wolfish grin. "You could always try on your outfit for tonight. I'm interested to see how you look in those 'formal panties' you're supposed to wear."

Lilli blushed fetchingly but she didn't seem reluctant. In fact, she nodded eagerly.

"I think that's a good idea," she murmured. "After all, I'm supposed to make sure they fit me just right."

"And *I'm* supposed to practice kissing them," Karn growled. Already he could feel his shaft rising at the thought. As a Kindred, there was nothing he loved more than kissing and tasting his female's pussy. And though he would technically only be kissing Lilli's panties, he had an idea his little Mistress wouldn't mind if he kissed a little more deeply than was technically necessary.

Lilli's blush deepened.

"Oh, do…you really want to do that?"

"Practice kissing your pussy? I mean your panties?" Karn lifted his eyebrows. "You have to ask, baby? Hell *yes*, I want to do it. Come on —let's go!"

And he ushered her quickly out of the study, making certain everything was in its place and the door was locked securely behind them. Part of his mission was complete and now it was time to tend to the other part—time to tend to his little Mistress and bring her pleasure.

Karn couldn't fucking wait.

# TWENTY-THREE

Lilli wiggled, trying to get comfortable in the formal panties. She was wearing the largest pair she'd been able to find and *still* they were tiny.

Instead of being a triangle shape, like most of her underwear, these panties—which were made of rich, gold lace—were V shaped. Which meant they dipped down in the middle and showed not only her bare mound, but also the top part of her pussy slit.

That might not have been so bad, except that the tingling sensation which Karn's seed had dampened for a while, had now come back with a vengeance. Even worse, it now appeared to have side effects. The side effects being the fact that her outer pussy lips were swollen and puffy and no matter how Lilli tried to keep them closed, they seemed to keep opening on their own to show her equally swollen clit.

*I look like I've been playing with myself for hours!* Lilli thought, staring down at the revealing panties in dismay. *Rubbing myself exactly where the Sisters at the convent told us we must never touch. Goddess, this is terrible! What will everyone think if I have to wear these out in public?*

"Mistress?" Karn called, breaking into her mortified thoughts. "Are you ready to come out of the closet and show me yet?"

Lilli bit her lip. Should she let her bodyslave see her in such an embarrassing state? Then again, how could she help it? He and everyone else was going to see her in a few hours when her mother came to take them to the awards ceremony.

Lilli wondered if she could make some excuse not to go. But no —she and Karn had a mystery to solve. She couldn't refuse to go because then he couldn't go either.

"Lilli?" Karn asked again and she knew she couldn't stall any longer. She would have to go out and face him.

Taking a deep breath, she stepped out of the large walk-in closet and into her bedroom where the big Kindred was waiting, sitting on her bed.

"Well?" she asked, biting her lip. "What do you think?"

Karn's mismatched eyes scanned her from head to toe, taking in the floating, feathery dress made of *u-liss* plumes dyed deep purple which dipped low enough to show her nipples at the top and was cut high enough to show the formal panties at the bottom. There were feather nipple drops to go with it, dyed gold to match the panties of course. They set off her pink points to perfection but it was between her legs that his gaze inevitably settled.

"Goddess, little Mistress," he growled softly. "You look fucking gorgeous but what's wrong with your little pussy? You're all slippery and wet and open."

"I can't seem to help it," Lilli admitted. She pressed her legs together but even that didn't make her pussy lips close enough to hide the pink button of her clit. It was standing out prominently and the awful pins and needles tingling had returned with a vengeance.

"What do you think is causing it?" Karn murmured. "You weren't like this earlier today when we took a shower together."

"I don't know," Lilli said desperately. "All I know is that when I woke up today, I was tingling in the place where they injected me with the quick-grow shot last night. And then the tingling seemed to move up to my…well, to my nipples and pussy," she finished in a low voice.

She thought about telling him that his seed made her feel better, but she felt shy about that. What if he thought she was asking him to come on her pussy again?

It had been one thing to make him spend in the shower when she was cleaning him—he was her bodyslave and she had to take care of him. But to ask him to pull out his shaft and come on her bare pussy for no other reason than because she wanted him to seemed wrong.

Plus, wouldn't his seed ruin her panties? At the very least it would be extremely visible and there was no way she could explain it. No, Lilli decided, she would have to keep the fact that his cream eased the tingling to herself.

"You say it started in the spot where they injected you." Karn's voice dropped to an angry growl. "I wish I'd been there with you last night, little Mistress. I wouldn't have let anyone stick you with hormones you didn't want!"

"I know you wouldn't, Karn." Lilli reached out and put a hand on his broad shoulder. "Which is probably why it's a good thing you *weren't* there. If you had interfered on my behalf, you might be on your way to the Diluthian mines right now."

"You might be right but I still would have stopped them." He looked her in the eyes. "I won't let anyone hurt you, Lilli—I swear it."

"Thank you, Karn." She stroked his cheek. She liked this, she thought—him sitting on the bed so they were closer to being face-to-face. He was so tall it was hard to reach him otherwise.

"You're welcome, baby." Turning his head, he pressed a soft kiss to her palm. "Now, do you think maybe this *problem* has to do with those hormones they injected you with?" he asked. "Your mother *did* say she was going to leave you some, uh, toys to help."

"I know." Lilli felt her cheeks get hot. Goddess, how embarrassing! "I…I don't want any toys," she told Karn in a low voice.

"You don't?" He frowned. "Why not, baby?"

"I…tried one. Once at the convent," Lilli confessed, her cheeks flaming now. "A friend of mine brought in a bunch of tiny little pleasure-button buzzers and gave them out."

Karn frowned. "This wouldn't happen to be the same friend who brought in the porno vid, would it?"

Lilli nodded.

"Uh-huh. Anyway, she brought them in and we all tried them but they were way too harsh for me. They *hurt.*"

"Hmm…" Karn nodded. "I see. You do seem to have a very delicate pussy. I was barely touching you this morning and you were twisting your hips all over the place."

"I don't know if you touching me again will help this," Lilli said. "I…I'm afraid it *already* looks like I've been touching myself for hours. Goddess, this is *so* embarrassing!"

"Don't worry about it, baby," Karn urged her. "I'm betting with all the high-class Mistresses is there, everybody is going to be more focused on their own appearance—not yours."

Lilli sighed.

"I hope you're right but all it takes is for one person to start talking about you…" She thought of Priss, who was terrible about starting rumors.

"Look, the only time anyone is going to be focusing their attention between your legs is when you get presented at the door and I kiss your panties," Karn said reasonably. "And I'll be sure nobody can see anything at that time because I'll hide you while I kiss you."

"You will?" Lilli looked at the big Kindred gratefully. "Thank you, Karn."

"You're more than welcome, little Mistress," he rumbled. "Do you think we should practice it now?"

"N-now?" Lilli stuttered. Suddenly her heart was bumping against her ribs. "I…I don't know, Karn."

"Have to practice sometime," he pointed out, his eyes half-lidded as he looked again at her barely-covered pussy. "And it's better to do it now than wait until everyone in a huge crowded ballroom is watching."

Well, he had a point there, Lilli thought. And hadn't they planned to let him practice kissing her panties anyway? It was just that she hadn't known how very small and revealing the formal panties would be when she'd made that plan. Still, Karn was right—it was better to be ready for tonight.

"All right," she whispered at last. "You...you can practice kissing my panties, Karn. But *just* my panties," she added, feeling that it wouldn't be right to let him kiss any other part of her. She had already gone much further with him than any Mistress *ought* to go with her bodyslave—it was time to rein things in.

If she could.

The words were scarcely out of her mouth before Karn was sliding off the bed to kneel at her feet. He slipped his big hands into the high front slit of her dress and stroked the backs of her thighs.

"Oh..." Lilli whispered, loving the touch of his big, warm hands.

"Little Mistress," Karn murmured, sliding his hands up to cup the full globes of her ass. He looked up into her eyes. "Just relax now and let me kiss your panties."

"Yes, all...all right." Lilli wished her voice didn't sound quite so breathless, but she couldn't seem to help it. Karn was so big and solid and muscular, kneeling before her as he was. He smelled so damn good too—that same spicy scent that seemed to draw her to him. Lilli was afraid if she wasn't careful, she would go way too far with him.

"Just relax," Karn repeated, leaning forward to rub his cheek gently against her inner thigh. "And open for me, little Mistress. Open and let me kiss you."

Lilli noticed that he didn't say he was going to kiss her panties this time—he'd just said her was going to kiss *her*. Nevertheless, she did as he asked and spread her thighs, presenting him with both the tiny golden V of her panties and her throbbing pussy with her clit on full display.

With a soft growl, Karn pulled her forward and placed a hot, open-mouthed kiss on the center of her panties. Lilli gasped when she felt the heat of his mouth bathing her clit but since he didn't actually kiss her *there,* she didn't feel she could say anything.

"There." Karn pulled back and looked up at her. "Did I do it correctly, Mistress?"

"I…I guess so." Lilli shifted her hips. Her clit was tingling and throbbing worse than ever. It was like that part of her body sensed what had *almost* happened and was longing for it now.

Karn frowned.

"But I'm not sure I did," he said. "I felt like maybe my kiss was off center—a little too low. Did you think so, little Mistress?"

Lilli nibbled her lower lip.

"I, um…maybe," she said at last. "I mean, maybe you could kiss just a *little* higher."

"I think you're right. Let me try again," Karn rumbled. Cupping her ass in his big hands, he pulled her close again.

This time his kiss landed squarely on her throbbing clit. Lilli gasped but didn't try to stop him as the hot, wet, warmth surrounded her aching little bud. Karn didn't try to lick her but she *did* feel just the tip of his tongue press lightly against her sensitive flesh. The sensation shot sparks of pleasure through her and made her hips buck in response.

"Oh!" she moaned as Karn pulled back at last. For a moment, the tingling between her legs had stopped—it was as though that tiny touch of his tongue had made her feel better, just the way his seed coating her inner folds had helped earlier.

"Gods, so sensitive," he growled softly, looking up at her. "No wonder you don't like toys, little Mistress. Your sweet little clit is too delicate for anything rough."

"You're…you're not supposed to be kissing my…kissing me there," Lilli pointed out breathlessly. "You're just supposed to be kissing my panties."

"Do you want me to stop then?" Karn arched an eyebrow at her.

"I…" Lilli bit her lip. "I don't know," she confessed softly. "No one has ever kissed me there before."

"I know, baby." His voice got deep and soft. "So why not let me be the first?"

Lilli almost said yes but then a stern little voice—a voice that sounded a lot like her mother's—spoke up in her head.

*You have to stop this, Lilliana,* it said. *Look at the way you've been acting ever since you got this bodyslave! You've let him suck your nipples and stroke your pussy—you even let him penetrate you with his fingers! What's next? Will you let him put his tongue inside you? His shaft? You know that's forbidden! You're going farther and farther down a road you can't retrace, no matter how hard you try. Stop now while you still can!*

"We shouldn't," Lilli said, listening to the little voice. "It's going too far."

He raised an eyebrow at her again.

"And having me shoot my cum on your pussy *wasn't* too far?"

"That was different," Lilli protested. "I...I had to wash you—wash your shaft. You're my bodyslave and I have to take care of you—that's all." She lifted her chin. "You have to understand that we have a certain relationship—one that can only go so far in...in a certain direction," she ended, rather lamely.

His face darkened.

"Your bodyslave. That's right—that's all I am." Suddenly he straightened up to tower over her at his full height. "Forgive me, Mistress," he said in a cold, formal tone. "I didn't mean to overstep the boundaries between us."

"Oh, Karn..." Lilli didn't know what to say. She felt terrible—clearly she had offended him. "Karn—" she tried again but he only shook his head.

"No, it's all right, Mistress. I understand. Do you have anything else you want me to do for you right now?"

"No," Lilli said miserably. "I...I guess you can go, if you want to."

"I'll be in the kitchens, helping H'rare prepare for your Midday Meal," Karn told her.

Then he turned and left the bedroom, leaving Lilli to feel miserable and upset without him.

# TWENTY-FOUR

*Just a bodyslave—that's all I am to her,* Karn thought angrily, as he sat in the back of the hover-ship that was flying them to the awards ceremony at the Zangelo Building.

He and Lilli hadn't said a word to each other, even while they were getting dressed. She had put on her outfit without help from him and Karn, likewise, had oiled his own shaft and put on the stay-hard strap he was required to wear along with the crotchless bodyslave leather trousers. There had been a mutual, silent agreement not to talk after their earlier encounter and Karn hadn't been willing to break it.

Damn it, why did her words hurt him so? He hadn't known the curvy little female that long and he had no intention of staying with her. So why should he care that she'd put the brakes on what was happening between them?

Or maybe nothing was happening between them—maybe he'd just convinced himself that it was. And maybe he was getting way off track—focusing on Lilli instead of his mission. He'd never had a female affect him this strongly before—never been so preoccupied that he'd been willing to stay in a dangerous situation, even after his mission was technically done.

What was wrong with him?

"Maybe I'm crazy," Karn muttered to himself.

At the muted sound of his voice, he saw Lilli's eyes dart up to the rear-viewer. She was sitting with her mother in the seat ahead of his, while he was sitting in the bodyslave compartment at the back.

Their gazes locked for a moment and he saw mute misery in her big brown eyes before she dropped them again and looked away.

That one look said it all—and it melted his heart.

*She's just a kid,* Karn thought to himself. *She might be of age but she's been raised in such a restrictive environment that she can't help but be naïve. She's caught between her strict upbringing, the hedonistic Yonnite lifestyle she's expected to embrace now, and me.*

He felt like a jerk. No wonder Lilli was confused. He saw now that she hadn't meant to hurt him. They had been moving awfully fast, considering how long they'd known each other—not to mention their proscribed relationship as Mistress and bodyslave. It wasn't surprising that she'd backed off and he shouldn't blame her for her reticence.

*Poor kid,* he thought, feeling a surge of compassion for her. *She's doing her best but she's not really cut out for this life at all. She doesn't like glitzy parties or catty Mistress politics and she's not an exhibitionist.*

He wished suddenly that he could take her home with him to the Mother Ship where she could live a normal life. A life where she didn't have to wear revealing gowns that showed her body so explicitly or navigate the snake pit that was Yonnite High Society.

That was impossible, of course. Lilli wasn't part of his mission and when it was over, he would have to leave her behind. But at least he could put her mind at ease and end the conflict between the two of them.

The next time he caught her eyes in the mirror, Karn gave her a wink. Lilli's eyes widened as though she wasn't sure what to think. He wanted to let her know everything was all right but it wasn't like he could say anything aloud. So instead, he just held her gaze steadily until she dropped her eyes and looked at her hands, an expression of confusion on her face.

*Damn.* Karn sighed. Well, he would make her understand once they got to the awards ceremony. Everything would be all right and he would try to remember her youth and inexperience from now on and rein in his own emotions for her.

After all, he was here to complete a mission—*not* fall in love.

# TWENTY-FIVE

Lilli wasn't sure what the wink meant. Had Karn forgiven her? Were they friends again? Had they been friends in the first place? *Ought* one to make friends with one's bodyslave?

Lilli was pretty sure you weren't supposed to do that and yet somehow she had made friends with Karn. Or maybe it was more than that. After all, she'd had plenty of friends at the convent, but she had never wanted to touch and kiss any of them the way she longed to touch and kiss the big Kindred. And she'd certainly never longed to press her body to theirs and feel their strong arms wrapped around her...

*No! Stop it, Lilli!*

She tried to push the naughty thoughts away because they made the tingling in her nipples and pussy so much worse. But she couldn't seem to help herself. Every time she managed to put the big Kindred out of her mind, their eyes would meet in the rear-viewer again and all she could think of was how good his big, warm hands felt on her body...

By the time they finally reached the Zangelo Building, where the Civic Awards Ceremony was being held, Lilli was in complete turmoil. Her body was throbbing—begging for attention. She felt like if she didn't have the big Kindred's hands and mouth on her soon, she was going to explode!

"Ah—here we are at last!" her mother exclaimed as the craft, driven by one of her most trusted bodyslaves, pulled up to the entrance, fifty stories above the ground. "Lilliana, be certain your dress is straight," she told her. "And you, Terx," she added to the bodyslave who was driving. "Put the ship in autopark so you can escort me in. I can't be announced without a bodyslave to kiss my panties."

"Yes, Mistress," the bodyslave said tonelessly. He did something to the controls and the craft paused long enough for all of them to climb out onto the walkway that led into the building, before flying away again.

The walkway was long and narrow and made out of clear plasti-glass—extremely strong but nearly invisible. When Lilli stepped out onto it, it looked like she was stepping onto thin air. Fifty stories below she could see the Yonnite ground traffic whizzing by in blurs of light. They looked like tiny insects buzzing down there and the people weren't even visible except as moving dots in the gathering gloom.

The sight gave Lilli a queasy feeling in the pit of her stomach. She had never liked heights, even when she could see what she was standing on. Walking on what appeared to be thin air above the ground made her feel dizzy.

"Lilliana, do hurry," her mother snapped, as she and her bodyslave took the lead. "What have I told you about shilly-shallying?"

"Sorry, Mother." Her words seemed to come from far away and Lilli wasn't sure if she had actually said them or only thought them. The ground, so far beneath her, swam under the too-high heels that went with her purple plume dress and everything began to look blurry and out of focus.

Suddenly the heels slipped on the slick plastiglass and she was fall-ing… falling…

Strong arms caught her and she was cradled close to a broad chest.

"Careful there, little Mistress," a familiar voice rumbled. "I don't think you've learned how to fly yet, so let's not go diving off the side of the building, all right?"

"Karn?" she blinked up at him, feeling dazed.

"Yeah, it's me." He gave her a concerned look. "Are you okay, baby?" he murmured in a low voice.

"I don't like heights," Lilli admitted. "They…they make me dizzy."

"So I see," he rumbled. "Come on—let's get inside so you don't have to see this crazy drop anymore."

He carried her down the long, nearly invisible entryway towards the lighted entrance of the building. As he walked, Lilli sighed and rested her head against his broad chest.

"Does this mean you forgive me?" she whispered, looking up at him.

"Nothing to forgive," he growled softly. "I should have known you were still finding your bearings in this crazy world and not rushed you."

"I shouldn't have pushed you away," Lilli told him. "I'm so sorry, Karn."

His mismatched eyes softened.

"Apology accepted, baby. And I'm sorry for acting like a jerk."

She frowned. "A what?"

"It's what Earth females call a guy who tries to take things too fast or acts like an asshole," Karn explained. "I think I did a little bit of both."

"I just wasn't sure…I'm still not sure…how much or how far…" She trailed off.

"How much you ought to get involved with your bodyslave?" he rumbled. "Probably not at all, at least according to Yonnite Society.

But it's up to you if you want to break the rules or not. I shouldn't be pushing until you're sure what you want."

"Oh, Karn…" Lilli looked up at him, heart pounding. "What I want is y—"

"Lilliana! What do you think you're doing?" her mother's shrill voice interrupted her confession. "Why in the world is your bodyslave carrying you? This is not the proper way to make an entrance at all!"

Lilli felt her insides clench tight, as they always did when her mother used that disapproving tone.

"Sorry, Mother—it's just that I almost fell!" she exclaimed, struggling to sit up in Karn's arms. The big Kindred placed her gently on her feet, keeping one hand unobtrusively on her lower back to help her balance as she stood upright.

"Fell?" Mistress Mirabella looked as though she didn't believe it. "Whatever are you talking about?"

"I just don't have much of a head for heights," Lilli said apologetically. "And we're so high up here." She motioned to the ground far below and the other skyscrapers rising all around them to illustrate her point.

"No head for heights? Well, chalk that up as yet *another* deficiency in my heir," her mother exclaimed. "No head for heights, no sense of fashion, no sense of politics… *Honestly*, Lilliana. Sometimes I wonder if the sperm the contraception center gave me when I got pregnant with you was defective! You don't act like a proper Yonnite Mistress at *all*."

"I'm sorry," Lilli said again, in a small voice. "I…I'll try to do better."

"See that you do!" her mother snapped. "Now I'm next to be announced and since you're a junior Mistress, you'll be some time after me. Stand here and wait your turn and be certain you don't embarrass me!"

"No, Mother. I won't." Lilli felt like crying. It seemed like no matter what she did, it was always wrong. Nothing was ever good enough for her mother. Lilli wasn't tall enough or thin enough or fashionable enough and she never did or said the right thing at the right time.

Not for the first time, she wondered how she would ever survive in this life for the long term. She'd only been home on Yonnie Six with her mother for about a week and they seemed to do nothing but make each other miserable.

"Hey…over here." Karn pulled her behind a huge potted *burnu* plant with bushy orange and green leaves that stood to one side of the lighted entrance. He lifted Lilli's chin and looked into her eyes. "You okay?" he murmured.

Lilli shook her head and sniffed back tears.

"I'm fine. It's just…nothing I do is ever good enough for her."

"Look at me." He stroked her cheek until Lilli looked up into his eyes.

"Yes?" she asked in a trembling voice.

"You're perfect, just the way you are," Karn told her. "Don't let anyone tell you different, Lilli."

Lilli smiled and sniffed again.

"How do you always know just the right thing to say?"

He gave her his crooked smile that showed one fang and shrugged.

"Dunno. Just an instinct I guess."

"Well, well—he*llo,* Lilliana."

They jerked apart and Lilli looked up to see Priss striding confidently across the invisible entryway with a new, muscular bodyslave in tow on a long black leather leash behind her.

"This is my new bodyslave, Randor," she said, yanking on the leash to make the male come closer. The leash was attached to a choke collar and the male gasped and stumbled forward. His lips turned blue for a moment before Priss let up on the pressure and he was able to stand upright again. He nodded stiffly at Lilli and said,

"Hello, Mistress," in a choked voice.

"There—isn't he impressive?" Priss demanded. "So much *better* than that other bodyslave you *stole* from me!"

"He's *most* impressive," Lilli agreed, to keep the peace. It was clear to her that the other girl had gone out and gotten the biggest bodyslave she could—possibly to compete with Karn. But though Randor was tall and broad through the shoulders, the big Kindred still had half a head in height over him and his shoulders were obviously wider. And there was no doubt whose shaft was bigger—Karn had him beat in that category as well.

Priss must have realized this too because as her eyes flicked over the two males standing side-by-side, her lips thinned down to a white line and her sharp blue eyes narrowed.

"So, how have you been, Lilliana?" she asked. "You seem to be getting awfully *cozy* with that Kindred bodyslave of yours."

Lilli tried to keep her face blank, though she couldn't help the guilty twitch of her mouth as she answered.

"I got dizzy on the plastiglass entryway and nearly fell. Karn caught me."

"Oh, well isn't that just *sweet.*" Priss sneered at her. "And here *I* thought the carnal cravings from the quick-grow injections were getting to you."

"Carnal cravings?" Lilli frowned at her.

"You know? The awful tingling? The need to be pleasured?" Priss grinned at her nastily. "We've *all* had the cravings, Lilliana. Just be sure you use a *toy* to satisfy them and *not* your bodyslave's shaft. Remember that allowing yourself to be penetrated by a male is the worst, lowest thing you could *possibly* do. Not to mention it's *completely* against the law."

Lilli felt her face flame with sudden heat.

"Oh, I didn't—" she began but Priss was already breezing past her, dragging her new bodyslave along behind her.

"Just be careful getting too cozy with that big Kindred," she remarked as she went. "It really doesn't *look* good and you wouldn't want people to *talk.*"

Then she was up at the podium and Lilli heard her say to the male servant standing there, "I don't care if I'm a junior Mistress—

you'll announce me *now* or you'll be out on the street within the hour!"

"Well, I guess now we know for sure that the stuff they injected you with is what's causing your problems," Karn murmured in Lilli's ear. "Is the tingling really bad, baby?"

"It's terrible," she admitted, pressing her thighs together desperately. "It's been driving me crazy for *hours.*"

Karn frowned.

"And nothing helps it?"

Lilli nibbled her lower lip. Should she tell him? Probably not, but she didn't want to hide her problems from the big Kindred anymore.

"It stopped for a minute back when you...when you kissed me. Kissed my panties, I mean," she admitted. "And before that when you...when I had your cream in me. But nothing else seems to help."

Karn nodded.

"Okay, well I can't exactly come on your little pussy right now but there is *one* thing I can do to help you."

"What's that?" Lilli asked. Just at that moment, the servant at the door called,

"Miss Lilliana, daughter of Mistress Mirabella? Are you here to be announced?"

"You'll see." Karn gave her that crooked grin and took her hand to lead her towards the entrance. "Come on, little Mistress—it's your turn."

# TWENTY-SIX

L illi went stiff with stage fright as she and Karn made their way up onto the announcing platform. It wasn't very big but it overlooked the grand, mother-of-pearl ballroom, filled with all the richest and most influential Mistresses in all of Opulex. She had always hated being the center of attention, and this was *way* worse than being in one of the morality plays the Sisters had helped the girls at the convent put on for the benefit of their classmates.

Lilli had only been in one of those plays—she'd been a supporting character with only one line. But when it had come time to speak her piece, she'd stumbled and bumbled and forgotten every word. In the end, she'd nearly fainted from mortification and misery.

This experience was *much* worse. This time it wasn't just other girls from the convent and the kindly Sisters watching. This time it was everyone who counted on Yonnie Six and all of them were judging her—*harshly*.

Lilli had seen the way Priss had preened and strutted and yanked on her bodyslave's leash, forcing him to kiss her panties. But there was no way she could act like that with Karn. All she could do was stand there, in the middle of the stage, feeling like she had back at the convent auditorium with everyone snickering and giggling and waiting for her to say or do something—anything at all—while she stood there, frozen.

"Mistress Lilliana," the announcer said and Lilli had the idea that he'd already said it twice before and still she was just standing there.

Suddenly Karn dropped to his knees before her.

"Mistress," he growled, looking up at her and taking her hands in his. "Allow me to pay obeisance to you."

"Oh, uh…" Lilli felt like her tongue was tied in knots.

"Look at me," Karn murmured, for her ears alone. "Lilli, look at me—just concentrate on me and forget what everyone else is doing."

"All right." She looked into his mismatched eyes and suddenly found herself drowning in their gold and blue depths.

"Mistress," Karn rumbled. "May I have the honor of kissing your panties?"

Doing as he had told her, Lilli forced herself to focus on the big Kindred and nothing else.

"Yes," she said softly, reaching out to stroke his cheek. "Oh yes, Karn—you may."

"Thank you, Mistress." And taking her hips in his big hands, he pulled her forward and kissed her.

Lilli bit her lip as she felt his mouth fall, not on the golden lace of her panties, but directly on her exposed and throbbing clit. She couldn't help moaning as Karn's hot, wet tongue slid around and around her tender little pearl and then found its way even lower, bathing her entire inner pussy.

"Oh, *Karn,*" she moaned, grasping his broad shoulders for support as he continued to lick and suck her avidly. He was sending sparks of pleasure through her entire body, making her feel weak in the knees. She forgot all about the fact that she was on a stage, forgot all the other Mistresses watching her. All she could concentrate on was the big Kindred and how much she loved his mouth on her.

She didn't know how long it lasted, only that when Karn finally pulled back—his mouth shiny with her juices, his eyes half-lidded with lust—she was so close to the edge it felt like even the slightest touch might tip her over into orgasm.

"Karn!" she begged. "Why…why did you stop?"

"Because there are other Mistresses waiting to be announced," he murmured and nodded at the servant who was announcing people. There was a line of women and bodyslaves behind him and the servant had his arms crossed over his chest and was frowning and tapping his foot impatiently.

But their performance—or rather, Karn's performance—seemed to have had a completely different effect on the watching Yonnite Mistresses. As Lilli and Karn pulled apart and the big Kindred rose to his feet, they began to clap.

"Oh!" Lilli put a hand to her heart, surprised as she looked out on the sea of approving faces. "Oh, are they clapping for *us?*"

"They're clapping for *you*, little Mistress," Karn murmured in her ear. "For training me so well."

"But I never trained you to do any of that!" Lilli protested. "You just, uh, *did* it."

"They don't know that," Karn pointed out. "So don't let them find out. Hold your head high and lead me like the dominant Mistress you are."

Lilli did her best to follow his instructions. Holding her head up, she made her way to a table in the back of the room where Yulla Yodermouth and Beelie and Bodie Bodypom were waving at her to come sit with them.

"Wow, that was really impressive!" Beelie said as Lilli seated herself and Karn took up his position behind her chair.

"Yeah—even better than Priss," Bodie said. "Don't tell her that, though," she added.

"Because here she comes!" Beelie finished for her twin.

*Oh, no!* Lilli had a sinking feeling in the pit of her stomach. If she'd known Priss was sitting at this table, she would have sat with her mother instead. Or *anyplace* there was a free chair, for that matter.

"Well, hello, girls. And hello again, Lilliana," she remarked as she seated herself beside Lilli. "How was your first formal announcement? I'm sorry I missed it but I had to run to the necessary room. I hope you didn't trip again, like you did outside, or do anything else *stupid*."

"Actually, Lilliana did really well," Yulla said, speaking up for the first time. "Everybody clapped for her and everything."

"What?" Priss narrowed her sharp blue eyes at Bodie and Beelie. "Is that true?"

"Uh-huh." They nodded in unison and Bodie said, "She really has her bodyslave trained *perfectly*."

"Is that *so?*" Priss glared at Lilli. "Well, then let me be the first to congratulate you on not tripping over your own two feet up there and acting like an *idiot,*" she snapped, nodding at the stage where someone else was currently being announced. "I know it must have been really hard for you to overcome your *natural inclinations..*"

Lilli didn't know what to say when faced with such open hostility. Such nasty manners hadn't been allowed at the convent, where everyone treated everyone else with respect and the Sisters insisted on mediating all conflicts, no matter how small.

"Um, where is the necessary room?" she asked the twins, deciding that getting away from the table completely was her best bet. "I need to find it before the ceremony starts."

"Running away, Lilliana?" Priss sneered at her but Bodie and Beelie seemed to have mercy on her.

"It's through that back exit," Beelie said.

"Right beside the elevator bank," Bodie added.

"Thank you." Lilli rose and nodded at Karn. "Come on, let's go." She nodded her thanks to Bodie and Beelie and, ignoring Priss, headed for the back of the huge, glittering ballroom.

# TWENTY-SEVEN

"Well, here we are. Do you really need to use the fresher?" Karn asked, looking down at Lilli when the two of them were finally clear of the ballroom and could talk normally instead of as Mistress and bodyslave. "Or were you looking for an excuse to get out of there so we can solve our mystery?"

"Oh, our mystery!" Lilli brightened at once. "That's right—we need to find out what happened with the Nightwalker Kindred!"

She'd been so preoccupied with the awful tingle—which Karn had finally soothed with his tongue—and then with Priss being nasty and awful, that she'd nearly forgotten the main reason she and Karn wanted to be here in the first place.

"Exactly—the mystery," he rumbled. "Are you up for it?"

"I'm up for anything that gets me out of that crowded ballroom with those awful people," Lilli said fervently. "Come on, let's go!" She waved her hand over the elevator's sensor and the shiny, mother-of-pearl door immediately slid open.

Lilli and Karn stepped in and Lilli said, "Take us to Mistress Zangelo's floor."

The elevator chimed and a smooth, artificial voice said,

"I'm sorry, that floor has been restricted as a crime scene area."

Thinking fast, Lilli said, "Override by order of Mistress Mirabella, member of the Sacred Seven."

The elevator seemed to take a while to process this but after a moment it chimed again and said, "Access granted."

Lilli sighed in relief as the doors slid shut and the richly appointed elevator began to hum quietly. Her mother would probably be upset if she found out Lilli had been taking her name in vain, but honestly—what else could she do? An innocent male's life might hang in the balance. And hopefully, her mother would never find out.

After a moment the elevator chimed again and the smooth artificial voice announced, "Zangelo residence."

The doors slid open and Lilli and Karn got out into a dimly lit, richly furnished apartment.

"What are we looking for?" Lilli found herself whispering, though she didn't know why. It wasn't like there was anyone else here—it was clearly deserted.

Karn shrugged.

"Clues, I guess. The Nightwalker was accused of killing his Mistress here. Let's see what we can find to either confirm or refute that."

"Okay, but let's stick together." Lilli shivered as she looked around the darkened living space. "This gives me the creeps!"

"I won't leave your side, little Mistress," Karn promised. "In fact, here…"

And he took her hand in his and intertwined their fingers.

Lilli felt better at once about walking into the dark apartment where a woman had been murdered. Karn was with her—he wouldn't let anything happen to her, she told herself.

They wandered past the richly furnished living area and through the well-appointed kitchens being careful not to touch anything. Nothing looked out of order until they came to a room off the kitchens which was filled with large metal cages.

"What's this?" Lilli asked blankly as Karn called for lights, which came on at once.

The big Kindred frowned.

"Looks like some kind of a kennel," he growled. "Did Mistress Zangelo breed any kind of animals?"

"No." Lilli felt her gut clench. "But I *do* think she might have kept rather a lot of bodyslaves."

"What a fucking way to live!" Karn shook his head as he looked at the empty metal cages.

Each one had a long chain affixed to the back of it, attached to a choke collar. Some had thin blankets lining their chain-link floors and some had nothing at all. A few discarded water and food dishes could be seen too.

"She treated them like animals," Karn muttered, glaring around at the cramped, bare cages.

"It's awful." Lilli felt hot tears prick her eyelids. "How could anyone treat other people this way?"

"Beats the Seven Hells out of me," Karn growled. "Come on, let's get out of here. I've seen as much as I want to."

"Wait!" Lilli caught his arm. "What...what's *that?*"

She pointed a trembling finger and he turned to follow her gaze. When he saw what she was pointing at, his face grew hard.

"Come on."

They walked up to the side of the abandoned metal cage and looked down at the dark streaks dried on its bars and the floor in front of it.

"Looks like dried blood," Karn said at last, frowning.

"Quite a lot of it," Lilli whispered. She couldn't seem to stop staring at the streaks and smears on the cage and the floor. "Do...do you think this is where he did it?"

"I'm still not convinced he *did* do it," Karn said, frowning. "Come on, let's go back this way and try to find Mistress Zangelo's bedchamber. According to the report I read, that's where the body was found."

"Okay." Lilli clutched his hand tighter and he gave her a reassuring squeeze.

"It's all right, little Mistress," he rumbled, looking down at her. "I'm not going anywhere."

"I know." It was the only thing that made Lilli keep going. She knew that if she'd been down here alone in the dim apartment where a bloody murder had been committed, there was no way she could have gone on after seeing those awful smears of dried blood. But being with the big Kindred made her feel safe.

She and Karn wandered around some more until they finally came to a large, circular room with what appeared to be a vast round bed in the middle.

"Do you think this is it?" Lilli looked doubtfully at the chamber. It wasn't set up like a normal bedroom, and the bed, which was covered in a vast black spread, certainly didn't appear to be a normal bed.

It was big enough to hold eight or ten people for one thing. For another, the bed seemed to be arranged very strangely. Instead of having pillows at the top of it—if a circular bed could be considered to have a top—it had seven or eight large, long, furry pillows arranged in a spoke-like pattern all around it.

The pillows were almost as long as Lilli was tall and they were covered in soft, thick fur in colors that ranged from deep magenta, to burnt umber, to turquoise. They stood out brightly against the black bedspread.

"What's the point of all this?" Lilli asked, stepped forward to look at the furry pillows in their strange, spoke-like pattern which almost made the circular bed look like some kind of a wheel.

"Don't know." Karn shook his head. "But look—" He pointed. "A surveillance room!"

Lilli followed his finger and saw that there was an open door at the far side of the strange bedchamber. She would have expected it to be the bathing chamber but instead, the glint of computing equipment could be seen.

"This could be what we've been looking for!" Karn's voice was excited. "Come on!"

# TWENTY-EIGHT

K arn couldn't believe his luck. The setup in the surveillance room was essentially the same as what Lilli's mother had in her secret home office. It was humming quietly to itself—clearly the Opulex authorities had neglected to turn it off when they had declared this apartment a crime scene area.

He took a seat and grabbed the manipu-cube at once, looking for files of the night the murder had been committed. Everything was encrypted but that didn't bother Karn a bit. After years in the Elite Espionage Corps, he was excellent at breaking encryptions. After a few moments, he figured out the rather simple code the programmer had used and he was in.

As he had hoped, the entire house was under surveillance with a hidden camera apparently secreted in each room—some rooms had more than one. He was looking for images from the bedchamber where the body had been found, but that file came up blank, along with many others.

*Looks like someone erased it,* Karn thought grimly. Who had done it? Was it the murderer, covering their tracks? Or some authority figure who didn't want to accuse a prominent Mistress of a heinous crime?

He was just about to despair when he found a file for the large kennel room he and Lilli had already visited. It had been hidden in an innocuous folder marked, *expendable assets,* which might explain why whoever had erased the other files had missed it.

He clicked on it and up popped an image of the kennel room.

"Oh!" Lilli whispered in shock as Karn played the footage. "Look at that! That *must* be the Nightwalker Kindred!"

"And *that* must be the murderer," Karn growled. They watched together as the scene played out. It was only a few moments long, but it was clear what had happened—the Nightwalker Kindred had been framed.

He pressed the spy device on the nail of his left ring finger again, hoping to record the data and send it on to Commander Sylvan and the Mother Ship—but there was a problem.

"There's a send-block on it," Karn growled in frustration.

"A what?" Lilli frowned. "What are you talking about?"

"Oh, uh…I wanted to send it to your Mother's computing device," Karn said, thinking quickly. Damn it, he had to be more careful around the little female! He had gotten entirely too comfortable committing espionage with Lilli in the same room with him.

"To my mother's device?" Lilli asked, clearly confused.

"So she can see the truth. She's the Archivist, isn't she? This ought to go to her," Karn said pointing at the screen. "But maybe I can record it instead—on this," he added, picking up a tiny drive at random out of a pile on the desktop. "Let's see what's on it— maybe we can erase it and put the scene from the kennel room on it instead. Then I can load it secretly onto your Mother's computing device. She'll wonder where it came from, but she'll have to act on it. After all, the case is in court—or going to court —very soon."

"Oh, and as the Archivist, she's supposed to supply the court with any relevant documents or evidence. Right!" Lilli exclaimed. "Good idea, Karn."

"Thanks, baby." He grinned at her and slipped the tiny, fingernail-sized drive into a slot in the manipu-cube.

He thought he'd take a quick look at the files on the drive before erasing them, but when the image popped up on the liquid crystal screen, he forgot all about that. Because what appeared on the screen seemed to be some kind of amateur porn—made right in the next room with the circular bed.

"Oh, my…" Lilli's voice was hushed as she looked over his shoulder at the screen. "What…what are they doing?"

The scene showed the same bed they had just seen, only this time it was occupied. Five Mistresses—all of them wearing masks, apparently for anonymity—were lying full length on the long, furry pillows. They had their skirts hitched up to their waists, showing bare bottoms and it was clear they had no panties on—not even the skimpy kind that Yonnite High Society favored. This was obvious because they had their legs spread and their knees were bent, resting on either side of the pillows they were lying on.

"Mmm," one murmured, rubbing against the fur of her pillow. "Lady Zangelo, this feels *lovely*."

"I told you—no names!" another of the masked Mistresses snapped. "And of course it's nice—it's fresh *zoola* fur. It costs a ridiculous sum, of course and it's doubly expensive since I have to throw all the pillows out and get fresh ones for every friction party. But *I* think it's worth it. Rub it against your nipples—the feeling is *quite* unique."

At this, all of the Mistresses pulled down the tops of their dresses —not that they had very far to pull in most cases—and began to rub their bare breasts against the long, silky fur of their pillows. There were appreciative moans from all of them and several congratulated Lady Zangelo on her very good taste.

"Now where are those bodyslaves?" another Mistress asked, frowning peevishly. "I'm getting quite chilly lying here all open like this!"

"They'll be coming in a moment. They just have to put on their friction sleeves," another Mistress told her. "Oh, Lady Z, did you ever get that one you just bought—that Nightwalker Kindred—trained enough to participate?"

"Not yet, more's the pity." Lady Zangelo sighed. "For he's hung like a Prosperian thunder-beast! But he's still completely savage—won't obey, though I used the pain collar on him fifty times a day!"

"Well, he'll come around," another Mistress said. "They always do. Maybe you'll get to feel that long, thick shaft of his during your *next* friction party, Lady Z."

"One hopes so," Lady Zangelo sniffed. "I swear that shaft of his is the only reason I bought him. That and that awful Mistress Bittlebum goading me and saying that he was completely untameable and nobody could handle him if *she* couldn't."

"Lady Bittlebum couldn't train a seventy-year old bodyslave with only one good eye and a limp—let alone a young, virile warrior," another Mistress said.

"It's not Lady Bittlebum I blame for the Kindred's savagery," Lady Zangelo said. "It's that old Mistress Hownow—the one who owned him in the first place. Do you know she actually raised him as her child without the use of any kind of collar or pain device?"

"She did?" Many of the Mistress's eyes widened behind their masks.

"Whatever for?" one of them asked.

Lady Zangelo snorted.

"Why, to be her *heir!* Can you imagine? A *male* heir?"

"No wonder he's so intractable," another Mistress remarked. "If she raised him as an equal to females. How perfectly ridiculous!"

"Nevertheless, I *will* break him eventually," Lady Zangelo said, frowning. "I have a new spiked neuro-collar that I ordered specially made for him, coming in tomorrow. Its spikes hook directly into the nervous system and stimulate the pain centers in the brain. *That* should make him behave!"

"Oh, how awful!" Lilli breathed behind Karn.

"Yeah, our Lady Z there seems to be quite a piece of work," he growled, nodding at her image on the liquid crystal screen. "Look—here come the bodyslaves."

As they watched, five bodyslaves—all very well hung—came into the camera's frame. Each of them appeared to be wearing some kind of covering over his shaft. Some of the coverings had raised bumps and ridges and one had tiny blunt nubs studding its surface.

"Those must be the 'friction sleeves' they were talking about," Karn murmured.

"I guess so," Lilli breathed.

At a signal from one of the masked women, the bodyslaves approached and took up positions behind their respective Mistresses.

"Is everyone ready?" Lady Zangelo asked.

"Just a moment—I must adjust," one of the Mistresses said.

The bed's height was such that it put most of the Mistresses in line with the cocks of their bodyslaves. But for a few, the distance wasn't quite right. Several of them did something to the tops of their pillows—possibly manipulating some controls hidden in the fur. The pillows rose and got plumper or flattened accordingly, lifting or lowering the Mistresses to the right height.

"All right—all good," one of them called.

"Good." Lady Zangelo's eyes narrowed in anticipation. "Then let the friction party begin!"

As if on cue, the five bodyslaves came up behind their Mistresses and did something which looked very much like penetration, though Karn knew that was strictly forbidden. It was hard to tell if they were actually inside their Mistresses or not, due to the angle of the camera which was recording the proceedings, but most of the women on the pillows wiggled and moaned in reaction to their bodyslave's actions and several of them began issuing orders.

"Pok, rub *faster*," one of them demanded. "I can barely feel you!"

"Use the vibration function," another Mistress told her bodyslave. "Ah—that's right—hold it *right there*," she added, squirming against his thick shaft.

"What are they doing?" Lilli asked in a shocked voice. "Are they letting their bodyslaves *penetrate* them?"

"I don't know." Karn looked up at her. "Why—what do you think about it?"

"I think they…" Lilli broke off, her cheeks going red. "I don't know *what* to think. Of course, you're *never* supposed to let your bodyslave, er, do that. But…"

"But what, baby?" Karn murmured, catching her eyes.

"Um…" She pressed her thighs together and he noticed that her little pink clit—which had been hidden for a while after he licked her on the stage—was now beginning to peep out from between her pussy lips as though begging for attention again.

"Are you starting to feel the tingling again?" Karn murmured.

"Well…" Lilli bit her lip. "Maybe…maybe a little bit."

"Do you need me to lick you again, baby?" he asked, his voice dropping to a low, lustful growl. He loved the sweet-salty taste of her little virgin pussy.

"I…I'm not sure if you should," Lilli whispered.

"But you want me to, don't you?" Karn asked. "Don't you, little Mistress? Don't be shy—you can tell me," he added gently. "If you need me to lick your soft little pussy, just say so. You know I fucking *love* the way you taste."

Just thinking of it made his shaft get even harder.

"You…you do?" Lilli asked, her big brown eyes growing wide.

Karn nodded.

"Couldn't you tell by the way I was kissing your 'panties' earlier? Fucking delicious," he growled. "And you must be in real pain by now. I've been touching and tasting you off and on ever since you woke up this morning but you still haven't had a chance to come."

"I *am* awfully tingly," Lilli confessed haltingly. "I mean, it's really driving me *crazy.*"

"Then why not let me lick you, baby?" he growled softly. "You don't have to be ashamed. Just bring that sweet little pussy over here and spread your legs for me. Let me lick your hot little cunt until you come all over my face."

"Oh, Karn…" Lilli blushed again but he could tell she wanted him to do what he was offering. "If…I mean, are you sure you don't mind?" she asked softly.

In answer, Karn lowered the chair he was sitting in until his face was level with her tiny gold lace panties.

"Come here, little Mistress," he growled. "Let me taste your sweet pussy again."

Pulling her forward, he brought her pussy to his mouth and yanked the skimpy panties down and then off. They might be tiny but he didn't want anything in the way of tasting her—and this time he was going to do it right.

This time he was going to lick her soft little cunt until she came all over his face.

"Oh!" Lilli gasped as he parted her outer pussy lips with his tongue and lapped her inner folds. She was hot and wet and trembling with need as he licked her. "Oh, *Karn,*" she moaned and he felt her clutching at his shoulders for a moment and then her fingers wove themselves into his hair.

He growled in approval, his cock throbbing, as she pulled him closer, riding his face. Gods, he loved to taste his female—loved to drive her crazy with his mouth!

Lilli was practically vibrating under his tongue, her swollen little clit throbbing in time with her heartbeat as she rubbed and pressed against him, giving in to the pleasure he was causing with his licking and sucking.

"Karn!" she cried again, and he knew she was near the edge. "Oh Karn, I'm so close! Please…*please* don't stop!"

He had no intention of stopping. This time, he was going to take her all the way, he swore to himself. This time he was going to make her come—come so hard she saw stars and rainbows and opened her thighs, begging for more—begging to have him inside her…

"Well, well, Lilliana—at least *now* we know why your slave is so good at kissing your panties! Clearly the two of you are doing a lot more than a Mistress and bodyslave *should!*" a nasty, familiar voice announced.

Lilli grew suddenly stiff in his arms and Karn heard his Mistress gasp, "Priss!" in a horrified voice.

They had been caught.

# TWENTY-NINE

"My, my—just *look* at the two of you!" Priss grinned at Lilli nastily. She had her bodyslave with her, as well as Bodie and Beelie and Yulla, who all had their bodyslaves trailing behind them too. "I don't think that's your *panties* your bodyslave is kissing, Lilliana," she remarked. "In fact, where *are* your panties, anyway? Oh wait—*there* they are!" And she pointed to the tiny scrap of gold lace which was lying at Lilli's feet.

"I...we..." Lilli felt frozen with mortification. Her heart was pounding and her mouth was dry. "I didn't...we weren't..." she began, but then couldn't finish.

"Well, I can see what got you all worked up, anyway," Priss remarked. Her sharp eyes had left Lilli and were focused on the liquid crystal screen, where Lady Zangelo and her cronies were still being pleasured by their bodyslaves. "My, my," she murmured. "I had heard a naughty rumor that Mistress Zangelo did this kind of thing, but I never thought I'd get to see it for myself!"

"What is it?" Yulla asked, frowning.

"Yeah, what's going on?" Bodie asked.

"Why, it's a *friction* party, of course!" Priss exclaimed as the people on the screen continued to writhe against each other. "Haven't you heard of them? They're so *naughty*. I've always wanted to go to one!"

"You have?" Beelie frowned. "But what are they about?"

Priss's sharp blue eyes flashed.

"They're about *pleasure*. Come on—I'll show you."

She led the way back into the large bedchamber and its huge round bed but Lilli hung back, her heart pounding unhappily against her ribs.

"Go on, little Mistress," Karn murmured to her. He was working rapidly with the cube, presumably recording the other information they had wanted to save. "I'm right behind you."

"Let's just leave," Lilli murmured, reaching down to scoop up her discarded panties. "I'll tell Mother I have a headache and I need to go home early. We can call a transport."

"Suits me." Karn rose from the chair. "We got what we came for." He leaned closer and murmured in her ear, "And I'd like to finish what we started—this time *without* an audience."

Lilli couldn't agree more. Despite the embarrassment of being discovered by Priss and her gang, she was still throbbing with unfulfilled need. As unobtrusively as she could, she peeked around the doorway. Priss and the other three girls had all settled themselves on their stomachs, lying on the long furry pillows and were in the act of pulling up their skirts.

*They look distracted,* Lilli thought hopefully. *Maybe Karn and I can just walk out past them.*

Moving as quietly as she could, she started to sneak out of the strange bedchamber. But before she had gone three steps, Priss called out,

"If you leave now, Lilliana, I'll tell your mother and my mother and *everyone* on the Sacred Seven exactly *why* your bodyslave appears to be so well trained."

"What...what do you mean?" Lilli froze in her tracks.

"I mean, if you're letting him lick your pussy without your panties on, no *wonder* he acts like he loves you and wants to serve you," Priss snapped, looking over her shoulder. "Now come here!"

Lilli walked over to her unwillingly.

"What do you want?" she asked, not sure what else to say.

"Why, I only want you to join in the fun!" Priss gave her a glittering smile that looked about as real as plastigold. "Pick a pillow and join the friction party."

"Oh, but…but I couldn't do that!" Lilli exclaimed. "I mean, did you *see* that vid? I think those Mistresses might have been letting their bodyslaves *penetrate* them!"

"Don't be ridiculous!" Priss snapped. "Their bodyslaves weren't penetrating them—they were simply *rubbing* against them. That's the point of the friction sleeves they were all wearing. They position their shafts between their Mistress's pussy and the pillow and just *rub.*"

"Oh…" Lilli murmured. That made sense, she supposed. No wonder the colorful sleeves the bodyslaves had been wearing over their shafts had all had nubs or studs or raised bumps on them—it was to stimulate their Mistresses when they rubbed against them.

"So that's what we're going to do? Let our bodyslaves rub their shafts against our pussies?" Bodie asked, frowning.

"Exactly." Priss smiled that fake smile of hers again. "We're going to do it *exactly* as the older Mistresses do! They think we're too young to have fun but what do they know?"

"But Priss," Yulla said timidly. "Our bodyslaves don't *have* friction sleeves. So won't they be rubbing their bare shafts against our bare pussies?"

"And isn't direct contact between a bodyslave's shaft and his Mistress's pussy against the law?" Beelie asked.

"Shut up and stop being so stuffy!" Priss snapped at all of them. "Haven't you ever wondered what direct flesh-to-flesh contact feels like? If it's against the law, it *must* feel good!"

"Better than a toy?" Bodie asked, frowning.

"We'll find out, won't we?" Priss said. "Come on—this is going to be fun! We don't need friction sleeves to enjoy ourselves. And *you…*"

she pointed at Lilli. "Pick a pillow and get into position. We're about to have the time of our lives and I don't want you missing it."

"But we shouldn't!" Lilli protested, although she kind of wanted to. But not in front of all the other girls—she would much rather have done this kind of thing alone with Karn in the privacy of her own bedchamber.

"Well, you shouldn't have been letting your bodyslave lick your pussy without your panties on, either," Priss said, smiling at her meanly. "Now get on the pillow or I'm telling your mother!"

Lilli exchanged a helpless glance with Karn. What else could they do but comply? Going as far as she could from Priss, Lilli found a long, furry, magenta pillow and lowered herself down on it.

The soft fur seemed to rub and tease her nipples—which were still bare and encircled with the nipple drops that matched her dress. It tickled the bare mound of her pussy too and she thought she had never felt so open and vulnerable as when she straddled the pillow, putting her knees on the mattress and her open pussy on display.

"That's better," Priss said, frowning. "Now, is everybody ready?"

"I guess so," Yulla said.

"Ready," Beelie and Bodie said together.

All three girls still looked uncertain but it was clear they didn't have the courage to go against Priss's orders. Lilli wished she could, but she feared what would happen if the other girl told on her. Oh, if only she hadn't caught her and Karn! If only—

"Bodyslaves, in position!" Priss ordered bossily, cutting off her thoughts. "You know what that means—position your shafts between the pillow and your Mistress's pussy. *No* actual penetration allowed, of course."

"Yes, Mistress," all of the bodyslaves rumbled—Karn included.

Lilli held her breath as she felt the big Kindred's thick shaft slide into position between her swollen pussy lips and the slick, silky fur. She bit her lip and couldn't help moaning as she felt the broad head bump over her aching clit before he settled into a resting position behind her.

"Now, hold it for a minute," Priss ordered. "Everybody wiggle against your bodyslave's shaft. See how it feels."

Lilli shifted her hips back and forth and up and down, rubbing against Karn's hot, throbbing thickness. She couldn't help the moan that rose to her lips at the illicit action. That morning in the shower she'd allowed him to shoot his seed over the inside of her pussy, but she'd never actually expected them to touch this way. It felt *amazing*.

"Feels pretty good," Bodie murmured and her twin agreed.

"My bodyslave has a really big cockhead," Yulla complained breathlessly, shifting her hips. "And it's rubbing right against my *clit.*"

"It's *supposed* to," Priss told her. "Now on the count of three, I want all of our bodyslaves to start thrusting. Work up some friction—that's what this party is all about. One…two…*three.*"

Lilli bit her lip as Karn gripped her hips and pulled slowly out until only the head of his cock was pressed against her slippery inner folds. Then he thrust forward, pressing his thick length against her inner pussy, the flaring crown of his shaft bumping over her tender clit as he went.

"Oh!" she heard herself moaning as he did it again…and again and again. "Oh, Karn, *yes!*"

"Gods, little Mistress, your pussy is so wet," Karn growled in her ear. "Love to rub against you like this—love to feel how wet and hot and open you are against my shaft!"

His dirty words made Lilli throb all over. Once more she was feeling close to orgasm. Once more the pleasure was building inside her, threatening to push her to the peak and then over the edge with the power of need and desire. If only he would just keep it up…

"Stop!" Priss exclaimed so loudly that everyone froze at once.

"What…what is it? What's wrong?" Beelie asked, panting.

"Yeah, Priss—why did you stop us? That was better than a toy!" Bodie pouted.

"I like the feel of flesh-on-flesh," Yulla declared, wiggling against her bodyslave's shaft. She turned her head. "And I forgive you for having a really big cockhead, Bolif."

Her bodyslave grinned and nodded. "Thank you, Mistress."

Priss didn't answer any of them. Instead, she turned her head and glared at her bodyslave who was frozen with a look of fear on his face.

"Randor," she snarled at him. "Just *what* do you think you're doing?"

Her bodyslave swallowed with an audible *gulp,* his Adam's apple bobbing nervously.

"Forgive me, Mistress," he muttered quickly. "I didn't mean to. It's just that you're so wet and slippery and—"

"Oh my Goddess!" Bodie's eyes went wide. "Did he actually *penetrate you,* Priss?"

Priss turned back to glare at her. Then she tossed her head defiantly.

"So what if he did? It actually feels really *good.*"

"You're lying," Yulla said flatly. "I was penetrated at the conception center and it *hurt.*"

"That's because the conception nozzle that impregnates you is really big and cold," Priss said loftily. "A bodyslave's shaft is warm and not nearly as big in diameter. So it feels *good* going in."

"Well, we'll take your word about that," Beelie said, frowning. "None of *us* is going to get penetrated by our bodyslaves."

"Oh, yes you are!" Priss snapped, glaring at all of them. "I'm not going to be the only one breaking the law here. If I get penetrated, you all have to, too!"

"But...I don't know how I feel about that," Yulla protested.

"I do—we could get in really big trouble if anyone found out!" Bodie exclaimed.

"But nobody is because we're going to take this to our graves!" Priss told her. "If we *all* get penetrated, then none of us can tell on the others because we all participated."

"But we *haven't* all been penetrated—just you," Lilli pointed out —and then wished she'd kept her mouth closed.

Priss turned on her.

"Well, you're *about* to be penetrated," she snarled. "Because if you're not, I'm going to tell on you. I mean, what would your mother say if she knew you were doing what we saw you doing with your brand-new Kindred bodyslave? I bet she might be *upset.* She might even send him to the Diluthian mines—don't you think?"

Lilli bit her lip in mute misery. Why was Priss so awful? And would she really tell Lilli's mother and get Karn sent to the mines?

"And Yulla—I'll tell your mother about the bracelet you stole at the Sundown festival," Priss went on. "Bodie and Beelie," I'll tell how the two of you are always changing places when you have to take tests in your finishing classes. I'll let her know that Beelie can't do a lick of math and Bodie can't string two words together to form a sentence because the two of you always switch off."

There was silence in the room and nobody could meet Priss's sharp blue eyes.

"You see?" she sneered. "I have something on *all* of you. Now spread your pussies wide for your bodyslave's shafts! And don't think you can cheat and just pretend, either. We're all going to be penetrated *right now.*"

She flicked a green gem on one of the many rings she was wearing and it popped open. Out of it flew something no bigger than a blood-gnat. It circled the room and suddenly a 3-D image began to form in the center of the bed.

"There—that's me," Priss said, as a close-up shot of her pussy came into view. Sure enough, her bodyslave's shaft was halfway inside her, clearly penetrating her entrance. "Now, let's see the rest of you," she snapped. "Come on, Bodie—you first!"

Bodie turned her head to look at her bodyslave.

"Go on," she murmured. "Just…don't go too deep."

"Yes, Mistress." The male nodded his head respectfully and then the tiny surveillance gnat flew in close and captured an image of him inserting the head of his shaft into his Mistress's pussy.

"Oh!" Bodie gasped, gripping the sides of her pillow as he slipped in. None of their bodyslaves had small shafts, owing to the fact that

Yonnite society used the size of a male bodyslave's equipment as a literal measuring stick for status.

"Are you okay?" Beelie asked, her eyes filled with concern for her twin.

"Yes, I...*think* so." Bodie wiggled some, which caused her bodyslave's shaft to enter her more deeply. "Actually, it doesn't feel too bad—once you get used to it," she told her twin.

"Good. Now it's your turn, Beelie. Spread your pussy and let your bodyslave penetrate you," Priss demanded.

She must have known that the twins wouldn't do anything without each other and she was right, because Beelie didn't even protest. She simply opened her legs wider and nodded at her bodyslave to do the deed. She moaned a little as he slipped into her, but didn't make anymore comment as the surveillance gnat showed that she had, indeed, complied with Priss's order.

"Good." Priss nodded in apparent satisfaction. She turned to Yulla. "Now it's your turn."

"But, Priss," Yulla protested. "Doesn't having a male's shaft in your pussy mean he's going to shoot his seed in you? And isn't seed what makes you pregnant?"

"You're *already* pregnant, you little idiot," Priss hissed. "It's not like you can conceive again! Not before the quick-grow heir you're already carrying is out, anyway!"

"Oh..." Yulla's rather dull face cleared and she nodded. "Okay then." She moaned a little and squeezed her pillow as her bodyslave entered her, but she didn't complain anymore.

"And now we only have one unpenetrated girl left," Priss remarked.

Lilli's heart was pounding as all eyes turned to her and Priss's surveillance gnat showed a picture of her sex. She couldn't help thinking that the mouth of her pussy looked awfully small and tight and the head of Karn's cock looked huge in comparison.

"Please," she whispered. "I...I don't think this is a good idea."

"No, it's *not*," Priss said, giving her a nasty smile. "After all, your bodyslave has the biggest shaft of all of them and I *know* they didn't let you play with sex toys at that stupid, backwards convent you were raised in. So he's going to stretch your pussy *way* out of shape when he sticks it in!"

"Also, she's not pregnant yet," Bodie pointed out. "All the rest of us are safe because we're already expecting. But what if Lilliana's bodyslave shoots his seed in her?"

"Well then, I guess she might have a little *problem* a few months down the road." Priss's nasty smile widened at the thought. "And what a shame *that* would be."

Of course, Lilli knew this wasn't going to be a problem because Karn was a Hybrid and unable to bond her to him or get her pregnant. But she was still frightened at the idea of his massive equipment breaching her untried entrance. But before she could say anything, Karn spoke up.

"I won't do this," he growled, frowning at Priss. "I won't rape my Mistress just for your pleasure."

Priss's eyes widened.

"How *dare* you speak to me, bodyslave! Just for that, I'm going to make you shove your shaft to the hilt in her tight little pussy! And if you don't, it's off to the mines for you."

Her threat left Lilli cold. She couldn't lose Karn that way—she just *couldn't*.

"It's all right, Karn," she said quickly, turning to face him. "It's not rape because I want you to do it. Go ahead—put…put yourself inside me."

He frowned.

"Are you sure, little Mistress? I don't want to do anything you don't want me to."

"I want you to," Lilli assured him again. "Just…be gentle, all right? You're awfully big and I'm awfully small."

Karn leaned forward and whispered in her ear.

"Remember that my precum has compounds in it to help you

open. So I won't hurt you." He stroked her back soothingly. "All right, little Mistress?"

His reassurances and the soothing touch made Lilli feel better.

"Yes, Karn," she murmured. "Go ahead then—put your shaft inside me."

Karn took himself in hand and then Lilli watched on the 3-D image the gnat was projecting as he rubbed the broad, flaring crown of his shaft against the swollen bump of her clit. The friction sent fireworks shooting through her nerves and she moaned softly and raised her hips, automatically giving him better access to her pussy mouth.

"Hurry up, bodyslave," Priss snapped. "Shove it in her! I want to see sweet little Lilliana skewered on that thick cock of yours that she's so proud of!"

But Karn refused to be rushed.

"My Mistress is a virgin," he growled. "I'll take my time with her."

As he spoke, he rubbed gently but firmly over Lilli's clit once more before slowly sliding down to fit the tip of his cock to the entrance of her pussy. He rubbed her there too, sliding around and around her opening and Lilli knew he was getting her ready by working his precum into her flesh to help her stretch to receive him.

*It's all right,* she told herself nervously. *Everything is going to be all right. Karn would never hurt me—he's being slow and gentle. I'm okay...*

Despite her self-reassurances, she bit her lip as she watched the 3-D image of the broad, flaring crown of Karn's cock slowly pushing inside her pussy mouth. She could see herself stretching wide to take him—wider than she would have thought possible.

And yet, it didn't hurt.

"Oh my Goddess," Beelie and Bodie murmured at the same time and Bodie asked, "How in the world is she taking so much? He's *twice* as big as my bodyslave and my poor little pussy feels stuffed!"

"Mine too!" Beelie exclaimed. "I thought she was an unpenetrated virgin!"

"I...I am," Lilli protested, huffing a little as Karn slid the head of his shaft fully into her. "Or…I *was*," she added doubtfully. She didn't suppose she could claim to be unpenetrated *or* a virgin now.

But apparently Priss disagreed.

"Don't be silly," she scoffed. "Penetration only counts if the male's shaft is all the way inside you and Lilliana's bodyslave only has the head of his shaft in her. I say he should go deeper—all the rest of us have our bodyslaves at least halfway inside us."

"Yes—I guess that *would* be fair," Yulla said, frowning.

"Mistress?" Karn murmured in Lilli's ear and she knew he was asking if she wanted him to go farther. She wiggled a little, trying to get used to his thickness piercing her so intimately. It didn't hurt but she *did* feel stretched to the limit. Could she take more of his thick shaft sliding into her little pussy? And did she want to?

The tingling in her pussy answered her question for her. She might never have considered doing this without being forced into it by Priss, but now she actually found she *liked* having Karn opening her…penetrating her, even if it was only a little bit. Now, Lilli found she wanted *more*.

"Go ahead, Karn," she murmured to him, looking back to meet his mismatched eyes. "You…you can put more of yourself in me."

"Yes, Mistress," he rumbled and then he was sliding deeper into her tightly stretched pussy.

"*Ohhhh*," Lilli moaned softly as she felt her inner walls opening to let him in. The 3-D image in the center of the bed showed the big Kindred's thick shaft getting deeper inside her, though he carefully stopped when he was halfway inside.

"Oh my Goddess," Yulla murmured. "I can't believe she took that much!"

"He's *huge*," Bodie said and her twin nodded in agreement.

"You must be satisfied *now*, Priss," Beelie said. "We've all been halfway penetrated—the same as you."

"Well, maybe I'm *not* satisfied," Priss declared. Twisting her head around, she looked at her bodyslave. "Randor, go all the way in," she commanded.

"Yes, Mistress." And with a long thrust, her bodyslave buried his entire shaft to the root in her pussy.

"Oh my Goddess," Bodie murmured unsteadily. "I can't believe you're doing that, Priss! I thought you said penetration didn't count unless the male's shaft was all the way inside you?"

"That's right—and now I've been *fully* penetrated." Priss wiggled her hips. "Mmm, it actually feels *good.*" She looked around the circle. "Well, what are you girls waiting for? Try it yourself and see."

Lilli saw Beelie and Bodie exchange a glance, but they must have liked the feeling too, because they nodded at their bodyslaves and moaned in unison as they were fully filled.

Yulla followed suit, though she didn't quite seem to enjoy it as much as the twins.

As before, Lilli was the only holdout.

"Well?" All of the other girls looked at her expectantly.

"Go on, Lilliana," Priss said, frowning. "Do it!"

"Mistress?" Karn asked again, his deep voice a rumble Lilli could feel throughout her entire body, now that they were joined together.

"Yes." Hanging her head, she widened her stance, trying to be open enough to take him all the way to the root. Well, almost all the way, she thought. There was no way she was going to take his mating fist inside her. Luckily, Priss didn't seem to notice. Or maybe she just didn't know that part of a Kindred should fit in a female also.

"Easy, little Mistress," she heard Karn say and then he was thrusting deeper into her—stretching her inner walls until she was certain she couldn't take much more.

But again, it didn't hurt a bit. She just felt more opened—more full—than she ever had in her life.

"Goddess," one of the twins murmured as the 3-D image showed Karn sliding home inside her. "How is she taking all that?"

Lilli wasn't sure herself. Though it didn't hurt, she never would have imagined her pussy would be big enough to accommodate a Kindred-sized shaft. Yet, here she was, stuffed completely full of her bodyslave's thick cock. How had this happened?

"Feels good, doesn't it girls?" Priss asked, grinning at all of them as she wiggled her hips. "No wonder it's against the law! If everyone knew how good it felt to let their bodyslave slide his shaft inside you, nobody would be doing anything else!"

Lilli rather thought she might be right. She had been horrified at the idea of letting her bodyslave penetrate her, but now that Karn was seated fully inside her, she found she *liked* being so filled. In fact, she wanted it to go on.

It wasn't just that she enjoyed the feeling of his shaft in her—it was the fact that having the big Kindred so deep inside her seemed to make the tingling stop, just as having him lick her or shoot his cream on the outside of her slippery folds did.

Plus, she had to admit that the forbidden pleasure of having Karn's shaft inside her was making her turned on. Just the idea that she was fully opened by his thick cock and the sight of herself stretched so tightly around him in the 3-D image made her shiver with desire.

But of course, Priss chose that moment to end it.

"All right," she said, sounding satisfied. "We've all been fully penetrated now, so we're all even. Everyone can have their bodyslaves pull out."

There were moans and sighs of disappointment all around but none of the other girls objected. Their bodyslaves pulled out and the girls all began sitting up and fixing their hair, getting ready to go back to the awards ceremony which was still going on upstairs.

"Well, that was interesting," Karn murmured, looking down at her as Lilli straightened her own dress and hair.

"Yes..." She blushed and found she couldn't quite meet his mismatched eyes. "I...I guess it was."

"Good thing Priss didn't make us go any farther," he growled.

Lilli nodded in agreement. She was actually surprised as well. She'd been certain the sadistic Mistress would force her and the other girls to submit to much more—maybe even to being fucked. It seemed strange that she would stop just when she did. But maybe she just wanted to make sure that all of them were even, so nobody could tell on anybody else.

Whatever the reason, Lilli wasn't sure if she was glad or sad that Priss had stopped things before they had gone any further.

She only knew she felt empty inside, now that Karn had withdrawn and she wished she could have him back in her again.

# THIRTY

K arn was throbbing as they rode home in Mistress Mirabella's
ship. Lilli seemed to be embarrassed by the intimacy that had
happened between them because every time he met her big brown
eyes in the mirror, she blushed and glanced away.

Gods damn it, he swore to himself. He hadn't wanted to hurt or
violate her! She'd said she wanted him to fill her, but he was afraid it
was only because Priss had been threatening to expose their secret and
have him sent to the Diluthian Mines.

*Rather be sent to the mines than hurt the female I care for,* he
thought, trying and failing to catch Lilli's eyes in the rear-viewer
again. He hoped he hadn't hurt her or scared her. If only they could
be alone and talk things out!

But the moment they got back to Lady Mirabella's mansion, she
decided to lecture Lilli about all the things she'd done wrong at the
awards ceremony. Karn would have stayed for moral support, but he
was sent from the room and had no choice but to go wait for Lilli in
her bedchamber.

He decided to take the opportunity to contact the Mother Ship, through the spy device fixed to his nail. Shutting himself firmly in the fresher, he locked the door and tapped in the special code that called home.

"Commander Karn? Are you well?" Commander Sylvan's face—or rather, a coin-sized image of it—appeared, hovering above the nail.

"I'm fine," Karn told him.

"Then why haven't you called for transport off of Yonnie Six?" Sylvan's eyebrows knit together in confusion. "You already completed your mission—good job, by the way—and we've been expecting your signal any time now."

"There's something else I have to see to here," Karn told him.

"Oh?" Sylvan raised one eyebrow quizzically. "What might that be?"

"There's another matter—a warrior who's been falsely accused." Rapidly, Karn explained about the Nightwalker Kindred who was being held in the Yonnite jail and was sentenced to execution.

"A Nightwalker? They're so rare!" Sylvan exclaimed. "And you say he's completely innocent?"

"Totally," Karn said. "And I have evidence to prove it—only it has a send-lock on it."

"I'll have to send someone to defend him in the Yonnite courts in order to get him out of there, anyway," Sylvan said. "One of our human female Councilors would be the ideal pick. Maybe you could physically give the evidence to her when she comes to Yonnie Six?"

"Sure." Karn nodded. "She can make some excuse to come to Mistress Mirabella's house. Or if that's too hard, we can rendezvous in Opulex. My Mistress is going there at the end of this week and I'm sure we can work something out."

"That would be perfect." Sylvan nodded. "Let me know when you have a more definite idea of your exact location."

"Will do." Karn nodded and heard the door of the bedchamber open. "Have to go, Commander—I'll be in touch," he murmured and quickly double tapped the spy device to shut it down.

Sylvan's image dissolved at once, just in time for him to hear Lilli call,

"Karn? Where are you?"

# THIRTY-ONE

"Here, little Mistress," she heard him call back. Going through her living area to the bedchamber, she found him waiting for her. He frowned when he saw her. "What's wrong, Lilli?" he asked softly. "Was your mother too rough on you?"

"Oh, not really." Lilli swiped at her eyes and tried to smile. She didn't like to admit how awful her mother could be sometimes. "She just…wants me to do things right, that's all," she said and sniffed.

But it seemed like Karn could see right through her.

"Yeah, I'll bet," he growled softly, frowning. "I heard some of what she was saying before she sent me away. You don't have to pretend with me, baby."

"Oh, Karn…" Lilli couldn't help herself anymore—the tears just overflowed. "Sometimes I'm not sure…sure if she loves me at all—or even *likes* me," she sobbed as the big Kindred took her in his arms.

"It's okay, just let it all out," he murmured, rubbing her shoulders and back soothingly. "Everything is going to be all right, sweetheart."

Lilli pressed her face against his broad chest and let herself be comforted. Karn was so warm and big and solid and he made her feel so safe, so cared for and protected.

At last, she was all cried out. With a trembling sigh, she took a step back and looked up at him with wet eyes.

"Thank you," she whispered. "Thank you for being there for me, Karn."

"There is no place I would rather be than here with you, Lilli," he murmured. Cupping her face in one hand, he swiped away the tears on her cheek with his thumb. "Come on now, let's go into the fresher. I'm going to take care of you tonight."

"You are? How?" Lilli asked uncertainly.

"You'll see." Karn gave her a hint of his crooked grin as he led her into the bathing chamber.

He undressed her, then drew her a warm bath and got into it with her so that he could wash her everywhere.

"I'm the Mistress, though," Lilli protested as he began to soap her arms and back. "*I'm* supposed to be washing *you.*"

"Not tonight, baby," Karn told her. "Tonight I'm taking care of you completely." His big hands ran down her sides and then gently cupped her bare breasts. "Do you want this?" he murmured in her ear. "If you're too tired—"

"No, I'm not too tired," Lilli said quickly. Now that the big Kindred had comforted her and helped her put her mother's mean words out of her mind, she was feeling that tingling ache again, spreading from the place she'd had the hormone shot to the tips of her nipples and her throbbing pussy.

"Mmm, didn't have to think twice about that, did you, baby?" Karn rumbled in her ear, sounding amused. "All right then…" His big hands came up, rubbing slippery soap over her bare breasts as he tugged lightly on her aching nipples.

"Ohhh!" Lilli moaned and leaned back against him, her head against his broad chest and her breasts thrust out as he caressed them. "Oh, *yes,* Karn!" she whispered.

"Gods, so hot and ready," he growled and then one hand was slipping below the water to cup her pussy. "I bet I could rub your hot little clit right now and you'd come for me in under a minute," he murmured in Lilli's ear. As he spoke, one long finger slipped into her inner folds and found the sensitive little button.

"Karn!" Lilli gasped and arched back against him, spreading her legs wider in the steaming water.

"That's right, baby—open for me," he murmured hoarsely in her ear.

But then, just a moment later when Lilli was feeling her pleasure start to build, he withdrew.

Lilli felt like she might scream with sexual frustration. All day long from the moment she'd woken up, Karn had been touching and teasing her in some way or another. And she *still* hadn't gotten to come. She felt like if she didn't reach orgasm soon she was going to *die*.

"What...why did you stop?" she gasped, looking over her shoulder at him.

Karn's eyes were blazing with lust.

"Because this isn't the way I want to bring you, baby—isn't the way I want you to come."

"How, then?" Lilli demanded.

But he only gave her that crooked smile and murmured again, "You'll see."

He pulled her into his arms and then rose easily and stepped out of the tub. After drying them both off, he carried Lilli into the bedchamber and laid her down on her bed with her lower legs hanging down over the end. Then he grabbed a pillow and positioned it on the floor in front of where she was lying.

Lilli looked at him uncertainly as he sank to his knees, resting on the pillow so that he was between her knees.

"What...what are you doing, Karn?" she asked, her heart pounding against her ribs. Both of them were naked and she felt open and vulnerable lying in the middle of the bed with the big Kindred kneeling before her.

"Finishing what I started," he growled. "So spread your legs and let me in, little Mistress."

Trembling, Lilli did as he said. Karn spent a moment rubbing his cheek against her bare pussy mound. Lilli didn't even have time to tense up before he was spreading her outer lips open and giving her inner folds a long, loving lick.

"Oh!" she cried and found that her hands were buried in his hair.

Karn wasted no time. He began with long, slow licks but quickly moved to sucking and lapping her swollen clit. Lilli, who felt like she'd been on the edge forever, bucked her hips up to offer herself more. She could feel the pleasure building and this time—*this time* —she was sure she would finally reach the peak.

A moment later, she finally did.

"Karn…*Karn!* she gasped as he circled her clit with his tongue. The pleasure rushed over her in a wave—so high and deep she was almost afraid she'd drown in it. She found that her thighs were clamped around the big Kindred's head and her back was arched with the force of her pleasure. Coming, she was finally *coming* and it was utterly and absolutely amazing—she never wanted it to end.

Finally, though, her clit began to seem too sensitive. She loosened her hold on the big Kindred's head and her hips started jerking away involuntarily.

Karn seemed to understand that she was done—at least for now. He raised his head—his mouth and lips shiny with her juices—and gave her a lustful smile.

"Better, little Mistress?" he growled.

Lilli nodded.

"That was…it felt so *good,*" she whispered hoarsely.

"Felt good to me too, baby," he murmured. "Now come on, let's tuck you in. It's been a long day."

Lilli didn't protest when he slid her, still naked, between the sheets and pulled the fluffy comforter up to her chin. But when he started to leave, she reached for him.

"Don't leave," she murmured sleepily. "Hold me tonight, Karn. I want to feel your arms around me."

"All right, but maybe I should put on some sleep trousers," he rumbled. "I'm naked, Mistress."

"So am I? So what?" Lilli murmured drowsily. "Forget clothes. Just get in bed and hold me tight."

Karn shrugged his broad shoulders.

"As you wish, little Mistress," he murmured and climbed in bed beside her.

Lilli sighed contentedly and snuggled against him with her back to his broad chest. She didn't even pull away when she felt the long, hard length of his shaft branding her ass.

"Um…" Karn shifted away.

"Wait, don't do that!" Lilli exclaimed, pressing back against him.

"I'm afraid me poking you all night is going to be uncomfortable for you, baby," Karn murmured in her ear.

"Then don't poke me," she said. "Here."

And lifting her top leg, she scooted back so that his thick shaft was nestled between her thighs with the broad head pressed right against her bare little pussy mound.

"Mmmm…" Lilli moaned contentedly. "That's *nice.*"

"Feels nice to me too, baby," Karn growled softly in her ear.

He shifted and suddenly he wasn't just rubbing *against* her pussy mound—he was rubbing *inside* her. For the broad, blunt head of his shaft found its way between her outer lips and slipped into her wet folds.

"Oh!" Lilli cried softly as the tip of his cock slid against her tender clit. Though she had just come not that long ago, she found she was ready for more—ready to feel her pleasure climbing again. Slowly, she rocked her hips back and forth, arching her back and sliding against the thick invader to send sparks of pleasure through her entire body.

"Better be careful, little Mistress," Karn rumbled, even as his big hands came around to cup her breasts and gently tug at her throbbing nipples. "If you're not careful, my shaft will slip into your pussy again, just as it did during the friction party."

Lilli felt her breath catch in her throat.

"Maybe…maybe that wouldn't be so bad," she whispered. "I mean, you've already penetrated me once, Karn. Would it really be so bad to do it again?"

"You tell me," he responded. "It's up to you, baby. What do you want to do?"

In answer, Lilli reached between her legs and found the long, thick shaft that was sliding against her wet folds. With trembling fingers, she grasped Karn and pushed him lower while she tilted her pelvis until she felt the broad, blunt head of his cock at the entrance to her pussy mouth.

"Maybe…maybe just the tip," she told Karn breathlessly.

"All right." With a slow thrust, he pressed up into her until Lilli felt the head of his cock breach her entrance and enter her pussy.

"Oh!" She wiggled against him, taking at least another inch inside herself. It felt really good, and it might have been enough if she hadn't had his entire thick length piercing her earlier that night. But she had and she couldn't be contented with just the head inside her now—she wanted more—wanted all of it, she admitted to herself.

Still she was embarrassed to admit as much to Karn.

"Karn," she murmured, wiggling so that even more of his thickness slipped into her. "Do you think…it's kind of tight, you know? So do you think you could…could maybe just move a little bit, just to get your, uh, shaft seated more comfortably inside me?"

"You mean by pulling out a little and pushing back in? Like this?" Karn growled in her ear. As he spoke, he suited actions to words by pulling back a tiny fraction and then thrusting forward so that his entire long, thick shaft slid deeply into her pussy.

"Oh!" Lilli moaned as she felt him touch bottom inside her. "Oh, yes, Karn—like that. *Just* like that."

"I'm glad I could please you, Mistress," he murmured, his deep voice half amused, half lustful. "Are you comfortable now?"

"Well…*mostly.*"

Experimentally, Lilli wiggled against him, letting a tiny bit of his thick shaft slide out and then slide back in again to the hilt. *Mmm,* that felt *nice!* Especially when she felt the head of his cock bump against the mouth of her womb.

"Careful, little Mistress," Karn growled in her ear. "If you do that much more, you'll be fucking yourself on my cock which we both know is forbidden."

"I...I guess you're right," Lilli whispered back, breathlessly. "It just...just feels so *good* to have you so deep inside me!"

"Feels good to me too but if you're not careful, I'll fill your sweet little pussy with my cream," Karn warned her. "So be still and stop fucking yourself on me."

At the forbidden thought of him coming inside her, Lilli's heart began to pound and her pussy got even hotter and wetter. She would never consider such a thing with a regular bodyslave, she told herself, but this was Karn—she cared for him.

*Maybe you even love him,* whispered a voice in her head.

Lilli tried to push it away but she couldn't help the feelings inside her. She knew a Mistress ought not to fall in love with her bodyslave but Karn was so kind and sweet and protective and handsome and his warm, spicy scent made her crazy with desire. How could she help the feelings that were growing inside her for him?

A new thought occurred to her.

"Karn?" she asked, turning her head to look up at him. "How many times does a Kindred need to come in a day?"

"What?" He rumbled laughter. "What would make you ask that, baby?"

"Well, it's just that you haven't come since this morning, even though we've been sort of, uh, teasing each other all day," Lilli pointed out breathlessly. "I know how desperate I was feeling to come before you, uh, licked me just now. And it just seems selfish that I'm the only one who got to have an orgasm if you need one too."

"Are you asking if I need to come inside your soft little pussy?" Karn growled in her ear. "Is that what you want to know, baby?"

"Well, I mean..." Lilli shifted against him again, causing several thick inches of his shaft to slide out of her tightly stretched pussy before sliding back in again. "I…I just don't want to be selfish," she whispered.

"You're very kind and considerate, Mistress." Karn tugged gently on her nipples again, making her moan. "I doubt any other Mistress would be so thoughtful as to let her bodyslave slide his shaft deep into her tight little pussy and fill her up with his seed when he felt the need to come."

"Goddess, Karn!" she whispered breathlessly, squirming on the thick shaft planted so deep inside her. "You don't know what it does to me when you say things like that!"

He looked down at her, giving her a slow, lazy grin that was pure lust.

"You mean you like it when I talk dirty to you, baby?"

"I…I guess so," Lilli admitted. "Is that what you call it? Dirty talk?"

"Mmm-hmm." Karn twisted her nipples gently and pulled out a few inches, only to sink his shaft deeply into her again. "For instance, I might tell you that I wanted to press the head of my cock against the mouth of your little womb and give your pussy a drink of my cream."

"Oh!" Lilli gasped as he pressed hard against the end of her channel. "Do…do you really want to?"

"Do I want to come in you? Hell yes, baby," he growled. "The question is, do you want me to? Do you want me to give you a creamy pussy and fill you up with my seed?"

"Oh, Karn!" Lilli wiggled restlessly against him. "I…I know I shouldn't want it because it's naughty and wrong but I can't help it—my pussy almost feels *thirsty* for your cream. Only…" She bit her lip and stilled against him.

"Only what, baby?" he urged gently, running his fingers lightly over her tight nipples to make her squirm some more.

"Only, would you have to…have to *fuck* me in order to make that happen? In order to come in me?" Lilli asked uncertainly. "Because I know that would be wrong and I shouldn't let you do it."

"So you don't mind me sliding my cock deep into your soft little pussy and filling you with my seed as long as I don't thrust in and out of you while I do it?" Karn murmured questioningly.

"I know it sounds silly but, well, it just feels like...like a line we shouldn't cross," Lilli whispered.

"Hmm...well, all right." Karn kissed her cheek gently. "Then let's define fucking. For instance, is it *any* movement in or out at all? Like the way you've been wiggling and 'adjusting' yourself on me?"

"No," Lilli said, biting her lip. "No, I don't...don't think that counts."

"Okay, well how about shallow thrusts like this?" Karn drew out about an inch and then thrust back in, grinding deep inside her and making Lilli moan with helpless pleasure. "Is that fucking?" he growled softly in her ear. "Or is it just grinding? Just pressing a little deeper to get all the way inside you?"

"*Ohh!*" Lilli gasped as his massive cock filled her to the limit. "No, that...that's okay too, I think," she whispered breathlessly. "I...I think you could do that, Karn. If...if you wanted to."

"Just trying to set some limits, baby," he rumbled. "So if you shifting around on me isn't fucking and me grinding deep inside you isn't fucking, then what about this?"

Lifting her leg, he pulled back until all but the head of his cock was outside of her pussy and then thrust forward again in one long, hard stroke. Then he pulled back and did it again...and again...

"Tell me, baby," he growled in her ear as he pounded inside her. "Is *this* what you mean by fucking?"

"Yes!" Lilli moaned, though she didn't try to stop him as his thick shaft opened her again and again, the head of his cock giving the mouth of her womb a rough, delicious kiss with every deep inward thrust. . "Yes, Karn! Goddess, yes—now you're...you're fucking me! Fucking me so deep and *hard!*"

He stopped as suddenly as he had started with a final deep thrust that seated his shaft all the way to the hilt inside her pussy. Only the thick ridge of his mating fist remained outside her filled channel.

"Good to know, baby," he rumbled. "Now that I know what you consider fucking, I won't do it again unless you ask me to."

"Oh, Karn…" she gasped breathlessly. "That felt so…it was…"

"It was fucking," he growled. "And *this* is coming."

Lilli felt the thick shaft inside her flex and grow even harder for a moment. And then something hot and wet spurted against the mouth of her womb, making her moan and gasp at the strange new sensation.

"This is me coming in you, baby," Karn growled hoarsely. As he spoke, one hand left Lilli's breasts and traveled downward. She moaned helplessly again as she felt his long fingers part her pussy lips and slip into her slick folds to caress her aching clit. "This is me filling you up with my cream," Karn told her as he stroked around and around her tender button and continued to shoot inside her. "Can you feel it? Can you feel me coming in you? And can you come for me too while I give you a creamy pussy?"

"*Ahhh!*" Lilli gasped, arching her back, trying to be more open for him. "Yes, Karn," she tried to say but the words got lost in a moan as another orgasm rolled over her in a warm wave of pleasure. It was deeper this time, maybe because her pussy was filled with his cock as he made her come. But for whatever reason, Lilli thought she'd never felt anything like it…and she never wanted it to end.

# THIRTY-TWO

They slept with his cock lodged firmly in her pussy. Karn was worried she wouldn't be comfortable, but Lilli protested whenever he tried to draw out. She liked having him in her, she said. Liked feeling him coming inside her—which he did several more times before they finally drifted off to sleep—though he didn't repeat the deep fucking motions he had made earlier.

It didn't matter if he was technically "fucking" her or not—it took every bit of Karn's willpower not to thrust a little deeper and slide his mating fist into her hungry pussy while he sank his fangs into her neck at the same time. He had the strong urge to try and bond her to him—an urge he'd never felt with any other female—but he knew he couldn't give in to it.

For one thing, the odds that he would be able to bond Lilli to him were about a thousand to one—if not more. And a failed bonding was painful. The other thing that stopped him was the fact that she was a Mistress of Yonnie Six. She had her own life to live here and she probably wouldn't be pleased to learn that her bodyslave was a Kindred spy who was planning to leave her at the end of the week, after he finished his mission.

The thought of leaving her made his heart fist in his chest but Karn tried to push the feeling away. He was a professional, he told himself. He'd been on countless missions for the Espionage Corps and he'd never allowed himself to get so close to a mark before. He had to ignore the deep protectiveness he felt towards the curvy little female, had to root out the feelings of tenderness and desire that had somehow taken hold and grown within him.

*But not tonight,* Karn told himself as he cradled her small, soft body close to his. *For tonight I'm just going to hold her and care for her. Tomorrow I'll start cutting off my feelings. Tomorrow is soon enough…*

# THIRTY-THREE

B ut when tomorrow came, he woke up with his shaft still lodged halfway in her tight, warm pussy and the sweet scent of her hair and skin in his nose.

"Morning, baby," he murmured in her ear.

"Good morning, Karn." Lilli sighed and pressed back against him, taking the rest of his rigid shaft inside her to the hilt. "Mmm, you feel so good in me," she murmured. "How many times did you fill me with your cream?"

"Think I lost count," Karn growled softly. "Though I think it's safe to say it might get pretty messy when I do finally pull out."

"Then don't pull out." Lilli turned her face up towards his and gave him a warm, sleepy, lustful smile. "Grind in me a little more, why don't you? Maybe give me a creamy pussy one more time before we get up."

"Mmm, nothing would give me greater pleasure, baby," he murmured. Slowly, he began making the shallow grinding motions that Lilli had deemed to be "not fucking" the night before inside her. Gods, she felt good inside! So tight and wet and welcoming as though she couldn't get enough of his cock filling her pussy...

"Oh, Karn!" she moaned, throwing her head back against his shoulder as he filled her. "Oh Goddess, that feels so *good!*"

Just then the com box above her bed crackled to life.

"Lilliana!" Her mother's voice was sharp. "Whatever are you doing still in bed?" she demanded.

Lilli froze against him and Karn felt her small body turn to ice in his hands. He frowned worriedly—he hated to see the effect her mother hand on Lilli. She was so cold, so cruelly disapproving of almost everything Lilli did. And it hurt his heart to see how badly Lilli took her mother's cutting criticism—it seemed to shatter her self-confidence and reduce her happiness to ashes every time.

*Well, not this time,* he thought to himself with sudden determination.

"It's all right, baby," he murmured in Lilli's little pink ear. "She can't see you and she can't hurt you if you don't let her. Just answer her calmly and you'll be okay."

He saw Lilli flick her eyes in his direction and then she nodded.

"I...I was just tired from the excitement last night, Mother," she called back, speaking to the com box. "Do...do you want me down for breakfast?"

"That's right—that's good," Karn murmured to her. He pulled his shaft out just a little way and then stroked back into her wet pussy as he spoke. At the same time, he reached between her legs and began to stroke her Goddess pearl.

Lilli bit her lip to stifle a moan but he could feel her loosening up around him, losing some of the tension that had frozen her to the spot the moment her mother's voice had crackled through the room.

"No, I've already had breakfast," her mother replied. "But I must leave for business soon and I wanted to give you instructions for while I'm gone."

"G-gone?" Lilli asked, her voice a bit breathless. "Where...where are you going?"

"I must go to the far side of the planet to deal with some Dream

Gas mining issues," her mother replied. "I'll be gone most of the week."

"Did…did you want me to go with you?" Lilli managed to get out. She was getting close—Karn could tell. But she wasn't asking him to stop stroking her clit or thrusting gently into her pussy. In fact, she was working her hips to catch his rhythm, helping him get deeper into her with every thrust.

"No, you'd only be in the way," her mother said heartlessly. "You must stay here and behave yourself. You may have some friends over if you like, but *no* wild parties!"

"Y-yes, Mother. I mean, no," Lilli panted. "No wild parties, I promise."

Karn frowned. Her mother really didn't know her at all. Lilli was the last person to invite a bunch of friends over for a wild time. She'd probably be happy to stay quietly at home, just the two of them.

"All right, good," her mother snapped. "And I'll be back the night before you go to Opulex to be certain you have your second quick-grow shot. You'll be staying at the Luxx by the way—it's the finest hotel in the entire city."

"Yes…all right!" Lilli's answer came out in a moan. "Have…have a good trip," she somehow added.

"Are you all right?" Her mother's voice was sharp. "You sound as though you're getting a cold or something."

"I'm…I'm fine," Lilli gasped. As a matter of fact, she was more than fine, as Karn knew intimately. He could feel her tight little pussy squeezing around his shaft as he pumped even more of his seed deep in her sweet depths. She was coming as hard as possible—it was a wonder she could carry on a conversation at all.

"That's right, baby," Karn murmured in her ear. "That's right—come on my cock. Come while I pump you full of my cream!"

Lilli bit her lip fiercely and he could tell she was trying not to cry out even as she clenched around him.

"Very well then," her mother said. "I'm off. And remember—no wild parties!"

"No…no parties," Lilli agreed but before she could say any more, the com box clicked off and her words dissolved into a moan of pure pleasure.

## THIRTY-FOUR

The rest of the week was what Karn had heard humans on Earth call a "honeymoon." They spent every day together, not as Mistress and bodyslave but as male and female—as lovers.

They read and watched vids together and swam in Lilli's mother's oversized anti-grav swimming pool where the water floated in mid-air and moving through it was more like flying than actually swimming. They ordered whatever they wanted for every meal—Lilli preferred plainer, more down-to-Earth food than the fancy and complicated Yonnite fare—and ate at the table together or sometimes just had the food brought up to her apartments so they could picnic together in her sitting room.

They didn't stay indoors all the time, however. Sometimes they took a hovercar and went hiking in the countryside. The parts of Yonnie Six that hadn't been strip mined for Dream Gas were actually quite beautiful and the weather was temperate—neither too hot or too cold.

And in between all these activities, they made love constantly. Well…in a way, anyway. Lilli still felt guilty about letting Karn actually "fuck" her, but she loved having his shaft inside her, grinding deep in her pussy and filling her with his seed. She claimed that the tingling caused by the first quick-grow hormone shot had gotten worse and she needed either his tongue or his shaft between her legs almost constantly to ease the sexual ache it caused.

Karn was happy to oblige her and he often thought it was damn lucky he was a Hybrid. If he hadn't been, he surely would have made her pregnant a dozen times over, considering how often he shot his seed inside her.

He still had a difficult time keeping himself from trying to bond her. Though he knew it was impossible, his body insisted otherwise and every time he sank his shaft deep in her pussy and came, he had the urge to thrust even deeper, to let his mating his fill her and to bite her and inject his essence at the same time. Only knowing that a failed bonding would hurt her held him back, because more and more, he wanted to keep the curvy little female with him forever.

Karn struggled with his feelings for Lilli. Should he tell her the truth about himself and ask if she wanted to come away from Yonnie Six and live with him on the Mother Ship? But how could he do that when he couldn't bond her to him? And how could he ask her to give up a life of wealth and ease to move to a small suite, only a little bigger than her bedroom apartments? The suites aboard the Mother Ship were comfortable and well-appointed with bathing pools and a fireplace in every suite, but they weren't as luxurious as the mansion Lilli was currently living in.

He still wasn't sure what to do when he spoke to Commander Sylvan and arranged the transfer of information about the Nightwalker Kindred later that week.

"We'll be staying at the Luxx—the most expensive hotel in Opulex," he told Sylvan, late one night after Lilli was asleep and he had gone into the sitting room alone to make contact with the Mother Ship.

"Excellent." Sylvan's head nodded on the 3-D holo projection. "We'll get a suite for the Councilor I'm sending to defend the Nightwalker in the Yonnite courts. You can 'meet' her in the lobby and hand her the drive with the information."

"I'll say something like, 'Excuse me, Mistress, I believe you dropped this,'" Karn agreed, nodding.

"Perfect," Sylvan said. "And then we'll have a transport standing by, waiting to take you right back to the Mother Ship. All you have to do is make an excuse to go outside and we'll take you directly home."

Karn frowned. "Ah, Commander, I don't think I can do that. I mean, I can't leave right away once the mission is completed."

Sylvan shook his head.

"I don't understand—why not?"

"Well..."

Karn tried to think how to explain it. How could he tell his commanding officer that he had allowed himself to fall in love with his Mistress? He couldn't, he decided. It would make him sound fucking unprofessional.

"I have...some obligations I have to attend to," he said, thinking of how he'd promised to go with Lilli to the conception center for moral support.

"All right. Then when do you want extraction?" Sylvan asked, frowning.

"Can I let you know?" Karn asked. "There are some loose ends that need to be tied up here and I'm not sure how long it will take."

"See that it doesn't take too long, Commander Karn," Sylvan said, his frown deepening. "You're one of our best operatives and I don't like leaving you in such a vulnerable position for any longer than I have to."

"I'll get things tied up as quickly as I can," Karn promised. "I'll message you with my device as soon as I'm ready for extraction."

"Just be careful," Sylvan warned him. "You know you're in hostile territory there, Commander. If the Yonnites found out you were more than just a bodyslave or that the pain collar you're wearing is a fake—"

"Karn, who are you talking to?"

Karn tapped the spy device on his nail quickly to end the conversation and turned to see Lilli standing in the doorway, yawning sleepily.

"I woke up and you were gone and then I thought I heard you talking to someone," she said, rubbing her eyes.

"Just watching a vid," Karn said easily, getting up from the couch where he'd been sitting. He was pretty sure she hadn't seen the tiny holo of Commander Sylvan—if she had, she'd be a hell of a lot more upset.

"Well, I miss you." Lilli yawned again. "Will you come to bed and hold me? I feel so lonely without you. Lonely and...and *tingly*," she added, looking up at him from under her thick lashes.

Karn felt his heart and his cock throb at the same time. How was it that this curvy little female had gotten under his skin so quickly? How was it that he wanted her so much that he would delay extraction from a dangerous assignment just to spend a little more time with her?

"Tingly, hmmm?" he murmured, walking over to cup one breast in his palm and thumb the tight pink nipple lightly. "And what can I do to help you with that problem, little Mistress?"

Lilli nibbled her lower lip, her breath already coming short as he teased her pink peak idly.

"Well," she said softly. "Maybe...maybe if you filled me with your cream again..."

"Mmm..." Karn leaned down to kiss her sweet lips. "But I just filled you right before you drifted off to sleep, baby."

"I know." Lilli looked down at her hands. "I'm sorry, Karn. It's just that the tingling seems to be getting worse instead of better. And I just feel like I want you in me *all* the time."

"Then it's a good thing I *want* to be in you, *all* the time," he murmured. Lifting her chin with one finger, he looked into her big brown eyes. "Hey, look at me, baby. You never need to be ashamed to ask for what you need," he told her. "You know I love to make love with you."

"I love it too," Lilli confessed. "I was just hoping you wouldn't get tired of me always wanting it."

"Are you kidding me?" Karn chuckled. "I'll never get tired of it—never get tired of *you,* Lilli." He bent to kiss her again and then, looking into her eyes he murmured, "Now would you like me to lick your sweet pussy first or do you need me to fill you up again right away?"

Lilli's cheeks got pink but she didn't drop her eyes.

"I love it when you lick me, Karn," she said softly. "But you know you, er, came in me not that long ago so I'm still kind of, uh, messy down there."

"I know it—I'm the one who made you messy," Karn growled, feeling his shaft surge again. "So why don't you let me clean you up with my tongue before I come in you again, baby? Would you like that?"

Lilli's blush deepened but she nodded eagerly.

"Oh yes, Karn—I'd *love* it."

"Then what are we waiting for?" Karn swooped her up into his arms and carried her back into the bedchamber.

He could decide what to tell her later, he told himself. Right now, she needed him to love her and that was all he wanted to think about at the moment...

# THIRTY-FIVE

L illi couldn't remember when she'd been more uncomfortable. The tingling that had been tormenting her all week had tripled, making her feel like her nipples and pussy were on fire with need—a need so deep and unrelenting she could barely stand it.

And it was all because of that second quick-grow hormone shot, she was sure of it.

"Now hold still, Lilli—this will only take a moment," her mother had commanded the night before when she'd finally come back from her business trip.

Lilli had been hoping she would forget the second quick-grow shot, but she'd had no such luck. The minute her mother walked in the door, she'd insisted on getting out the second syringe and injecting the bright green, poisonous looking liquid into Lilli's inner thigh. She'd barely even stopped to say hello first!

"Now, you're ready to conceive," she'd said, nodding with approval as Lilli winced at the bite of the many tiny sharp needles. "You're scheduled at the Primary conception center in Opulex tomorrow at three sharp, so see that you're not late."

"But...what if I *don't* conceive?" Lilli had asked timidly, hoping to plant the idea of a conception failure, as it was often called, in her mother's mind.

But her mother shook her head firmly.

"That's not going to happen. These quick-grow shots make a female *extremely* fertile. Why, a stiff wind could make you pregnant!" She nodded approvingly. "You'll have a baby-bump and be in fashion along with all your friends before you know it."

Lilli didn't want to point out again that Priss and her crew weren't her "friends," so she simply nodded.

"Yes, Mother," she said submissively. She didn't know how she would explain her failure to conceive when her mother was so set on it, but she would worry about that later. For now, she just wanted to get away from Mistress Mirabella.

Life with just Karn for the past four days had been heavenly. With her mother back in the mix, everything was up in the air again. The tension which had left her body when she spent time with the big Kindred alone was back. It made her neck and shoulders feel tight and she seemed to have a hard time getting a deep enough breath.

Being around her mother was like being around a volcano that might explode and spew criticism and cruelty at any moment.

*I just want to get away from her,* she thought. *I don't like spending time with her at all!*

She felt guilty, having such thoughts about her own mother. But once she had admitted to them, she couldn't take them back. Her mother was awful to be around—always critical and overbearing and never kind or loving, as a mother was supposed to be. At least, Lilli *thought* that was how a mother should be—it was how Karn said his own mother had been.

And speaking of Karn, all she wanted right then was to curl up in the big Kindred's arms and let him take care of her.

But of course, that wasn't possible. After the injection, Lilli's mother insisted on the two of them having dinner together. She told Lilli about her business trip, expecting her to know all about the family business—which bored Lilli to tears—and randomly inserted pieces of criticism about Lilli's hair, figure, face, and style of clothing.

By the time the dinner was over, Lilli had felt both physically and emotionally exhausted. She had excused herself as early as possible to go back to her room, saying that she had to get a good night's sleep so that she could get an early start on her trip to Opulex the next morning.

Her mother seemed to want to stay up and criticize some more, but at last she relented and let Lilli go to bed.

True to her word, Lilli *had* made an early night of it. She'd cried in Karn's arms—though she tried not to, her mother's sharp words cut her like knives and she couldn't help bleeding. The big Kindred had held her close and then given her a soothing bath to help her relax. For once Lilli hadn't felt the tingling and so they had simply fallen asleep in each other's arms without even making love that night.

It wasn't until the next day, when she and Karn had finally escaped the house and were in the hover ship flying to Opulex, that the tingling had come back with a vengeance.

One minute there had been nothing and the next moment —*wham!* Lilli gasped in dismay at the sudden need that nearly overwhelmed her—the need to be penetrated, to be *filled.*

She shifted on the seat, feeling like she might go crazy with the fierce desire. Her nipples were tight little points under the thin pink top she wore. She had on a demi-cup support garment which cupped and held the under-curves of her large breasts without covering the nipples. Suddenly the transparent shimmer-silk that covered her breasts seemed to be rubbing her sensitive peaks in an almost unbearably erotic way.

Down below, things were even worse. Lilli had on a pink, split skirt that matched her top and tiny pink silk panties. The little triangular panel that covered her pussy was suddenly soaked with her juices and her clit was throbbing with need. Worst of all, her pussy suddenly felt so *empty.* Lilli felt her inner muscles clench, as though begging for something to hold on to. Her channel wanted desperately to be filled and deep within her, her womb was begging to be bathed with seed.

"Oh!" she moaned, doubling over as the terrible needs attacked her all at once.

"Mistress?" Karn, who had been sitting beside her and holding her hand low on the seat and out of the sight of the bodyslave who was driving the vehicle, turned to her quickly. "What is it?" he asked, looking at Lilli anxiously. "What's wrong, little Mistress?"

Unfortunately, he wasn't the only one looking at her, Lilli saw. Yarks, who was one of her mother's most trusted bodyslaves, was driving them to Opulex. He was staring suspiciously through the thin, smoked glass barrier that separated the driver's from the passenger's seat. Lilli wasn't sure how much he could hear but she thought it might be a fair amount, since she'd seen her mother speaking through the glass barrier and directing her bodyslaves on various occasions when they flew.

So she couldn't explain exactly what was happening to Karn—not without arousing more suspicion from Yarks. But she was in such deep need, she didn't know what to do. She looked at Karn beseechingly.

"I'm all right. I just had a…a sudden cramp," she said, hoping he would understand.

"A cramp?" he frowned. "What kind of cramp?"

"It…it's hard to explain," Lilli faltered. "But I think it might have, uh, something to do with that second shot. The one mother gave me last night?"

"*Oh.*" Understanding grew in his mismatched eyes. "I see, little Mistress," he said formally, clearly also speaking for Yarks' benefit. "Well then, is there anything I might do to ease this, er, cramp of yours?"

If they had been completely by themselves, Lilli would have begged him to take her. Her pussy was aching to be filled and her nipples were so tight and hard they hurt. But what could she do about it with her mother's bodyslave watching them from the rear-viewer? He had already been giving them disapproving looks because Lilli had told Karn to ride with her instead of back in the bodyslave compartment and now he was glaring suspiciously at the two of them through the smoked glass as they talked.

Suddenly Lilli had an idea. Several times when she'd been out at events with her mother, she'd seen Mistresses having their bodyslaves massage them when they were tired. Mostly just their shoulders and backs but once or twice, she'd seen a Mistress require her bodyslave to give her a breast massage. Maybe she could do that with Karn now while still avoiding suspicion.

"Karn," she said, frowning at him imperiously. "All this riding for so long and jouncing up and down has made me tired and sore. I require you to give me a breast massage to ease the pain I'm feeling."

Karn seemed to understand what she was saying at once.

"Of course, Mistress," he said formally. "Might I suggest that you sit on my lap, so that I can reach around and massage you more easily?"

That sounded like an excellent idea to Lilli. After all, the big Kindred was wearing the tight black leather trousers with no crotch, which was usual for a bodyslave who was going out in public and who would be on display. That meant his long, thick shaft was fully out in the open and fully engorged, thanks to the stay-hard ring fastened around the base of his shaft, right above his mating fist.

*Which means I can at least rub against him,* she thought desperately. She knew she probably ought to wait until they got to their hotel room in Opulex, so they could make love properly. But honestly, she *couldn't* wait—the tingling aching need was so strong she felt like she might go crazy.

So she climbed willingly into the big Kindred's lap, sitting with her back to his front and trying to look bored, as she'd seen the other Mistresses look, when they made their bodyslaves massage them in public. Apparently it was all right to have your bodyslave's hands on you, as long as you didn't look like you were enjoying it too much.

"Here now, little Mistress," Karn murmured in her ear as he reached around to cup her breasts and began a slow, teasing massage. "Is that better?" he asked as he kneaded her full mounds and then tugged gently at her nipples through the thin material of her top.

"Some," Lilli said. "You can…can massage me under my top, Karn," she told him. "I think it would be more effective that way."

"Of course, little Mistress." He tugged up her top, baring her breasts completely, before he went back to tugging and teasing her nipples. "Is that better?"

"A…a little," Lilli whispered breathlessly. As she spoke she was shifting on his lap and tilting her hips back to try get more contact with his long, thick shaft.

Obligingly, Karn did some adjusting of his own so that instead of pressing against her ass, his long cock was between her thighs. Lilli sighed and sank down further in his lap, so that the hard ridge of flesh was rubbing against her tender outer pussy lips through the thin material of her panties.

"How about this, then, little Mistress?" he murmured, twisting her nipples as he worked his hips to rub his shaft against her pussy lips in long, slow strokes.

"It's nice but…it could be better." Reaching down with trembling fingers, Lilli pulled her panties to one side. There wasn't much to pull —the front of her panties was just a tiny triangle and the back was a single string that didn't cover anything at all. But once the string was out of the way, she was able to sink down more fully on the big Kindred's shaft and feel it rubbing inside her pussy lips.

"Yes, Mistress. I understand," Karn growled softly. Slowly—almost imperceptibly—he was thrusting against her so that the broad, mushroom-shaped head of his cock slid into her slick, inner folds and bumped over her throbbing clit.

Lilli had to bite back a gasp as a bolt of pleasure shot through her. She was well aware that Yarks was still staring at them suspiciously from the driver's seat. But she also knew that he couldn't see anything below the waist in the rear-viewer. So she felt safe in letting herself grind against the hard ridge of Karn's cock as he slid it slowly back and forth between her swollen pussy lips.

But as good as it felt to rub against him while he tugged her tender nipples, Lilli still needed *more.* The only question was, how to get it? Then she had an idea.

"You know, Karn," she murmured, still rubbing against him as he twisted her nipples and massaged her breasts. "I had…the most delicious breakfast today. The kitchen served Carnathian sausage. Very thick and juicy."

"Is that right, little Mistress?" Karn growled in her ear. "And did you like the sausage?"

"Mmm." Lilli nodded. "It was delicious. So good in fact, that now I wish I had more. I'd love to have more of that thick sausage in my belly right now."

It was clear from the low growl of lust in her ear that Karn had taken her hint.

"Is that right, little Mistress?" he growled softly. "Right in your belly, right *now?*"

"Right now," Lilli agreed breathlessly, rising up ever so slightly so that the broad head of his cock slipped down from her tender clit to find the slippery entrance to her pussy.

Karn tilted his hips and she bit her lip as she felt the familiar sensation of his thick shaft slipping into her as her inner walls stretched to take him.

*"Oh,"* she gasped as he finally bottomed out inside her. "Deep in my belly, Karn. So *deep."*

"Yes, Mistress," he growled. Gripping her breasts more firmly, he pulled halfway out and then slid deep into her again…and again and again and *again.*

He was fucking her, Lilli realized as he continued the slow, deep movements. Not hard and fast as he had that first night for only a few strokes, when they were defining exactly what fucking was. But deep and long and slow, and all the while maintaining the guise of giving her a simple, innocent breast massage.

Though she had only let him enter her and grind inside her until he filled her pussy with his seed before, not actually thrust in and out, Lilli couldn't find it in her to protest. After all, she told herself, he wasn't fucking her hard and fast so maybe the long, deep strokes didn't even count. At any rate, it seemed to help the desperate needy ache inside her so she welcomed him eagerly, spreading her thighs a little wider and tilting her hips to help him get even deeper into her.

The delicious thrusting inside her continued as Lilli tried her best to maintain a bored expression and not notice the suspicious glances Yarks was throwing their way through the smoked glass partition.

She mostly succeeded, except for a pocket of turbulence they hit, when they were nearly to Opulex. The sudden patch of bumpy air, caused her to jounce and jiggle on Karn's shaft, drawing a gasp from her lips as the head of his cock gave the mouth of her womb several deep, hard kisses in a row.

"Are you all right, little Mistress?" Karn growled in her ear—he must have felt her inner muscles clenching around his thickness, Lilli thought. It felt so *good*—and yet she still needed more.

"I…I'm fine," she said, her voice coming out more breathless than she thought. "I was just…just thinking of breakfast again."

"Oh?" Karn murmured, twisting her nipples. "Thinking more about the sausage, were you?"

Lilli shook her head.

"No, about the delicious Kurthian cream I had in my morning tea. I…I wish I could have some more of it now—deep in my belly."

"Really, Mistress?" Karn sounded doubtful. "But if you poured too much cream in your tea, wouldn't it, er, spill out and make a mess?"

Lilli knew what he was saying—he was trying to warn her that if he came in her now, his seed would be running down her thighs and wetting her panties when they went to get out of the ship. It was a valid concern, considering that Kindred seemed to produce much more seed than other kinds of bodyslaves.

How often in the last week had Lilli finished making love with the big Kindred, only to have a gush of his cream come out and stain the bedclothes the moment he withdrew from her? They had begun laying down towels before they made love, just for that reason.

But just at the moment, she didn't care about that—didn't care that his cream would ruin her panties and wet her thighs right before they went out in public. She only knew that her pussy was crying out to be filled—that her womb was thirsty for a drink of his seed. She had to have it and she had to have it *now*—she couldn't wait.

"I'm not concerned about the mess the cream might make, Karn," she told him, squeezing his thick shaft hard with her inner muscles. "I only care how delicious it is and how I want it *right now.*"

"Very well, little Mistress," he growled in her ear. "If that's what you want…"

"It is," Lilli assured him breathlessly. "I want a big dose of cream, right in my belly."

"Yes, Mistress," he growled and then she felt him flexing inside her as his shaft grew even larger and thicker. Then something hot and wet bathed the mouth of her womb and she knew he was coming— coming inside her just as she had ordered him to.

She tried to keep a bored expression on her face, but just then they hit another patch of turbulence and he was thrust even deeper inside her.

With a little gasp, Lilli looked down between her legs and saw that the thick bulge of his mating fist—which had always remained outside her before when they made love—had slipped into her pussy along with the rest of his massive shaft.

*Oh my Goddess, how did I stretch to take so much?* she wondered dimly. But the sensation felt so good, she didn't even care. Somehow the pleasure of him penetrating her was even deeper this way—deeper and more fulfilling.

She felt as though her womb had opened, almost like another mouth within her—opened to suck the head of his cock as he thrust inside her. And now the big Kindred was coming directly into her womb, filling her completely with his seed as that other mouth inside her sucked him hungrily and drank every last drop he spurted deep inside her.

*Is this what it feels like to be impregnated? To conceive?* Lilli wondered hazily. Of course, she couldn't be getting pregnant by Karn, since he was a Hybrid. But it certainly *felt* like he was seeding her womb—or doing his best to, anyway.

Karn seemed to feel it too, because he murmured urgently in her ear,

"My mating fist slipped inside you, baby, and it's going to take a little while to get it out again. Tell him to fly around the city and show you some of the sights before he drops us off at the Luxx. I won't be able to pull out of you for a while."

Lilli nodded imperceptibly and, still trying to keep her face impassive, ordered Yarks to give them a tour of Opulex.

He frowned at her in the rear-viewer.

"But aren't you due at the conception center at three, Mistress? Mistress Mirabella told me to be certain you weren't late."

"I'll be fine, Yarks," Lilli said crisply. "This trip isn't just for the purposes of conception—it's my coming-of-age present and I want to see the city! So take the ship around and give me a tour—if you don't, I'll see that my mother finds out."

"Yes, Mistress," Yarks muttered sullenly, and steered the ship away from the pearly pink spire of the Luxx hotel, where they had been headed.

Lilli pretended to look out the window and tried not to moan as Karn continued to fill her. Having his mating fist inside her seemed to make her more sensitive and there appeared to be a part of it which rubbed against and stimulated her throbbing clit. She couldn't help herself—during the next pocket of turbulence, she came hard on the big Kindred's shaft as Karn continued to grind deep inside her.

She bit her lip to hold back her moans as the orgasm rippled through her and her inner walls clenched hard around the big Kindred's cock. In response, Karn, too, began to come in her again. With her new, much more open position, Lilli could feel every hot spurt of cream he shot deep into her thirsty womb and she couldn't help thinking that it really was going to be a terrible mess when he finally pulled out.

But just at the moment, she couldn't care about that. All she wanted was for this to go on forever—for Karn to never stop making love to her and making her come on his long, hard cock.

They flew around the city again and again, for the better part of two hours, with the big Kindred's mating fist still lodged firmly in her tightly stretched pussy. It wasn't until Karn finally murmured in her ear that it was safe to land that she told Yarks to take them to the Luxx so she could check into the suite her mother had rented for her.

The moment they touched down in the landing area beside the huge, shiny pink building, Yarks started to get out of the ship to open her door. But Lilli stopped him with a glare.

"Stay where you are, Yarks," she ordered him, hoping she sounded as imperious as her mother when she ordered bodyslaves all around.

"But Mistress, I must open your door for you," he protested, frowning.

"Never mind about that—Karn will get the door for me," Lilli said imperiously. She just hoped she and the big Kindred could extri-cate themselves from their intimate position without arousing anymore suspicion.

"Yes, Mistress," Yarks said sullenly, sinking back into the driver's seat.

"Thank you." Lilli turned her head. "Karn, we're here. Let's go check in," she told him.

"As you wish, little Mistress," he growled. Placing his hands firmly on her hips, he helped her off his lap before opening the door.

Lilli had been expecting a gush of cream down her thighs, espe-cially considering how long they'd been making love and how many times Karn had come inside her. He'd shot deep in her pussy five or six times by her count and she had felt every single spurt of his cream deep in her inner core.

But to her surprise, there was barely a dribble of wetness when the long, thick shaft slid out of her. In fact, her panties weren't even ruined!

Lilli frowned as she looked down at herself and surreptitiously rearranged the little pink triangle of her panties to cover herself more fully. Where was the gush of cream she'd expected? Where had all the seed the big Kindred had shot deep inside her gone to?

She didn't know but she had no time to worry about it at the moment. Karn climbed out of the ship, his long shaft still hard and shiny with her juices, and held out a hand to her.

"We're here, little Mistress," he rumbled.

"Oh, thank you." Lilli murmured, taking his hand and stepping out of the ship. She turned to Yarks. "Excellent driving," she told him. "You may leave us now. We won't need you again until tomor-row, after I'm finished at the conception center."

"Yes, Mistress." He nodded woodenly and then the hover-ship rose up into the air and whooshed soundlessly away.

# THIRTY-SIX

They checked in at the lobby, speaking to a large pink insect who was manning the front desk. Lilli had expressed a wish to actually tour the city before her appointment at the conception center at three, but Karn knew he needed to keep them in the lobby a little while longer in order to make his rendezvous with the Councilor whom Commander Sylvan was sending to defend the Nightwalker Kindred in court.

In order to do that, Karn got his Mistress seated on a round, richly padded desk in the lobby and asked to kiss her panties. What he really wanted to know was where all the seed he'd shot into her pussy had gone to. He had come in her again and again—especially after the pocket of turbulence had forced not only his shaft but his mating fist deep inside her tight little channel.

The feeling of being so deeply buried inside her had been almost more than Karn could bear. He'd felt his fangs go razor sharp and it had been all he could do not to sink them deep into the tender flesh of Lilli's throat and inject his essence.

The urge to try and bond her had been so strong, he'd barely contained it. Only the way Yarks was staring at them suspiciously through the smoked glass partition had kept him in line. But though he wasn't able to inject his essence, he *had* been able to inject his seed —spurt after spurt of it, deep in her hungry little pussy. Yet, when he'd finally pulled out of her after hours of fucking and coming, hardly a drop had leaked out—where in the Seven Hells had it all gone?

Lilli was willing enough for him to kiss her panties, though she put on a show otherwise, since they were in public.

"Now, Karn," she exclaimed, giggling as he buried his face between her thighs and inhaled deeply, breathing in her scent. "Stop it! You know you mustn't kiss my panties in public unless we're being announced somewhere!"

"But my Mistress," Karn told her. "I just love to make my obeisance to you. How else can I show my reverence?"

"Well…" Lilli bit her lip. "Maybe…maybe just a *little* kiss then. If you must."

"I must," Karn growled. "Spread your legs, Mistress, and let me show how much I love and respect you."

Diving between her thighs, he tugged down her panties and explored her pussy thoroughly with his tongue. Lilli moaned breathlessly and threaded her fingers through his hair, tilting her hips and letting him thrust his tongue deeply into her wet depths.

Karn frowned inwardly as he tasted her. He could taste a trace of his seed in her pussy, but not nearly as much as he knew he had spurted inside her. Where had the rest gone?

Regardless of the mystery, he loved tasting her. He spent several long, delicious minutes lapping and sucking her sweet pussy, enjoying the moans and gasps she gave and the way her hot little cunt quivered under his tongue.

Karn wondered if it was turning her on that they were doing this in public, in the middle of the hotel lobby with other Mistresses and bodyslaves walking by. Technically he shouldn't be kissing her "panties" unless they were being formally announced, but since other

Mistresses were also using their slaves for pleasure in the opulent lobby, nobody seemed to pay much attention to them.

Nobody but a girl dressed in conservative clothes from Earth, Karn saw from the corner of his eye. She had lovely dark chocolate skin and long, black braids gathered into a conservative bun at the back of her neck. Her dark, almond shaped eyes were wide as she watched him interact with his little Mistress.

Karn excused himself for a moment and walked over to the female—who looked exactly as Commander Sylvan had described her.

"Excuse me, Mistress—I think you dropped this," he said, leaning over and pretending to pick something up off the floor. As she thanked him, he pressed the fingernail-sized drive into her palm and murmured, "the Nightwalker's name is J'are and he is in desperate trouble."

Then, leaving her behind, he went back to Lilli, who was squirming on the round, padded bench.

Karn knew that look—she was in need again. Damned if that second hormone shot her mother had insisted on giving her hadn't made the sexual desire that had been tormenting his curvy little female even worse.

Lilli confirmed his suspicions when she asked to go to their suite instead of exploring the city, as she had originally intended. Karn was worried that they might miss her appointment—though she didn't actually intend to go through with the insemination, she had to at least sign in to make it appear as though she had. But the look of need in her big brown eyes convinced him and he followed her willingly up to the luxurious suite they were staying in during their trip to Opulex.

After all, meeting his Mistress's needs was his first priority.

# THIRTY-SEVEN

Lilli couldn't help herself—she needed more. Even after hours of sitting on the big Kindred's lap with his shaft buried deep inside her, she still wanted and needed more of him.

"Karn," she begged softly as soon as the door was shut and they were alone. "I feel like I'm going crazy! This tingling is almost more than I can stand."

"I noticed you were feeling the need, baby," he said dryly. "Tell me what I can do to make it better."

"Maybe…" Lili shifted her hips. "Maybe lick me some more?" she said, looking up at him. "I was…was so close down in the lobby just now. I was sure you were going to make me come."

"Didn't want you to get embarrassed in public," he growled softly. "But you think it would make your little pussy feel better if I licked you some more and made you come all over my face?"

"Yes!" Lilli squeezed her thighs together, trying to ease the ache she felt there. "Oh yes, Karn—please! I know we don't have much time before my appointment at the conception center…"

"We always have enough time for me to lick your pussy," he

countered. "Come on, baby—take off those little panties and let's get on the bed."

Lilli did as he asked and soon she found herself in a strange new position she'd never tried before. Karn lay on his back on the luxurious bed and lifted her so that she straddled his face.

At first she was afraid she might crush him, but after a moment Lilli relaxed and let herself come down to ride his tongue as he commanded. Moaning and holding tightly to the headboard, she felt him lash her tender clit and then thrust his tongue deep inside her. She gave in to the pleasure he was giving her and came over and over, riding his face as he reached up to stroke and tug her nipples at the same time.

At last she collapsed beside him, spent and exhausted. She knew that in a moment she had to get up and go to the conception center, but just then she wasn't capable of doing anything but lying there and trying to catch her breath.

Karn rolled on his side and looked down at her, his mismatched eyes blazing.

"Gods, your pussy tastes so sweet, baby," he growled. "Do you feel better now?"

"Mmm, for now, anyway." Lilli stretched luminously on the thick gel-foam mattress and glanced over at Karn.

Her gaze caught his erection, which was still long and hard and ready, sticking out of the crotchless black leather bodyslave trousers he wore. Despite the fact that he had just fucked her for two hours straight, he looked achingly hard and needy again.

"But what about you?" she asked, nodding down at his shaft.

"What about me, baby?" he asked, giving her a lazy smile.

"It's not fair for me to come and not you," Lilli said, frowning. "Do you need to slide your shaft deep in my pussy and fill me with your cream one more time before we go?"

Karn gave her a hungry smile.

"I'd love to, but I'm afraid we'll be late for your appointment.

Besides, I just filled you with my cream for the past two hours on the way over here and I'm still not sure what happened to it."

"That *is* strange," Lilli admitted. She rubbed her belly, which seemed a little rounder than it had—maybe his seed was still deep inside her and that was why her lower tummy seemed a bit bigger than it had been. "I thought for sure when you, uh, pulled out of me that your seed would go *everywhere,*" she said.

"I thought so too." He shrugged. "I guess your little pussy was just really thirsty for a drink of my cream."

"Mmm..." Lilli smiled and snuggled close to him. "I wouldn't mind another drink right now, Karn." She sighed and rubbed her cheek against his broad chest. "I'm so glad you're a Hybrid and you can't get me pregnant. Having your seed in me makes the tingling from those awful shots *so* much better and of course we couldn't risk it any other way."

"Of course not," he agreed, stroking her hair. "Although, lately I've been wishing I *wasn't* a Hybrid, baby."

"Really?" Lilli looked up at him in surprise. "Why? Do...do you *want* to get me pregnant?" she asked uncertainly.

Karn chuckled.

"Don't get me wrong, sweetheart—planting a baby in that sweet little belly of yours would be a pleasure. But mostly I wish I wasn't a Hybrid so I could bond you to me. So we could have the closeness other Kindred have with their mates."

"Oh, Karn..." Lilli felt a lump in her throat as she looked up at him. "I wish that, too," she whispered.

He stroked her cheek.

"It's not every Mistress who wants to be bonded to her bodyslave, you know," he murmured.

"I doubt any other Mistress feels for her bodyslave like I feel for you," Lilli said and then bit her tongue. Why had she put it that way?

Karn looked at her for a long moment and then murmured, "And how do you feel, Lilli?"

"I...I feel like I've been waiting for you all my life," she whispered, unable to help herself. "I know that doesn't make sense but I feel...complete when you're with me. When you're *in* me." She kissed his broad chest gently. "I know we haven't known each other long but, well, I guess I love you, Karn. Is that crazy?" she asked in a small voice.

"Not crazy at all, baby," Karn assured her. "I love you too."

"Oh, Karn!" She leaned up to kiss him on the mouth. "I was so afraid to say it. I'm so glad you feel the same way!"

"Never felt this way for any other female," he told her. "And because I feel so much for you, baby, there's something I've been meaning to tell you—something really important."

"What is it?" Lilli looked at him, her heart pounding. She knew a Mistress shouldn't fall in love with her bodyslave but how could she help it when Karn was so big and strong and gentle and sweet and loving? How could she not want to be with him forever as more than just a Mistress and bodyslave?

"I wanted to tell you—" Karn began but just then the jeweled chronometer strapped to Lilli's wrist began to go off.

"Lilli, this is your mother!" a pre-recorded message from Mistress Mirabella announced. "If you're not already at the conception center, you *should* be!"

They jumped apart guiltily and Lilli looked at the chronometer. Oh dear—she was supposed to be at the center in less than twenty minutes!

"We'd better go," Karn said, also looking at the time. "Don't want to be late for your fake appointment."

"Exactly." Lilli nodded. She looked up at him. "But I still want to hear what you were going to tell me, Karn."

"Later, baby," he murmured, stroking her cheek. "Let's get this appointment thing over with and then we can spend all night in each other's arms. I'll tell you then."

Lilli felt a warm glow suffuse her entire body.

"That sounds wonderful," she whispered, leaning up to kiss him. "I guess we'll have more time to do things right after I get finished at the conception center."

"We'll have all the time in the world," Karn promised her.

Neither of them knew their time together had almost run out.

# THIRTY-EIGHT

"I don't like the look of this place," Karn growled as they stood outside the tall metal door of the conception center. The dark gray plastisteel the building was constructed of was forbidding and it didn't help that there wasn't a single window in sight.

"I don't either," Lilli said. She lifted her chin, looking determined. "But we only have to go in for a minute. Just long enough for me to check myself in and pretend I've had the procedure done. Right?"

"Right." Karn nodded, but he still didn't like it. He felt instinctively that there was danger lurking here—something that might harm his female.

The feeling was so strong he almost took Lilli by the arm and pulled her away.

*I could tell her everything now,* he thought. *We could call the Mother Ship for extraction and run away together and never see this cursed planet again.*

After Lilli's declaration that she loved him, he was certain she'd go with him. The only thing that held him back was the fact that he wouldn't be able to bond her to him.

*But she doesn't seem to mind about that,* he told himself. *And we're in love—this feels right. Maybe the priestesses in the Sacred Grove can ask the Goddess to give us some kind of special blessing to help us grow closer together even if we can't bond.*

It was a hopeful thought and the only thing that kept him from speaking it out loud was the fact that he wanted time to explain everything to Lilli in detail before he asked her to go with him.

*We'll just get this over with quickly,* he thought, looking up at the conception center, which rose like an accusing gray finger towards the Yonnite sky. *Then we'll go back to the hotel and order something nice from room service and make love and I can lay all the facts out for her. Then she can make up her mind.*

After all, this was a decision which couldn't be rushed.

He had no fear that Lilli would try to keep him as her bodyslave or turn him in to the authorities or anything like that. And he had little doubt that she would come with him. Her mother's mansion might be nice, but Lady Mirabella herself was a nightmare. Karn had seen the way her cruel words reduced the tenderhearted Lilli to tears. She would probably prefer a life with him, even if it wasn't as drenched in glitz and wealth—at least he hoped so.

*I'll ask her later, after all this—after I have time to explain myself,* he told himself again. *I'll—*

The beeping of Lilli's chronometer interrupted his thoughts. It was time for her appointment.

"Well...I guess I'd better go in." Lilli's cheeks were pale and her eyes were big as she stepped towards the gray, windowless building.

"You mean *we'd* better go in, baby." Karn took her hand and entwined their fingers. He gave her a reassuring squeeze. "You're not going anywhere without me."

"Thank you, Karn." She shot him a grateful look and took a deep breath. "Okay, then let's go."

Together, they stepped into the building.

# THIRTY-NINE

Inside it was cold—meat locker cold, Lilli thought, wishing she'd worn something warmer than the flimsy pink top and skirt. She shivered and wrapped her arms around herself.

But in addition to not being warm enough, the skirt no longer seemed to be fitting her correctly. The slight roundness in her belly, which she'd noticed briefly back at the hotel room, seemed more pronounced now. It made the skirt feel tight and uncomfortable and this was *already* an uncomfortable situation.

Lilli thought of how the other girls had described the insemination process—how the metal probe that went into you felt like an icicle—and shivered. She was *really* glad she wasn't going to actually have to go through with this!

The room they had walked into was rather small—sort of a lobby, Lilli thought. The walls were a stark white—blank and forbidding with no decorations except for a single viewscreen mounted on one of them.

"This must be where we sign in," Lilli whispered to Karn. She didn't like the way her voice echoed and wished she hadn't said anything at all.

"Well sign in and let's get the Seven Hells out of here," he growled. "This place gives me the fucking creeps."

Lilli couldn't have agreed more. She went up to the viewscreen and reached out to touch it, tentatively, with one finger. The screen came to life at once, turning from blank black to stark white, like the walls. In the middle of it hovered a single name in bold black print—Lilliana Mirabella

Lilli touched her name and watched as the black letters turned suddenly blood red. She wondered if that was all she had to do. Now that the system had acknowledged her, could she just go?

"Is that it?" she asked out loud and Karn shrugged.

"Must be."

But he was wrong.

Suddenly, a door at the far side of the room opened and a woman with dark purple hair done up into an elaborate series of curlicues came out. She was wearing a businesslike dress which barely showed her breasts and panties at all. She must be one of the lesser Mistresses, Lilli thought. The ones who didn't have enough money to own their own buildings in downtown Opulex and so made their livings by serving others, higher in the social order, as doctors and legal Councilors and things of that nature.

Of course, any Mistress was free to use the conception center so maybe it was this woman's turn and Lilli was intruding.

"Excuse me," she said quickly. "I didn't mean to interrupt your appointment. I'll just be going now."

"Oh, no, my dear Ms. Lilliana." The woman shook her head. "I'm not here for me—I'm here for *you.*"

"You...you are?" Lilli looked at her uncertainly. Beside her, she could feel Karn bristling protectively. "But...who are you?" she asked. "I'm afraid I can't remember your name or where we met."

The woman laughed briskly.

"Well of course not because we've never met. My name is Mistress Martinet—I'm the personal sperm consultant your mother hired to meet you here and help you through the insemination procedure."

"You…you are? You mean you report directly to my mother?" Lilli's heart sank down to her shoes. She'd been planning to get in and out of the conception center without anyone seeing her—let alone someone who could tell her mother if she actually had the procedure done or not. What was she going to do now?

"Of course! I've been waiting for you but I'm afraid…" Mistress Martinet looked at the plain black chronometer strapped to her wrist. "You're about three and a half minutes late. Which means we have to be moving along since another Mistress has an appointment scheduled here in a little less than an hour."

"Oh, well maybe I'd better go then—since I'm late," Lilli said quickly. "I wouldn't want to interfere with another Mistress's appointment and we can always reschedule for another day."

"Nonsense," Mistress Martinet said sharply. "Your mother tells me that you've only just had your second quick-grow shot yesterday which means you should be at peak fertility *now.*" She tapped her chronometer again, as though for emphasis. "So we need to get your impregnated *today.*"

"But—" Lilli tried to protest.

"Never fear." Mistress Martinet was already taking her by the arm. "What usually takes the longest is choosing which sperm you want to be impregnated with. But that's where I come in—I've already narrowed down your choices to several candidates your mother deems appropriate. So you've only got to choose one and we'll get you pregnant like that!" She snapped her fingers and smiled brightly at Lilli.

"I…I don't even get to choose my own sperm?" Lilli asked as the other woman dragged her through the door and further into the conception center.

"Yes, of course you do—out of the three acceptable candidates your mother already approved," Mistress Martinet said briskly.

Lilli turned her head and saw with relief that Karn was with them. Mistress Martinet noticed it too because she frowned and turned her head to look back at him.

"You're not needed, bodyslave. I'll take good care of your Mistress and deliver her back to you in the lobby in no time," she told him.

Karn glared at her.

"Where my Mistress goes, *I* go," he growled.

The fierce look in his mismatched eyes must have unnerved Mistress Martinet because her face went noticeably paler.

"Well…as long as you stay well back and don't touch anything," she said at last. "Ah—here we are!"

They had been walking down a corridor and now she opened a black door at the end of it and led Lilli into another small room. Inside were more blank walls and another black viewscreen. Mistress Martinet tapped it lightly with one long nail and it came to life.

"Now then," she said, turning to Lilli who still felt numb. "I've taken the liberty of creating some models of the way your DNA would mix with the DNA from the three sperm candidates your mother has chosen. Have a look and see which one you like the most."

She tapped the screen again and a baby's face appeared. It had a shock of black hair and big blue eyes. Mistress Martinet tapped it again and it changed to a child of around one, then ten, then fifteen, and finally it became a young woman about Lilli's age.

"This is what your daughter will look like if you choose Candidate number one," she told Lilli. "As you can see, the genes are extremely dominant—it was the only way to get blue eyes when yours are brown. This child will be quite beautiful as you can see, but also strong tempered and willful—something to bear in mind if you intend to raise her yourself. However, your mother tells me that you'll probably be engaging the services of a nannybot, so you don't need to worry about her personality for at least twenty years, until she comes of age."

"I don't know that I want a nannybot," Lilli protested. "I don't think it's right to give your child to someone—or some*thing* else—to raise."

"Oh?" Mistress Martinet's purple eyebrows rose in apparent surprise. "Well then, maybe *this* child will be more to your liking."

She tapped the screen again and a new baby face appeared. This one had brown hair and the eyes were brown like Lilli's own.

"This daughter will be much more pliant and easy to deal with. She won't want to disobey and will be subservient to you and do what you tell her."

Mistress Martinet tapped again as she spoke, showing the child growing up in different phases, as she had with the first image.

"However," she continued, "Those were the same characteristics your mother chose for *you*, and now she tells me she rather regrets it. She told me to instruct you that you do not want a 'spineless' daughter—you need one with some willpower and stamina to follow you into business."

"My…my mother said I was spineless?" Lilli felt the familiar ache in her heart.

"Oh, not in so many words, my dear," Mistress Martinet said quickly. "She just wanted you to consider that in order to make your way in the cutthroat world of Yonnite business, one needs a little, ah, how can I put it? A little—"

"Bullshit," Karn said harshly.

"I *beg* your pardon?" Mistress Martinet glared at him. "That wasn't at all what I was going to say. And how dare you interrupt?"

"I said, this whole process of planning some kind of designer child is bullshit," Karn growled, not backing down a bit. "How can you pick out babies so coldly like this? You ought to take what the Goddess gives you and be grateful for it."

Lilli wondered if he felt like that because he knew himself to be incapable of fathering children. Maybe this seemed like an extravagant waste to someone who just wished they could have kids and would have been happy with any child as long as they were blessed to have one.

"If you continue to interrupt I'll…I'll have you thrown out,"

Mistress Martinet warned him, though her face was pale when she said it.

"By who?" Karn glared at her. "I don't see anyone else around. I'm here to protect my Mistress and I'm not going anywhere. So stop messing with her mind."

"I'll just show you the last Candidate," Mistress Martinet said, turning back to Lilli and ignoring the big Kindred, though she cast a fearful look over her shoulder from time to time to see if he was still watching. He was.

She tapped the screen a third time and yet another baby face appeared. This one had red hair and brown eyes.

"Now, this candidate will be a good mixture of tractability, beauty, and intelligence," she told Lilli. "This is actually your mother's first choice, though she wants you to know you can pick for yourself among the three of them."

"I...I don't know." Lilli felt sick. She didn't want to pick *any* of the sperm candidates to be impregnated with. She just wanted to go home and forget any of this had ever happened. But how could she? Mistress Martinet was standing right there, ready to tell her mother if she backed out of the insemination. There would be no hiding it or pretending the process hadn't worked because her mother would know all the details already.

*I think I'm actually going to have to go through with this,* she thought, and felt like crying. She wasn't ready to have a baby yet! Not all by herself! She wanted someone to help her raise it. Someone to love it and care for it—not a cold, lifeless nannybot which was only programmed to take care of it and couldn't really have any feelings for it.

*But I have Karn now,* she thought, glancing at the big Kindred. *Maybe **he** can help me raise the baby. Maybe I won't be alone after all.*

"Well, if you can't decide, we'll go with your mother's choice," Mistress Martinet said briskly. She tapped the screen again and said loudly, 'Prepare the sperm of Candidate three for insemination."

"What?" Lilli gasped, but the other woman already had her by the arm again and was leading her out of the room.

"Down this way," she said to Lilli. "It won't take but a minute and then you'll have that cute little baby bump in less than an hour."

"Baby bump?" Lilli's hand stole down to her lower belly automatically and she wished again that her skirt fit better. What was wrong with it, anyway?

"Oh yes—you'll start showing almost from the moment of conception. The quick-grow formula makes certain the baby developing inside you grows at an exponential rate."

As Mistress Martinet spoke, she was leading Lilli into yet another room behind another black door. Only this one was much larger and had more than just blank walls and a view screen.

# FORTY

The room was divided into two sections by a clear plastiglass barrier. On one side of the barrier were several chairs. On the other was also a chair, but a much different kind of chair than Lilli had ever seen.

It was padded in bright red leather and it looked like it reclined but the bottom part of it appeared to be split into two long sections.

*Is that where my legs go?* Lilli wondered, feeling sick with dread as she remembered the tales she' heard. *Is the chair split so they can be spread apart while I get inseminated?*

Opposite the padded red chair was a tall silver box with lights blinking on the front of it. What was *that* for?

"Now then," Mistress Martinet said briskly. "Lilliana, let's get you into the insemination chair so the procedure can begin."

"No!" Karn said, frowning. He took Lilli by the arm. "Little Mistress," he said urgently. "I need to talk to you *alone.*"

"What are you saying?" Mistress Martinet demanded. "We must get moving along here. I insist that you let go of Mistress Lilliana so that she can make her appointment time."

"Fuck her appointment time," Karn growled. He tugged urgently on Lilli's arm. "You don't have to do this, Lilli! Just give me a minute to talk to you about it—*please.*"

Lilli shook her head sadly.

"I'm sorry, Karn, but there's nothing to talk about. She's won…I'll have to go through with it." She could feel her eyes starting to sting with tears so she blinked rapidly, trying to keep them back. "It's going to be okay," she told the big Kindred. "I…I'll just have to raise the baby as best I can. And maybe…maybe you can help me?"

She looked up at him hopefully.

"Baby—" Karn began but at that moment, Mistress Martinet interfered.

"I must *insist* that we get Mistress Lilliana into the insemination chair *now.* Once the sperm is thawed, it must be used *immediately.*"

Lilli let herself be led through a glass doorway and into the side of the room with the scary looking, red padded chair. She saw Karn start to follow her but she shook her head.

"It's all right, Karn. It should…should be over in a minute," she said dully.

He frowned but sank down into one of the chairs on the other side of the plastiglass barrier to wait for her.

"Very good, Mistress Lilliana," Mistress Martinet said approvingly.

She shut the door firmly and there was a soft clicking sound, as of a lock sliding into place. Then the plastiglass around the cracks of the door sealed itself—it was almost as though the door had never been there to begin with, Lilli thought with a shiver. She was stuck in here —completely cut off.

"Now, if you'd take off your under-things please, and we'll just get you settled…" Mistress Martinet said.

Lilli slipped out of her pink panties and sat reluctantly in the chair. She had the sudden urge to jump up from the chair and run to Karn but it was too late, the wheels had been set in motion and there was no going back now.

"What's that silver box?" she asked, nodding at the forbidding looking rectangular monolith which now seemed to be looming over her.

"Why, that's the insemination bot," Mistress Martinet said brightly. "You don't need to worry about it, Mistress Lilliana. All you have to do is hold still and let it do its job. Now let's get started, shall we?"

She pressed a button on the back of the chair, somewhere behind Lilli's head, and suddenly straps came out of the red padded arms and wrapped around Lilli's wrists.

"Hey!" Lilli gasped, looking down at her immobilized arms. "That's—"

But before she could finish, straps shot out of the lower part of the chair and immobilized her legs as well.

"Just relax," Mistress Martinet said briskly. "You'll make the process much more difficult if you struggle."

"But why do I have to be strapped down?" Lilli asked in a trembling voice. She was feeling more and more unsure about this—she wished she would have gone with Karn when he said he wanted to talk to her in private.

Speaking of the big Kindred, he was out of his chair and standing on the other side of the plastiglass barrier, watching her with a worried look on his face. She tried to smile at him reassuringly but Mistress Martinet's next words wiped the expression off her face entirely.

"You have to be strapped down so that the insemination needle doesn't go astray," she said.

"I'm sorry, the *what?*" Lilli demanded.

Just at that moment, a small door in the tall, silver insemination bot opened and a long metal arm slid out of it. At the end of the arm was a thick, bulky, phallic-shaped object, also made of metal. And on the end of that was…

"A needle!" Lilli gasped in horror as she saw the long silver needle shoot out of the end of the metallic phallus.

"Yes, the insemination needle, as I said," Mistress Martinet said briskly.

"But…but you can't put that thing up inside me!" Lilli gasped. "What if it stabs me?"

"Oh, it's going to. But it won't hurt—much—as long as you hold still," Mistress Martinet told her. "You see, what happens is this: The insemination phallus enters you until the tip of it is pressing directly against the opening of your cervix. Then, when the bot determines that the alignment is right, the needle shoots out—as quick as a wink —and slides right into your womb. That way when the sperm you picked is deposited inside you, it has a much better chance of making you pregnant."

"That's awful!" Lilli exclaimed, her gut clenching in fear. "You can't do that to me! I've talked to lots of girls who got impregnated recently—none of them said anything about a needle!"

"Oh, the needle is optional," Mistress Martinet assured her. "But your mother decided it would be best to use it to be certain you conceived. It adds a five percent chance of success to the entire procedure."

"Only five percent?" Lilli gasped. "My mother decided it was all right to let a machine stab inside me with a needle for just an extra *five percent?*"

Mistress Martinet frowned.

"You're very lucky your mother cares so much about your chances for a successful conception."

"No!" Lilli shook her head wildly. "I don't want this—I don't care what you or my mother say. *I don't want this!*"

She started fighting against the straps, trying to get her arms and legs loose. But it did no good at all—the straps were too strong. She could barely even twist her hands and feet at all, let alone slip them loose.

"Now, Lilliana…" Mistress Martinet frowned at her, as though she was a naughty child refusing to take her medicine. "As long as you lie still, the bot should have no trouble getting the needle in the right place. If you start shifting around, however…" She shook her head and made a *tsking* sound with her pursed lips. "Well, in *that* case, I can't promise the needle might stab you someplace else—which would be much more painful than the regular procedure, I promise you."

"But I don't *want* to be stabbed inside with a needle!" Lilli gasped. She could feel tears stinging her eyelids and this time she couldn't hold them back. "I agreed to be impregnated but please, *don't use the needle!*"

"I'm sorry," Mistress Martinet said coldly. "But your mother didn't pay me to go soft the minute I saw a few tears. If you'll just hold still, the whole thing will be over momentarily."

She pressed another button and the bottom half of the chair split abruptly, parting Lilli's legs though she tried desperately to keep them closed. The seat of the chair arched up, tilting her pelvis and opening her even more.

"Now look," Mistress Martinet said, frowning. "I'll retract the needle for now, at least." She pressed another button and the long, silver needle slid soundlessly back into its phallic sheath. "It won't come out again until the tip of the insemination phallus is right against your cervix," she promised.

This did little to calm Lilli down. Mistress Martinet was simply telling her she would be stabbed later on, rather than right away. It didn't really matter because either way, she was going to get stabbed—and in a terribly sensitive place, too!

"No!" she moaned as the thick silver probe began moving towards her unprotected pussy. "No, *please!*"

Outside the plastiglass barrier, she could see Karn shouting and pounding on the glass. But it was too strong. She couldn't even hear him through it, let alone see any cracks in the impenetrable shield between them.

When his fists didn't work, the big Kindred reached for the metal chair he'd been sitting in. Lifting it over his head, he swung it as hard as he could against the plastiglass.

The chair bounced off harmlessly—though it did leave a small crack in the barrier, Lilli saw hopefully.

Mistress Martinet saw it too.

"That's enough of that!" she exclaimed. Reaching around Lilli's neck, she snatched off the chain which held the remote to Karn's pain collar.

"No!" Lilli gasped in horror as she turned and pointed it at the big Kindred.

"I've had enough of this," Mistress Martinet said through clenched teeth. She shot Karn a triumphant look and pressed the big red "pain" button on the remote as hard as she could.

Nothing happened.

Well, nothing but Karn picking up the *other* chair and hurling it at the plastiglass barrier as well.

"What's wrong with this thing?" Mistress Martinet jammed her finger down on the button again and again, still with no results. Karn kept raging, shouting so loudly that Lilli could hear him, even through the soundproof plastiglass.

*"Hurt my Mistress and I'll fucking **kill you!**"* he was shouting. His mismatched eyes had gone a blazing, blood-red.

Lilli was hopeful that Mistress Martinet might think she needed to stop the insemination procedure due to Karn's attack on the plastiglass. But when the small crack he had first made didn't grow any bigger—no matter how many times he slammed the chair against it —she appeared to decide to get back to business.

"Now, just hold still and it will be over before you know it," she said to Lilli, pressing another button.

This caused the long metal arm—which had frozen in midair for a moment—to start moving again. It snaked towards Lilli, the thick metallic phallus at its end glimmering ominously in the bright overhead lights.

Lilli shifted her hips from side to side, trying to avoid the damn thing. But the metallic arm moved in a snake-like fashion, anticipating her moves and finding her entrance anyway.

"No!" she moaned as the ice-cold tip of the phallus probed at the mouth of her pussy. "No, I don't want this!"

"Just *hold still,*" Mistress Martinet told her, through gritted teeth. "Honestly, your mother is *not* paying me enough! I've never had such a troublesome client—*never.*"

"Please!" Lilli begged as the phallus began forcing its way inside her. It was horribly thick and freezing cold, just as she had been warned. If she hadn't been making love with Karn so much in the past week, it never would have gotten inside her. As it was, the awful thing was still a tight fit. Maybe because it was completely dry and all of Lilli's own natural lubrication had dried up—possibly with fear.

"Please!" she begged, her inner muscles clenching in protest as the blunt silver probe nosed its way inside her. "Please! Karn!"

"Your bodyslave can't help you now," Mistress Martinet snapped. "And if you don't stop shifting your hips around, the insemination needle is going to stab you in the wrong place. So *be still!*"

Lilli tried but it was as if her body had a mind of its own. Her hips kept twitching and her thighs kept trying to close as her inner muscles tried desperately to expel the invader. But it was no use—before she knew it, the ice-cold tip of the metallic phallus was all the way inside her, pressing against the mouth of her womb.

Finally, Lilli froze.

*Oh no!* she thought, squeezing her eyes shut and clenching her fists on the padded arms of the chair in awful anticipation. *Now it's going to stab me! Oh Goddess, I wonder how much it's going to hurt? And how long is it going to take? How long is the needle going to be inside me? What am I going to do?*

But instead of stabbing her, the snaky, metallic arm of the insemination bot suddenly stopped moving. The bot beeped loudly and then said, in a tinny, robotic voice,

"Insemination impossible."

"What?" Mistress Martinet glared at it. "What are you talking about?"

"Insemination impossible," the bot said again. And to Lilli's immense relief, the metallic phallus began to withdraw.

"Oh, thank the Goddess!" she sobbed as it slowly slid out of her.

But Mistress Martinet wasn't ready to concede defeat.

"Damn it, do your job!" she snarled at the Insemination bot, mashing down on the buttons again.

But the Insemination bot did not respond. It just kept withdrawing slowly but surely from Lilli's channel.

"Why, then?" Mistress Mirabella demanded desperately. "Give an explanation for your behavior, bot! Why are you not impregnating Mistress Lilliana?"

The bot beeped and said in a metallic voice, "Insemination is impossible because insemination and impregnation have already been achieved."

*"What?"* cried Mistress Martinet and Lilli at the same time. And Mistress Martinet said, "That's impossible! She *can't* be pregnant already!"

"Affirmative," the bot proclaimed. "Subject is impregnated." It paused for a moment, and then beeped again. "The fetus she is carrying is male."

# FORTY-ONE

L illi felt numb as the metallic phallus withdrew on the end of its long, snaky arm and the thick straps released her arms and legs. How could she already be pregnant? And how could the baby be male? Unless…

She looked through the plastiglass barrier where Karn was standing there, still panting with rage. His eyes weren't as red and he had stopped throwing chairs now that the phallus had withdrawn from her, but there was still tension in his broad shoulders and his big hands were clenched into fists at his sides.

Could it be that *he* had impregnated her?

*But he told me it was impossible! He promised he couldn't make me pregnant without bonding me to him and he said that Hybrids can't bond,* Lilli thought wildly. How could this happen? How could Karn have lied to her so blatantly?

"Here. Put on your panties," Mistress Martinet said coldly. She was looking at Lilli as though she was nothing but scum on the sidewalk. "You aren't fit to be in a conception center where good, honest Mistresses come to get a legitimate heir after what you've done."

"After what I've done?" Lilli asked blankly. "What…what are you talking about?"

"You know good and well what I'm talking about," Mistress Martinet snapped. "You've been inseminated and impregnated already and the child is *male*. There's no way that could happen unless you let a male *penetrate* you!"

"But…but aren't there mistakes sometimes at the conception center?" Lilli faltered.

"Not for years—not since they got their new sperm sorting software upgrade," Mistress Martinet said nastily. "But I know perfectly well you've never been to a conception center before—your name wasn't in the system until your mother made your appointment earlier this week."

"But—" Lilli started.

"And I can tell by the way that bodyslave of yours acts towards you that *he's* the father," Mistress Martinet went on relentlessly. "Calling you 'baby' and acting so possessive and overprotective—all the hallmarks of a male who has sunk his sexual claws into a female! Not to mention sunk his shaft into her," she went on, rather crudely, Lilli thought.

But crude or not, she was absolutely right about Karn.

The thing Lilli couldn't understand was how she herself could have been so wrong about him.

*How could he lie to me like this?* she wondered numbly as she waited for Mistress Martinet to unseal the plastiglass door and let them out. *How could he say he couldn't get me pregnant and do this to me? How could he say he loved me and then act this way?*

What was she going to tell her mother?

"Baby!" Karn rushed to her the moment she came out of the plastiglass insemination chamber. He took her by the shoulders. "Are you all right?"

Lilli shook off his hands and looked up at him.

"How could you, Karn?"

"How could I what?" He looked at her with confusion in his

mismatched eyes and she realized he hadn't been able to hear anything that was said on the other side of the plastiglass.

"How could you *penetrate* your Mistress and make her pregnant? You disgusting *male*." Mistress Martinet looked at him with utter loathing. She raised the pain collar remote, which she was still holding, and pointed it directly at him while pushing the button.

Nothing happened.

"What is *wrong* with this?" Mistress Martinet shook the remote. "I thought the plastiglass barrier was blocking the signal but it *still* isn't working!"

Karn ignored her.

"Lilli," he said urgently. "What are you talking about? What did that thing do to you?"

"The insemination bot didn't do anything—well, it didn't make me pregnant, anyway." Lilli looked up at him, tears stinging her eyes. "Because *you* already did that. You made me pregnant even though you said you couldn't. And everyone is going to know because the baby is a *male*."

"*No one* is going to know."

The new voice from the doorway was horribly familiar.

Looking around, Lilli saw her mother standing there. And she was pointing a blaster straight at Karn's chest.

# FORTY-TWO

"Whoa, hang on there. Let's just think this through." Karn put up his hands at once in a "don't shoot" gesture. "Mistress Mirabella—"

"Don't speak to me, bodyslave." Her voice was like ice but she was looking at Lilli, not him. "So you've disgraced me yet again—and in the worst way possible," she said. "How could you do this to me, Lilliana? Do you know how difficult this is going to be to keep quiet?"

"Mother!" Lilli put a hand to her throat nervously. "How...why are you here?"

"I'm here because I got a very damning vid message on my personal communications device about an hour ago," her mother snapped. "It was from Priss Tempertant and it showed you and that...that *Kindred...*" She waved the blaster at Karn. "In the middle of an unnamable activity!"

Lilli went white and Karn felt a growl rise in his throat. No wonder that little bitch, Priss, had insisted on making him penetrate Lilli! She'd been filming the whole thing! And no doubt she had edited out herself and all the rest of her group, leaving Lilli and himself as the only ones engaged in the illicit activity.

"Mother—" Lilli started but Mistress Mirabella shook her head.

"I don't want to hear a word. You're coming with me. And you," she added, looking directly at Karn for the first time, "Are going straight to the Diluthian mines!"

"What?" Lilli looked at him in shock. "But, Mother, you can't—"

"Oh yes I can!" Mistress Mirabella said grimly. "Give me the remote to his pain collar!"

"It doesn't work," Mistress Martinet said, speaking up for the first time since Lilli's mother had come into the room. "I've tried it twice since your daughter and her bodyslave got here. He is *completely* out of control."

"I'll speak with you later," Mistress Mirabella snapped at her. "Just keep all this to yourself and you'll be compensated accordingly. But if you breathe a word of this to *anyone…*" She turned a menacing glare on the other woman which caused Mistress Martinet to blanch.

"I understand," she said quickly. "Not a word, Lady Mirabella—I swear it."

"Good. Now get out." Mistress Mirabella jerked her chin at the door.

While her attention was momentarily distracted with the other Mistress, Karn decided to act. This looked like the only chance he was going to get. As Mistress Martinet headed for the doorway, he lunged for the blaster.

"Not so fast!" Mistress Mirabella jerked away before he could grab the weapon and threw a handful of small, metal beads at him. They stung when they hit him but they didn't bounce off, as he would have expected. Instead, they began to flatten out and grow at the same time. Almost before he could blink, they had covered his entire body in a series of interconnected metal plates.

"What the fuck?" Karn growled, looking down at himself. He tried to pry one of the silver plates free, but his arms were already immobilized by the metal holding him in place. In fact, he realized with growing concern, his entire *body* was immobilized. Except for his face, he was completely encased in the interlocking metal plates—and it had taken less than three seconds!

"I thought I might have some problems with you, Kindred," Mistress Mirabella snapped, glaring at him. "And since you'd seduced my daughter, I surmised that she might have disabled your pain collar. I'm not surprised to see that I was right—it's a good thing I brought the Obedience Skin with me."

"Obedience Skin?" Karn frowned. "What the fuck is that? These metal plates all over me?"

"Exactly. The metal plates which now control how your muscles can and will move—according to what *I* say," Mistress Mirabella snapped. "Now come with me—we're getting out of here before anyone else enters the conception center and sees us."

To his horror, Karn found his legs obeying her orders. Though he wanted to protest, he found that the metal plates around his limbs moved his arms and legs whether he wanted to move them or not. It didn't do any good to fight them, either—it was like fighting with a plastisteel wall. The smart metal of the Obedience Skin just kept going, even when he tried to stop it.

He felt fucking horrible as he walked unwillingly behind Lilli and her mother. Lilli's head was down, her shoulders shaking with silent sobs. Could what she said be true? Could she actually be pregnant with his child? With his son?

The thought made his heart soar and plummet at the same time. Deep down, he'd always wanted a mate and a son—a family like other Kindred warriors had. But he'd never admitted it to himself because he thought it was impossible. Now it had proved to be not only possible but a reality—he had gotten the woman he loved pregnant!

But in doing so, he had betrayed her in the worst way possible.

"How could you, Lilliana?" her mother demanded as she stalked stiffly down the corridor. "How could you degrade and debase your-self so far as to let a male penetrate you?"

Lilli's reply tore at Karn's heart.

"He…he said he loved me," she whispered in a broken voice. "And he claimed he couldn't…couldn't get me pregnant!"

"I didn't think I could!" Karn protested. "Lilli, please—I would never—"

"Silence!" Mistress Mirabella made a gesture at him and suddenly one of the thin metal plates grew over his mouth.

"Mmmph! *Mmmph!*" Karn protested, but he couldn't get another word out—not a single one.

"That's better," Mistress Mirabella snapped as they stepped out of the conception center. "You can rant and rave all you want once you get to the Diluthian mines but you'll not say a single word more to my daughter!"

She nodded at the curb, where two different transports were waiting. One was the fancy, sleek, silver one they had driven in on the way to Opulex earlier that day. The other was an ominous dull black and it had guards waiting outside of it, holding heavy-duty stunners and pain prods.

"What are you doing out of your transport?" Mistress Mirabella hissed at them. "Do you want everyone to *talk?*"

"Sssory, Mistresss," one of them hissed and Karn saw they were Horvaths—green, scaly, lizard-like humanoids which the Yonnites often used for distasteful duties they didn't want to undertake themselves.

*Like transporting prisoners to the Diluthian mines, apparently,* whispered a little voice in his head. *How long do you think you're going to last there, Karn? Probably not more than a week.*

But it wasn't the thought of going to the mines that upset him the most—even though it would certainly mean his death. No, what was killing him was that Lilli thought he had betrayed her and hurt her on purpose.

*I love you!* he wanted to shout, but there was no way with the damn metal plate practically welded to his mouth.

"We thought he might possse a danger to you, Mistresss," the other Horvath guard hissed, breaking his miserable train of thought.

"I can take care of myself. I came prepared, as you can see," Mistress Mirabella snapped.

"I sssee." The first guard sounded impressed. "I didn't know a fine lady such asss yourself had accesss to an Obedienssse Sssskin."

"I have access to anything I want," Mistress Mirabella said shortly. "Except an heir I can be proud of," she added, glaring at Lilli.

"I'm sorry, Mother. So sorry." The words were a low sob and they twisted Karn's heart. "I...I thought he loved me," she whispered again.

*I do!* he wanted desperately to shout, but of course he couldn't. He could only stare at her, hoping she would lift her head and meet his eyes.

"You little fool!" Her mother sounded both disgusted and exasperated. "This is one reason I wanted you to have a quick-grow heir! I thought if she grew fast enough, I might be able to replace you with someone who actually had a decent head for business on her shoulders. But I never dreamed you'd do something like *this!*"

Lilli absorbed her words like a physical blow, her steps staggering for a moment as though her mother had actually struck her. Karn felt a murderous rage sing through his veins. If only he could get out of this damn metal plating, he would show Lilli's mother exactly how much she had hurt her daughter. He would—

The first Horvath guard cleared his throat.

"Excusse me, Mistresss," he hissed. "But will you be wanting the Obedienssse Ssskin back?"

Karn held his breath. If he could get this fucking metal suit off, he could press the communications device embedded in the nail of his ring finger and call for help! It would mean the difference between life and death. How much did the damn Obedience Skin cost anyway? He hoped it was extremely expensive so that Mistress Mirabella would ask for it back.

But Lilli's mother only shook her head.

"Keep it," she said shortly. "Leave it on him and let him starve, for all I care."

"Starve?" Lilli's head jerked up. "Mother—"

"Silence!" Mistress Mirabella hissed. "If you dare say one word in defense of that *male* I'll disinherit you! I ought to do so right now but I still need you to get me a decent heir, since I'm too old to carry another child myself. Now get in the ship! We're going home."

Karn watched as Lilli hung her head and followed her mother into the sleek silver hover-car ship where he and his little Mistress had made love only a few hours before. How had things changed so drastically so quickly? And how had he gotten her pregnant without bonding her to him?

Karn had no answers. He only knew that the woman he loved was about to fly away from him and he would never see her again.

At the last moment, Lilli turned her head and he managed to catch her eye. He tried to convey how he felt with a look, but she shook her head and turned away.

The door of the silver ship closed behind her and she was gone.

# FORTY-THREE

"Go up to your room and think about what you've done," her mother said coldly the moment they arrived back at her mansion. "I've got to make some vid calls and clean up this mess you made. I hate to *think* of the amount of money I'll have to put out to shut up Mistress Martinet—not to mention Priss Tempertant! You're going to cost me a ridiculous sum, Lilliana—far more than you're worth, that's for certain!"

"I never meant to shame you, Mother," Lilli said in a small voice.

"You've shamed *yourself*," Lady Mirabella spat back. "Having you has been the biggest disappointment of my life! But you'll make it up —I can promise you that. Tomorrow morning we're going back to Opulex to get that *thing* inside you removed. And then you'll be implanted properly with a daughter—a new heir for me—made *exactly* to my specifications."

"What?" Lilli's hand went protectively to her lower belly. "You're going to make me get rid of Karn's baby?"

"It's a *male!*" her mother snapped. "Of *course* we're getting rid of it! A Mistress of Yonnie Six cannot have a male child! The shame of it would ruin our family name forever!"

"But—" Lilli began.

"*Go to your room!*" her mother snarled. "*Now,* Lilliana—I mean it! I don't want to see your face again until I come to get you tomorrow morning."

Tears running down her face, Lilli turned and fled up the grand staircase.

She didn't stop until she was in her own room. She flung herself on the bed and pressed her face to a pillow, sobbing so wretchedly it felt like the pain inside her might tear her apart.

But the pillow she had picked was Karn's. When she breathed in, the big Kindred's spicy scent invaded her senses, which caused a fresh round of sobbing.

"Oh Karn," she whispered brokenly. "How could you lie to me like that? How could you put me in this awful position?"

She turned her head away from his pillow, to get away from his scent, but everywhere in her room she seemed to see him. Sitting or laying on the bed beside her, laughing his deep, rumbling laugh when they joked around, having an indoor picnic, just the two of them, on the carpet, talking long into the night…

"I still love him," Lilli whispered to herself despairingly. "I can't help it. Even after he deceived me, I still love him. And now he's gone to the mines. He…he's going to…to *die.*"

The words came out in a choked sob and she pressed her face to the pillow once more and breathed in his scent. This was all she had left of the big Kindred, and soon it would fade too…

Just as the thought came to her, she felt a strange sensation in her lower belly. It was so odd and unexpected that Lilli stopped crying and rolled onto her back. There…there it was again! A *fluttering* in her lower belly—almost like a flutterbye was waving its wings inside her.

Lilli pulled down her skirt and put one trembling hand to her belly. She felt the fluttering again and something moved under her fingers. It was a motion so slight she wouldn't have felt it if she hadn't been so attuned to it. But it was most definitely there.

Suddenly, she realized what it was.

"His baby," she whispered, a feeling of wonder filling her. "It's Karn's baby—his son—and it's alive inside me!"

*It won't be for long,* whispered a nasty little voice in her head. *Not if Mother has her way. You'll be losing it tomorrow, Lilli, so don't get too attached.*

A wave of fierce love and protectiveness swept over her and Lilli put both hands to her belly, cradling the tiny life there.

"No!" she whispered, stroking the barely-there bump. "No, I won't let her kill you! I'll protect you—I swear I will!"

But how?

Lilli had to face the facts—she was stuck in her mother's house with no way to leave. She had a bit of money in her account, but what could she do with it? If only she knew how to fly a ship she might be able to get away, but that wasn't a skill they taught at the convent where she'd been raised. Also, where would she go, even if she did get away?

"To the mines," Lilli whispered to herself. "I'd go to the mines and save Karn, if I could."

But again, it was impossible. Though the Diluthian mines weren't that far away—they were just located on one of Yonnie's Six's moons —they might as well have been on the other side of the universe.

"Because I can't fly," Lilli whispered to herself. "And I have no one to fly me. Oh Karn, if only I could get to you! I'd forgive you for what you did and we could fly away together and make a life for ourselves and our son…"

It was a beautiful dream but that was all it was—just a dream. She had no way to get to him—she was a prisoner in her own home. Her mother would make her get rid of Karn's baby so she could be impregnated with a daughter—an heir who would take Lilli's place.

*But I don't want a daughter—I want a son—Karn's son! The one growing inside me now,* Lilli thought desperately.

"I don't want to lose him," she said aloud. Curling on her side, she cupped her barely swelling belly with both hands. "Oh please, can't anyone help me?"

*"I will help you, daughter."*

The warm, powerful, feminine voice which filled her room surprised Lilli so much she almost fell off the bed.

"H-hello?" she stuttered, looking all around. "Who…who is that?"

*"I am the Goddess the Kindred worship—the Mother of All Life—including the tiny life now growing within you,"* the voice told her. *"And I say to you now, my daughter, that you shall not lose your baby."*

"But how?" Lilli asked, her voice trembling. Karn had spoken to her of the Kindred Goddess, the female deity his people worshiped, and it had been clear that he really believed in her. But Lilli had never expected to actually *speak* with her!

*"Do not worry about how—only be on the lookout and help will come to you,"* the Goddess told her. *"Seize the opportunity when you see it, for it will only be offered once."*

"All right," Lilli said, nodding her head to the unseen presence. "I promise—I'll take it. But…" She bit her lip. "But what about Karn? You're his Goddess—can't you save him too?"

*"You shall save him yourself, my daughter,"* the Goddess told her. *"Do not ask how, for you will know when the time comes. And remember…do not be afraid to attempt the impossible."*

Then the voice and the warm, feminine presence that accompanied it faded. It left behind only a fresh, sweet scent that seemed to lift Lilli's spirits and make her feel like a new person.

"Thank you," she whispered, though she sensed the Goddess was gone. "Thank you so much for giving me hope." She put her hands on her belly again. "Thank you for me…and for my baby."

## FORTY-FOUR

L illi waited anxiously, but no help came. The hours ticked by on her chronometer and nothing happened. She just stared at her walls and wondered where Karn was now and if he had reached the mines yet and if he was all right. Maybe she had imagined the voice and the presence. Maybe the stress of the situation and her deep desire to protect her baby had made her have a hallucination.

Maybe she was going crazy.

She kept feeling the fluttering in her lower belly—Karn's son telling her he was alive and well—but the tiny movement made her feel hopeless.

"How can I protect you if I can't get the two of us out of here?" she whispered, rubbing her belly. "And how can I rescue your father so you can know him instead of just hearing about him after he's already dead and gone?"

She was about to give up and go to bed to have another good cry, when there was a knock at the door of her apartments. Swiping at her eyes, Lilli padded to the door and opened it, only to see a vaguely familiar bodyslave standing there with a tray.

"Your dinner, Mistress," he said, bowing respectfully. "Would you like me to put it down on the table for you?" He nodded at the low table before the couch where she had so often eaten with Karn, while they were watching a vid.

The thought made her sad all over again and Lilli was about to send the dinner away and say that she had no appetite when she took another look at the bodyslave holding the tray.

"You're Priss's bodyslave, aren't you?" she asked uncertainly. "You're H'rare—right?"

"Yes, I am. And I *was* hers until you and Karn won me from her, Mistress," he said. "I can't tell you how grateful, I am." He dropped his voice. "Or how sorry I am for what happened to Karn—he was a good male."

"Yes, he was." Lilli felt a lump in her throat. "He told me that if we didn't try to save you, you'd be sent...sent to the mines." She could barely get the words out.

"He was right about that," H'rare said solemnly. "Mistress Priss threatened me with the mines twenty times a day while she owned me." He shook his head. "Never thought Karn would end up there while I stayed here safe in the kitchens."

Lilli had a sudden thought—a hope so wild she was almost afraid to speak it. Trying to sound off-hand, she said,

"H'rare—while you were Priss's bodyslave, did you ever fly her anywhere?"

"Fly her in a shuttle or a hover-ship you mean?" He raised his eyebrows. "Oh yes, Mistress. Lady Priss insisted that her bodyslave be able to do everything and anything for her, from massaging her toes to fixing her favorite rasta-bean smoothie to flying her to downtown Opulex for shopping whenever the notion took her."

"I see." Lilli opened the door wider. "Come in so you can put down that tray, H'rare. Let's talk."

"Of course, Mistress," he said, frowning. "But talk about what?"

"H'rare," Lilli said in a low voice. "How would you like to be free?"

"*Free?*" He looked around, as though he was afraid someone

might have heard the forbidden word. "I don't know that I rightly understand you, Mistress," he murmured.

"Come inside," Lilli said again. "And let's talk about it…"

She felt that flutter in her belly again, but this time the feeling brought hope, not despair.

*The Goddess was right,* she thought. *I will find a way to save you, little one. To save all of us…*

She hoped.

# FORTY-FIVE

Gods he was hot. And thirsty. And so damn tired he felt like he could drop in his tracks—but he couldn't because the fucking Obedience Skin just kept on going.

Karn swung the pickaxe again and felt the reverberations all the way up his arms as it hit solid stone. He would have liked to rest, but the skin wouldn't let him. Hell, it would barely let him breathe, since the metal plate still covered his mouth.

The Horvath guards had dropped him off at the mines, given him the tool he currently held, and simply said, "Work." The Obedience Skin had taken over from there and he had been chopping and hacking away at the greenish-gray rock face of the open Diluthian pit for hours now.

He wasn't the only one working of course—there were hoards of unlucky slaves pounding away at the rock. None of them had tried to speak to him—not that he could have spoken back even if they had.

The toxic odors of the Diluthian being unearthed all around him stung his nostrils and made his throat raw. He wanted to retch but he was acutely aware that if he threw up, he would die. With his mouth blocked, he would choke on his own vomit. So he held onto his gorge grimly and tried to ignore the way he wanted to gag every time one of his blows unearthed a new vein of Diluthian and the more foul odors were released.

*I'm going to die here,* he thought, not for the first time. If it hadn't been for the Obedience Skin, he would have escaped easily. He could have pressed the communicator on his nail and called for help at once. But his fingers were encased in the fucking skin—the same skin that forced him to keep working, even when the other slaves were allowed a five-minute break and a swallow of water.

Karn wondered what would get him first—the thirst, the toxic gasses he was breathing in, or simply exhaustion. He was well aware that if he hadn't been in excellent physical shape, the grueling non-stop work for hours on end would probably have caused his heart to give out. But even the strongest heart couldn't keep going forever.

And even the strongest heart could be broken.

*Oh, Lilli—I'm so fucking sorry,* he thought, his eyes stinging as he pounded away at the rock face. *I didn't know what we did together would hurt you. I just wanted to love you, baby. I'm so sorry…*

The thoughts of her and the baby they had made together, growing inside her, tormented him, but Karn comforted himself that he wouldn't be sad for very much longer. Soon his heart would give out or he would die of thirst or the toxic fumes would damage his lungs so badly they would no longer work well enough to send oxygen to his body. Then he would flicker out like a candle flame and hopefully go to be with the Goddess.

He wondered grimly if the Obedience Skin would keep working, even after he was dead. Would it go on lifting his arms and swinging the pickaxe, even with him dead inside it? Would he be like a zombie corpse, still animated by the suit even after his soul had left his body? Would he—

"There—that's the one. That is the bodyslave I want!"

The imperious voice was vaguely familiar but when Karn looked up—the skin *did* allow him to turn his head at least—he didn't recognize the face attached to it. Maybe because it was covered by a thick black respirator mask.

"That's the one," she said again to the Horvath guard standing beside her. "Bring him to my ship at once!"

# FORTY-SIX

L illi's heart was pounding as she barked out orders the same way she'd seen her mother and Priss do on numerous occasions. She was pretending to be her mother, and hoping that the Horvath guards wouldn't question her.

*Oh please!* she thought, as she waited for the guard who had accompanied her from the central control station to respond. *Please, let them believe me! Please let me get him safely away!*

Sneaking out of the house with H'rare had been a ticklish business. They'd waited until midnight, when she was certain her mother was fast asleep along with the rest of her bodyslaves. Only then had they dared to enter the docking bay and steal a ship.

Lilli had chosen the long-range vehicle to take with her. H'rare said he could drive it and it was the biggest and most expensive one. Maybe she and Karn could sell it and live on the proceeds wherever they ended up.

*Which won't be anywhere unless this guard believes I'm Mother and releases Karn to me,* she thought desperately. *Oh, please...*

"I said, bring him to my ship," she snapped at the guard, who seemed to be hesitating.

"You—ssstop working," the guard said to Karn.

But the big Kindred kept going, hacking mercilessly at the steep, gray-green wall of stone that rose above them on all sides.

"Ssstop!" the guard insisted, but Karn wouldn't. Was he mad at her, Lilli wondered? Would he prefer to stay here than coming with her? Or maybe he just didn't know who she was—she did have on the black respirator which covered her entire face, after all. She hated for the big Kindred to be in any doubt about who she was, but she couldn't risk any of the Diluthian fumes getting into her lungs and possibly harming the baby.

"Make him stop!" she shouted at the guard. "At once, do you hear me? *At once!*"

"Er…" The Horvath hissed uneasily. His long, forked tongue ran out and swiped nervously over one yellow-slitted eyeball. "I cannot release him to you, Mistresss Mirabella," he said at last.

"What? Why not?" Lilli demanded. "Do you doubt my authority to take him?"

"No, no—of coursse not, Mistresss." The guard held up his green, scaly hands. "But the Obedienssse Skin—it has clearly malfunctioned. I have ssseen thisss happen once before. When the skin isss made to do only one action for hoursss on end, it some-timesss ssstops responding to ordersss."

"What?" Lilli was horrified. "But…is there no way to stop it?"

The guard shrugged his scaly shoulders.

"It isss DNA activated. Only the touch of the one who put the Skin on in the first place can make it cease itsss current motion." He looked at her. "Asss I understand it, *you* are the one who put it on him, Mistress. So only *you* can ssstop it."

Lilli felt as though someone had dumped a bucket of ice cubes into the pit of her stomach. Should she try touching the Obedience Skin? She had, of course, half of her mother's DNA so it *might* work. But if it didn't, her cover would be blown. The Horvaths would prob-ably detain her and report her and then Karn would die and she would be sent back to Yonnie Six and have her baby killed so she could incubate an heir her mother liked better.

Her mind was pulled in two directions. On one hand, she loved Karn desperately and wanted to save him. But on the other hand, she also felt fiercely protective of the new life inside her. She *had* to save her baby! What should she do?

Suddenly the Goddess's words came back to her.

***"Do not be afraid to attempt the impossible,"*** she had said. Also, she had promised to send Lilli help to escape and she *had* done it.

*I need to trust,* Lilli told herself. *The Goddess wouldn't have brought me this far only to let me fail now. She means for me to rescue Karn **and** our baby. She's with me now—I will not be afraid.*

Taking a deep breath, she reached out with one hand and laid it lightly on the silver plates that covered Karn's broad back.

"Stop," she said in a clear voice. "Stop working and come with me."

Karn's arms stopped in mid-swing and he abruptly dropped the pickaxe to the ground. He turned and faced Lilli, clearly waiting to follow wherever she led.

Lilli let out a breath of relief and thought, *Thank you, Goddess!*

"Very good," she said, trying to keep her voice strong, though inside she was as weak as jiggle-jelly with relief. "Let's go to my ship. Thank you, guard," she added, as the Horvath began to accompany them. "That will be all—you can go now."

"Yessss, Mistress Mirabella," the guard hissed and slunk off, his long lizard-like tail dragging in the greenish-gray Diluthian dust as he went.

"Come," Lilli said to Karn and started for the ship. She was determined not to break character until they were safely underway, just in case any of the other Horvath guards might be watching.

He followed obediently as she led the way, his heavy footsteps puffing up little jets of dust as they walked. She was glad again that she was wearing protective gear. This stuff was completely toxic. In fact, she would have to remove the Obedience Skin just before he stepped aboard the ship—she didn't want any of the Diluthian dust in the air circulating system once she took off her mask.

As soon as they reached the ship, she waved at H'rare to open the door and turned to the big Kindred, who had stopped obediently just in front of her. She wished she could read his face, but the bottom half of it was still obscured by the metal of the Obedience Skin and his eyes simply looked tired. No, more than tired—weary almost to death, Lilli saw with concern.

She touched his chest, letting her hand rest over the metal of the skin and said, "Skin, remove yourself from this male."

She had no idea if this order would work and, indeed, at first it didn't seem to. Karn just stood there, looking at her with those dead-tired eyes and for a moment Lilli was worried that he might collapse right in front of her.

Then the metal of the skin began to heat up—just a little at first, but soon it was so hot Lilli could barely stand to keep touching it. She held her hand there anyway, right over the big Kindred's heart and repeated her command.

"Come off him, Skin!" she demanded. "Come off *now!*"

Abruptly the metal plates began to separate and melt away. Soon they were nothing but a handful of hot silver balls cupped in the center of Lilli's palm. With a gasp, she threw them away, not wanting anything to do with the thing that had hurt the man she loved.

"Karn?" she asked, looking up at him. "Karn, are you all right?"

"Is it you the, little Mistress?" he rasped and then began to cough.

"It's me," Lilli told him. "But I have to keep the mask on as long as we're near the Diluthian dust and gasses. I can't risk it hurting the baby."

"The...baby." His mismatched eyes filled with wonderment. "My...son," he said hoarsely.

And then he collapsed at her feet.

# FORTY-SEVEN

"In here—get him in the ship! Hurry! And bring me some water, H'rare! Oh please—we have to get out of here!"

Karn was vaguely aware of the flurry of activity around him—the grunts of effort on the other bodyslave's part as he dragged Karn into the ship and Lilli hovering around, begging him to hurry.

*Sorry,* he wanted to say—wanted to apologize for collapsing and for being unable to get himself into the ship. But after hours and hours of unrelenting hard labor with no breaks and no hydration, his body was too weak to do anything but lie there as H'rare and Lilli dragged him aboard.

He blacked out for a moment but something cold and refreshing rubbing all over his face brought him around. Opening his eyes, he saw Lilli bending over him. Yes, it really was his sweet, precious Lilli and not her mother, as he had originally feared when she came to get him. No doubt she'd pretended to be Mistress Mirabella in order to fool the guards. But now, with the black mask off, there could be no doubt.

"Lilli," he rasped. "Baby…"

"Shhh, don't try to talk." She wiped the cool cloth over his forehead gently. "Just rest. And drink. If that awful skin was over your mouth this whole time, you must be so thirsty!"

She held a squeeze bulb of cold, fresh water to his lips and Karn thought he had never tasted anything so wonderful in his life. The finest bubble wine from Zinzu Tertia couldn't touch it—not even the nectar of the Goddess herself could be as good as the deep, life-saving draughts he sucked from the bulb Lilli held.

"Careful," she told him, her lovely brown eyes anxious. "Don't make yourself sick."

Karn wanted to tell her that he was fine now—that just seeing her was the best medicine any male could ask for. But he had to say something else first.

"So…sorry, baby," he got out, his voice still hoarse. "Didn't know I could…get you pregnant without a bond."

"It's all right." Lilli put a hand protectively over her lower belly, which was definitely rounder than it had been the last time he'd seen her. "I'm keeping him," she said, lifting her chin defiantly. "I don't care if he is male—I already love him." her eyes softened. "Just like I love his father."

"Oh, Lilli…" He started to pull her down, wanting to wrap her in his arms and never let her go, but H'rare's voice from the front of the ship stopped him.

"Mistress Lilli," he called anxiously. "We're being tracked! And your mother is on the viewscreen!"

# FORTY-EIGHT

L illi felt like her heart had stopped dead in her chest.

"My...my mother?" she wheezed, barely able to get the words out.

"I'm afraid so." H'rare sounded both apologetic and frightened. "And she's demanding to talk to you."

Wondering if her legs would hold her, Lilli got shakily to her feet and made her way from the passenger compartment to the front of the ship.

On the viewscreen, to H'rare's left, was a full-color image of her mother. And Lady Mirabella had a *lot* of color at the moment—most noticeably in her face, which was nearly purple with rage.

"How dare you?" she said in a low, dangerous voice as soon as Lilli came into view. "How *dare* you disobey me you insolent girl? How dare you steal my best ship and go after that no-good male who you allowed to penetrate you?"

Lilli raised her chin.

"I love Karn, Mother," she said, trying not to let her voice tremble. "And I love his baby too—*our* baby." She put a hand protectively over her belly. "I don't want to lose either one of them. I...I won't let you kill them!"

Mistress Mirabella's eyes flashed.

"I'll kill all *three* of you if you don't turn that ship around *right now* and head for home," she snarled.

"Just let us go," Lilli pleaded. "You don't like me anyway, Mother —you never have. You always thought having a daughter was a chore. Just let me disappear and I swear you'll never have to see me again."

"What?" her mother nearly shrieked. "Just let you go—just like that?" She snapped her fingers. "Lilliana, I am a member of the *Sacred Seven*. Do you know how it would look if anyone found out that I had allowed my daughter to run off with her bodyslave and have his wretched male baby? Do you know what people would *say?*"

Suddenly Lilli saw red. She'd never dared to get angry at her mother before, no matter what awful, cutting things Mistress Mirabella said to her. But finally, after a lifetime of derogatory comments and nasty words, she felt she's had enough.

"That's *all* you care about, isn't it?" she demanded. "What people will *say*—how things *look*. Well, let me tell you something, Mother—I don't care anymore. It doesn't matter to me if I ruin my reputation, your reputation, *and* our family name. I don't even care if you get kicked out of the Sacred Seven! I'm in love with Karn and we're going to go someplace where people care about more than just appearances. Where they care about more than who's got the most money or the highest building or the most expensive dress or bodyslave or hover-car. We're going to go someplace where people value what's inside and we're going to raise our son there *together*. And you can just...just *go to Hell!*"

Throughout this speech her mother's eyes had been getting wider and wider but when Lilli finished they narrowed to slits of rage.

"You're not going anywhere but straight home, young lady," she informed Lilli. And if you don't, the two ships I have on your tail will shoot you out of the sky."

"What?" Lilli felt sick. "You wouldn't!"

"Oh, wouldn't I?" A cruel smile curved Mistress Mirabella's thin lips. "I'd rather have people think that my heir died in a tragic crash than let them know she was running off with some male in order to have his baby!"

"Mistress Lilli," H'rare said hoarsely. "We really do have two ships on our tail—both military grade with laser cannons!"

Lilli felt sick. What should they do? If they turned around, both her baby and Karn would be killed. But if they went on, *all* of them would die, including H'rare whose only crime was being brave enough to leave with her and pilot the ship when she asked him to.

*Goddess,* she prayed, *where are you now?*

There was no answer and her heart sank. She looked at H'rare who looked back at her anxiously, his hands hovering over the complicated-looking controls.

"What do you want to do, Mistress?" he asked in a low voice.

"I don't know." Lilli bit her lip. "I don't…don't know where we can go."

"There's nowhere you can go but *home,*" her mother snapped from the viewscreen. "Come home and surrender yourself at *once,* Lilliana or face the consequences!"

"I don't think so." The deep, familiar voice behind her made Lilli whirl around.

Karn was standing there, still looking weary around the eyes, but standing tall and strong nonetheless.

"You say we have nowhere to go?" he said to Lilli's Mother.

"Nowhere but back to the Diluthian mines," she spat at him. "Only this time I'll make *sure* they kill you!"

"I'm not going back to the mines and Lilli's not going back to you, you abusive bitch!" Karn growled. "You've hurt her for the last time."

"Not quite the last." Mistress Mirabella's thin lips curved into that cruel smile again. "If you don't come back, I'll have you shot out of the sky and *that* will be the last time I hurt her. It will be terminally final but also *extremely* satisfying."

*"You will kill no one."*

The deep, resonant voice filled the cabin, making them all jump. On the viewscreen, Mistress Mirabella was looking all around.

"Who said that? Who's there?" she demanded in a high voice. "Is this some kind of trick?"

There was no answer but suddenly, right in front of them, a swirling blue vortex opened in the blackness of space.

*"Fly, my children,"* the warm, feminine voice told them. *"Go quickly, you are in great peril!"*

"Who is that?" H'rare gasped, looking all around. "Who said that?"

"The Goddess," Karn and Lilli said at the same time and Karn roared, *"Fly!"* and pointed at the swirling wormhole in front of them.

At the same time, Lilli could hear her mother shouting, "FIRE!"

There was a blast of light behind them and she felt the ship rock dangerously. Sliding to one side, she nearly fell, only to be caught by Karn's long arm around her waist.

*"FLY!"* he roared again and then they were diving nose-first into the swirling blue void of the wormhole and leaving Lilli's mother and everything she had ever known behind forever.

# FORTY-NINE

"Well, your baby is just fine, thank goodness!" Olivia, the doctor who had met them at the docking bay of the Kindred Mother Ship, ran her scanner wand over Lilli's belly and smiled.

She and Lilli were in the exam room together while Karn paced anxiously outside, speaking to his commanding officer, whose name was Sylvan. He was also a doctor and had been examining the big Kindred as Liv examined Lilli. Apparently, though he had inhaled a lot of the Diluthian dust, Karn was going to be all right as well.

The fact that her bodyslave wasn't actually a bodyslave at all and was, in fact, a Kindred spy had been news to Lilli. At first, when Karn had admitted it, she'd simply stared at him with her mouth hanging open. But the vast white bulk of the Mother Ship, orbiting a strange moon she had never seen before, convinced her. It had just appeared like magic, the moment they exited the wormhole and that was when Karn had admitted everything.

Lilli wasn't upset to learn the man she loved was a spy. Mostly, she was just glad they had someplace to go. She'd had visions of them roaming around the galaxy, looking for a place to hide where her vindictive mother couldn't find them. Now, it turned out that Karn had a safe home and people of his own—very nice people, if Liv was any indication.

"So you're sure he's okay?" she asked anxiously.

"Perfectly okay," Liv assured her. "Though he appears to be growing like a weed—I do believe he's a few centimeters longer than he was just a minute ago!" She shook her head in wonder.

"It must be the quick-grow hormones I was injected with," Lilli told her. "They're supposed to make a pregnancy three months long instead of nine."

"Well, when you're pregnant with a Kindred baby, you usually end up being pregnant for *twelve* months," Liv told her. "So I guess that means you'll only be pregnant for four of those—lucky you! It's miserable to be pregnant for a whole year—which is one reason I only have one kid." She grinned at Lilli and then she got serious. "It's *also* why the Goddess sent you that wormhole. Karn had called us and Sylvan was about to bend space for you, but pregnant women can't travel through the rift."

"They can't? Why not?" Lilli asked.

Liv shook her head. "It's bad for the baby. Karn knew that, of course, but what could he do when your ship was about to be blown out of the sky? But then the Goddess intervened and came to your rescue."

"I'm so grateful she did," Lilli said sincerely. "You know, Karn had told me about her, but I didn't know she really existed until she spoke to me from out of nowhere."

"Yeah, she can surprise you like that." Liv grinned at her again. "It's pretty shocking the first time it happens to you and you just hear her voice out of thin air. It's wonderful too, the way she watches out for her children."

"I guess I'm one of her children now, since I'm carrying Karn's baby," Lilli said, smiling. "Speaking of which…" She leaned forward on the exam table and looked at Liv earnestly. "Karn told me he couldn't er, get me pregnant unless we were bonded. And he said he couldn't bond me to him because he's a Hybrid. Was any of that true? Because…look at me." she pointed to her slightly rounded belly. "I'm pregnant but we're not bonded—at least, I don't *think* we are."

"Can you hear his voice in your head and can you send your own mental voice into *his* head?" Liv asked.

Lilli gave her a shocked look.

"No! Why, is that part of being bonded?"

"It is." Liv nodded and smiled. "A wonderful part, actually. When you bond with a Kindred, your souls touch and you just have this wonderful, deep understanding of what the other person wants and thinks and needs and feels."

"And you have that, with your mate?" Lilli sighed longingly. "That sounds *amazing.*"

"It is," Liv assured her. She shook her head. "But I've never heard of any Kindred being able to get a girl pregnant *until* he bonded her to him. So you'll have to forgive Karn—he must have been as shocked to learn that you were pregnant as you were."

"Everybody was pretty shocked," Lilli said grimly. "Shocked and appalled in the case of my mother."

"She doesn't sound like she treated you very well," Liv said tactfully.

"If you call trying to shoot the ship I was on out of the sky and kill me 'not treating me very well' then yes, that's true." Lilli tried to snort, but it turned into a sob. She gulped and put a hand to her mouth. "Sorry. I just…can't believe she tried to do that. But she's never liked me very much—I was a disappointment to her because I'm too nice and I don't have a head for business or care about material possessions and always having the best of everything the way other Yonnites do."

"Well, you don't have to worry about her anymore," Liv said firmly, putting an arm around Lilli's shoulders. "You've got a new home now—here with us. And I promise you, here on the Mother Ship we *like* nice people."

Lilli gave a half-laugh/half-sob and hugged her back.

"Thanks. I don't know why I'm feeling so emotional."

"You've been through a lot of trauma," Liv said soothingly. "And you've got crazy preggy-lady hormones. That will make *anybody* emotional, hon."

"I guess so." Lilli sniffed and swiped at her eyes. "I'm just so glad my baby is all right and Karn is okay and we're all together. I only wish…" She trailed off, biting her lip.

"Wish what, hon?" Liv asked gently. "Go on, you can tell me."

"I only wish I could have that bond with Karn—the soul-bond you were talking about," Lilli admitted. "It sounds so wonderful. Can't a Hybrid *ever* bond?" she asked Liv wistfully.

"Well, you know what, I actually know several that have," Liv said thoughtfully. "It's usually impossible but sometimes the Goddess intervenes and it happens."

Lilli felt her heart jump and she heard a little voice in her head murmur, ***"Do not be afraid to attempt the impossible."***

"I see," she said, nodding. "Thank you, Liv—you're a wonderful doctor." She ducked her head shyly. "And an even better friend."

"We *are* going to be friends," Liv said, grinning at her. "As soon as you get some rest and feel up to it, I'm going to introduce you to a group of girls you're just going to *love*."

"A whole group?" Lilli asked uncertainly.

"Well, sure." Liv looked at her anxiously. "Why, does that upset you?"

Lilli bit her lip.

"It's just I, uh, had a group of girls that were supposed to be my friends on Yonnie Six—but really they were just the daughters of my mother's friends. And they were *awful.* That's how Karn and I got caught—one of them made a vid of us, uh, being intimate and sent it to my mother."

"How awful!" Liv exclaimed indignantly. "I promise you, Lilli, that friendship is nothing like that here on the Mother Ship. We love and support each other and if anybody has a problem, they talk it out."

"Okay, well…thank you, then. I'd love to meet your friends," Lilli said, smiling. "They sound more like the group of girls I grew up with at the convent than the ones I knew on Yonnie Six."

"You're going to love them," Liv promised her. "My best friend, Kat, is going to want to throw you a baby shower and my cousin, Lauren, is going to want to make the cake and give you all kinds of cupcakes—anything your pregnant cravings can dream up, she can make. And my twin sister, Sophie, is going to be thrilled to meet you too. And there are so many, many more—even another Mistress from Yonnie Six, Neh'sa—but she's really nice, don't worry. She and her man didn't like it there, either—that's why they ended up here."

By the time they finished talking, Lilli's head was spinning. Liv sent her away from the Med Center with strict instructions to rest and said that she would want to see her every other day, to chart the course of the quick-grow pregnancy.

"Normally I'd only want to see you a couple of times a month and then once a week when you got close to delivery," she told Lilli. "But this is unprecedented—the baby's growing so quickly I'll need to check on him more often."

Lilli was happy to promise to come back soon. She really liked Liv and was excited and a little nervous to meet the other women she'd talked about. Maybe here on the Mother Ship, she could finally have the kind of life she'd dreamed of—a nice, normal life with supportive, caring friends and a mate she truly loved.

There was only one thing missing. But maybe, just maybe she could have that too.

*"Do not be afraid to attempt the impossible…"* The voice of the Goddess rang in her head.

Lilli was through being afraid—she was ready to reach for what she wanted. And what she wanted was Karn—completely.

She just hoped she could have him.

# FIFTY

The suite Karn brought her to was charming. It was furnished with oversized furniture, obviously meant to hold a huge male of his size, and it had a cozy little living area with a fireplace, as well as a lovely deep bathing pool to relax in. Yet, he seemed anxious about it as he showed her around.

"I know there's no anti-grav pool or flo'jamon courts," he rumbled, as Lilli looked around. "And no servants to cook and clean for you—"

"I don't need any of that," Lilli interrupted him. "We didn't have any of that at the convent, you know. We did all the chores ourselves and we certainly never had any fancy amenities."

"But at your mother's house—" he began.

"Is my mother," Lilli finished for him. "And all the gold and jewels and fancy tech and servants in the world couldn't make living with her bearable." She blinked, trying to hold back the tears that suddenly threatened. "She was awful, Karn!"

"I know she was baby," he rumbled, drawing her close and rubbing her shoulders and back soothingly with his big, warm hands.

"But you don't ever have to see her again. We're together now and she can't hurt you."

"Or you. Or our son." Lilli put a hand protectively over her belly.

"Gods, I still can't believe I got you pregnant." Karn shook his head wonderingly. "That's supposed to be impossible without a bond. It must have been those crazy quick-grow hormone shots your mother gave you. It's the only way I can think it could have happened."

"Oh?" Lilli tilted her head and gave him a mischievous look. "I can think of a way it happened—maybe you filling me with your shaft and your seed over and over and over again for the past week?"

His mismatched eyes were suddenly half-lidded.

"Well, yeah, that too," he growled softly. Leaning down, he cupped her face in his hands gently and took her mouth in a long, hot kiss.

As their lips met, the tingling need came back in full force. Lilli nearly gasped with the sudden desire, which reminded her of how she had felt on their journey to Opulex. It was like her body was hungry for his cream—hungry to be plowed and planted by his seed yet again.

"Karn," she begged, the moment the kiss broke "Make love to me, right now! No, don't just make love to me—*fuck* me."

He gave her that charming, lopsided grin of his—the one that showed only one fang.

"We're barely alone for a minute and you're already asking for sex? I thought Dr. Olivia told you to rest."

"She did," Lilli admitted breathlessly. "But I can't seem to help it —I need to have you in me. I…I think I'm still feeling the effects of those awful hormone shots."

He raised an eyebrow at her.

"Is it the tingling again, baby?"

Liv nodded.

"It is. And it's making me feel *crazy*."

She went to the bed and lay on her back. Lifting her top to show her naked breasts and taking off her panties, she spread her legs to offer him her open pussy.

"Please, Karn," she whispered. "Fuck me—fuck me *hard.*"

His mismatched eyes went half-lidded and a low growl of desire rose in his throat.

"I'd love to, but what about the baby?"

"He's safe," Lilli promised him. "I asked Liv about it and she said we could, er, do what we wanted."

Her cheeks got hot at the admission. It was one of the last questions she'd asked her new friend before leaving the Med Center and it hadn't been easy to ask, but she'd had to know. Now she was happy to report that it was safe to do exactly what she wanted with her man.

"Well, as long as the doctor says it's okay...as my lady wishes," he rumbled, coming to stand between her thighs. "But first, I need to taste you again."

He dropped to his knees between her legs and looked up at her.

"Is this okay, baby? I want to check you out and be sure that damn metal phallus at the conception center didn't hurt you."

"It didn't." Lilli bit her lip. "It felt awful inside me, but it didn't wound me any—though I think it might have if you hadn't, uh, stretched me out some before I went there."

"It made me crazy to see you so upset on the other side of that plastiglass barrier and not be able to get to you," Karn said hoarsely. Leaning forward, he rubbed his cheek gently over her bare mound. "Sweet baby," he murmured. "Just want to heal you and make you feel good."

"Oh, Karn..." Some of her desire melted into tenderness and she reached down to stroke her fingers through his long, thick hair. "I love you," she whispered. "Thank you for being so sweet to me."

"Of course, baby." Gently, he kissed the apex of her mound and then ran just the tip of his tongue tenderly down her slit.

Lilli moaned and arched her hips as her desire flared again.

"Karn..." she whispered, tugging at his hair. "Please..."

He gave her a wolfish grin.

"Can't wait for me to spread your hot little pussy with my tongue again, little Mistress?"

"You don't have to call me that anymore, you know," Lilli pointed out breathlessly as he opened her outer pussy lips with his thumbs and kissed her aching clit.

"I know I don't," he rumbled, grinning up at her as she writhed in pleasure. "But maybe I want to, sometimes. I fell in love with you from the first minute you bought me, you know. I don't want to forget that part of our time together."

Lilli started to answer but at that moment, he started to lap her pussy. With long, slow strokes that started at the mouth of her channel, he bathed her inner folds with his tongue, tasting her juices and teasing the ripe bud of her clit until she thought she might go crazy.

"Oh, Karn…*Karn!*" she moaned, arching her back to ride his face. "Oh yes, please—that feels so *good.*"

"Feels good for me, too, baby. Gods, I love to lick your pussy," he growled and went back to lapping and sucking her clit until Lilli thought she was going to explode with pleasure. She could feel her orgasm hovering just over the horizon, like a thunderstorm threatening to break. If the big Kindred would just keep licking…

Karn did. He seemed to know exactly which spots to concentrate on and once he'd found the right place, he kept licking steadily, never varying the speed until Lilli's hips were bucking in a regular rhythm and her breath was coming fast and short.

"Karn!" she moaned, gripping his hair even harder and grinding against his tongue. "Oh yes, there! *Right there!*"

The thunderstorm broke and a hot rain of pleasure overwhelmed her. It felt so good—so *right*—and yet Lilli still needed more.

"In me!" she begged, tugging at his long hair as the pleasure of her first orgasm at last began to fade. "Please, Karn, I need you *in me!*"

He got on the bed with her and pulled Lilli into his lap so that she was straddling the long thick shaft of his cock. His mouth was still shiny with her juices and his eyes were blazing.

"Is this how you want it, baby?" he growled. "Face to face?"

"Yes." Lilli nodded eagerly. "Face to face. And… and I want it really deep—just how it was in the ship on the way to Opulex. I…I want your mating fist inside me again. I really liked that," she admitted, feeling her cheeks get hot again with a blush.

"That wasn't supposed to happen," he told her but he was already fitting the head of his cock to her wet pussy mouth once more. "It was dangerously close to bonding, you know, baby."

"I thought you *couldn't* bond me to you," Lilli whispered and then moaned softly in pleasure and relief as he filled her once more.

"I can't. But I wanted to try—my body sure as hell did, anyway," he growled, seating himself to the hilt inside her—all but his mating fist, Lilli noticed with disappointment.

"Deeper," she begged, wiggling against him. "I want to feel you all the way in me again, Karn! In fact, I want you to pretend like you're bonding me—like your breeding me and trying to get me pregnant," she told him.

He frowned down at her.

"You want me to pretend like I'm planting a baby in your belly? But I already did that."

"Do it again!" Lilli moaned eagerly. Goddess, just the thought of how he had made her pregnant made her pussy clench all around his shaft with need! She had never wanted a baby before this, but now the idea of the big Kindred planting one inside her turned her on so much she could barely breathe!

"Please, Karn," she begged raggedly. "Put yourself all the way inside me and come deep in my womb!"

A low growl of desire rose in his throat and he thrust forward. Lilli moaned as she felt his thick shaft fill her completely and his mating fist slip into her unresisting pussy. Goddess, it felt good—felt right to have him so deep inside her!

"Karn!" she moaned and leaned forward to put her neck directly against his mouth. She could feel the sharp points of his fangs as he kissed her there—they skated dangerously over her skin but never quite drew blood.

"Gods, baby," he groaned, as he thrust inside her. "You feel so good wrapped all around me. Love to feel your soft little pussy clenching around my shaft!"

"Come inside me," Lilli begged breathlessly. "I want to feel you shooting in me, Karn. And…and bite me while you do."

He pulled back, frowning.

"Baby, if I bite you, my body will think I'm trying to bond you to me and we might end up with a failed bonding. That hurts—hurts a hell of a lot."

"But it *might* work," Lilli pleaded. "After all, you weren't supposed to be able to get me pregnant but you did that! Please, Karn, can't you just *try* to bond me to you? If it doesn't work this time, I promise I'll never ask again but please? Can't you just try?"

"Gods, baby," he growled. "Almost from the first minute I saw you, all I wanted to do was sink both my shaft and my fangs in you at the same time."

"Really?" Lilli looked at him with wide eyes. "You've wanted to bond me to you before this?"

"Hell yes," he growled. "I've been fighting the urge for days." He sighed. "I shouldn't but if you're really not afraid…?"

"I'm not," Lilli said eagerly. "Please, Karn—let's just try."

"As you wish, little Mistress," he murmured. "All right then, spread your legs wide and let me get really deep into you—then bare your throat for my fangs."

A shiver of pure desire ran through Lilli. She did as he said, opening her thighs even wider as she felt his thickness stretching and filling her. At the same time, she pulled her long blonde hair out of the way and pressed the side of her throat to his mouth once more.

"Bite me, Karn," she whispered. "Bite me and bond me and make me yours forever."

Her words seemed to have an electric effect on the big Kindred.

With a low growl, he sank his razor-sharp fangs deep in the vulnerable side of her throat.

Lilli gasped as a short, sharp pain went through her. Then the pain turned abruptly to pleasure—a pleasure so deep it made her earlier orgasm look like dipping your toes in the ocean as opposed to being drawn in and drowned by it.

With a low moan, she began to come, her inner muscles squeezing around the thick shaft buried deep inside her. And as her pussy clenched around the big Kindred's cock, she felt the now-familiar sensation of his cream shooting deep inside her, filling her completely, making her his forever…

*"Yes, you are mine forever—and I'm yours, baby,"* a deep, familiar voice growled in her head.

If Liv hadn't told her this was a side effect of bonding with a Kindred, Lilli probably would have screamed. As it was, she simply moaned and sent back a message of her own.

*"It worked!"*

*"Yes, it worked."* Karn pulled her even closer. Withdrawing his fangs from her throat, he looked down into her eyes. "You're mine now, baby," he growled softly. "Mine forever and I'm never letting you go."

Then he thrust into her once more, filling her with himself and sealing their love as they continued to claim each other over and over again.

Lilli hung on tight and reveled in the new bond she felt—the deep, wonderful closeness that told her their two souls were entwined.

*Thank you, Goddess,* she prayed as her heart overflowed with joy. *Oh, thank you so much! You're so good to me!*

She had a whole new life now—away from her controlling, hypercritical mother. A life with a mate who loved her and new friends and a baby on the way.

And all because Karn had insisted on…Protecting his Mistress.

# EPILOGUE

"So how is the baby?" Karn was hanging anxiously over Liv's shoulder, watching on the monitor as she waved the wand over Lilli's lower belly again. "We didn't er, hurt him, did we?" he asked in a low voice.

"No…" Liv was frowning. "You didn't hurt him," she said, reassuring them when Lilli and Karn exchanged anxious looks. "But, well…this is strange."

"What's strange?" Lilli asked quickly.

"Well, it's just…I'm reading *two* heartbeats, here." Liv shook her head. "I could swear there was only one little guy in there yesterday. But now there seem to be *two.*"

"Twins?" Lilli gasped and Karn growled, "A double blessing!"

"Let me just get Sylvan to double check this," Liv said. "Oh, Sylvan?" She poked her head out of the exam room. "Would you mind coming in here for a moment?"

"Of course. Karn, it's good to see you again." Sylvan offered Karn a warrior's clasp. "And this must be your lovely mate, Lilli."

"Mate in every sense of the word," Karn informed him proudly.

"We're bonded now, though I always thought it would be impossible."

Sylvan's eyebrows raised almost to his hairline.

"Truly, you are blessed by the Goddess!"

"Possibly doubly blessed," Liv told him. "That's what I want you to check—do you see two heartbeats in there, Sylvan?"

Sylvan took the wand and waved it over Lilli's belly as he studied the monitor for himself. After a moment, he nodded.

"Yes, definitely. Though one baby seems less developed than the other. He appears to be about…oh, about a month younger than his brother."

"But there was only one baby yesterday—I'm sure of it!" Liv protested. "How could this happen?"

"Well…" Sylvan put down the wand and rubbed his chin. "Didn't you tell me that Lilli, here, had been injected with extreme fertility hormones?"

"Quick-grow hormones—yes." Lilli nodded.

"There're all the rage on Yonnie Six right now," Karn said dryly.

"I see. So that's probably how you got pregnant in the first place," Sylvan told Lilli. "Because of the extreme hormones. But do you think they might still be in your system?"

Lilli thought of the persistent tingling and sexual need she'd begged Karn to help her with the night before and blushed.

"Maybe," she admitted, feeling her cheeks get hot.

"Mmm, I see." Sylvan nodded. "So these hormones make it much easier to get pregnant and they make the fetus grow extremely fast."

"That's right," Karn said.

"And *when* exactly did you get bonded?" Sylvan raised an eyebrow questioningly.

"Last night," Lilli said, her cheeks getting hotter.

"All night long," Karn added, with his lopsided grin.

"Well, I think that solves the mystery of your first baby's little brother," Sylvan said dryly. "Apparently these hormones you were given are so potent that you continue to release eggs that can be fertilized even after you're already pregnant."

"Oh my!" Lilli put a hand to her mouth. "Does that mean we shouldn't, uh…do what we did to get bonded anymore for a while?"

"Let me run some blood tests," Sylvan told her. "It should be safe again as soon as the hormones are out of your system. But until then, unless you want triplets, I'd lay off the, er, bonding activities."

"Understood," Karn told him. "Two is enough for us."

"It's *more* than enough." Lilli looked at Liv. "How in the world am I going to manage two at once?"

"You'll have your hubby to help you," Liv said firmly. "Kindred make *excellent* fathers. And don't forget I'm going to introduce you to my friends. My own sister, Sophie—who's married to Sylvan, by the way—had twins."

"A boy and a girl." Sylvan smiled proudly.

"And my best friend, Kat, had triplets," Liv went on. "Of course, she's got *two* husbands to help her raise them, but still—they're a handful."

"I bet!" Lilli murmured. She promised herself she was going to try and control the extreme sexual desire she felt—she had to unless she wanted to wind up with a whole *bunch* of babies inside!

"But will the second baby be all right?" Karn asked anxiously. "I mean, will he be born on his older brother's due date and won't that be too early for him?"

"Please don't worry." Sylvan shook his head. "We can give your mate compounds to help delay her labor until both of your sons are ready to be born." He patted Lilli's hands. "We're going to take good care of her and your babies."

"Thank you," Karn said gratefully. "I really appreciate it, Commander Sylvan."

"It's the least I can do after you risked your life on such a difficult and dangerous mission," Sylvan said gravely. "Why, without you, the Nightwalker Kindred you discovered in the Yonnite System would have been put to death by now."

"Oh—is he going to be all right?" Lilli asked anxiously. When he was telling her about being a spy and not a bodyslave at all, Karn had also admitted his role in trying to save the other warrior. She was glad she'd been involved in helping him find the evidence that would hopefully set the Nightwalker Kindred free.

"He's going to be, if the Goddess wills it," Sylvan said grimly. "I've spoken to the Councilor who's helping him in the Yonnite Court System. She's up against some big challenges but she's a very determined young woman—I know she'll prevail."

"Imani, right?" Liv asked, raising an eyebrow. "The one who took Councilor Allisandra's place?"

Sylvan nodded. "Exactly. She's on Yonnie Six right now, fighting for the Nightwalker's freedom. Though I think there have been a few complications in the case..."

"Whatever it is, the Goddess will lead her through it," Liv said confidently and Lilli nodded her head in agreement.

"She certainly took care of Karn and me—and our baby," she pointed out.

"*Babies*," Karn corrected, grinning at her. "I never thought I'd even have one son—and now we're going to have *two!*"

"Two sons," Lilli murmured—she was still trying to wrap her head around the idea.

She vowed to herself that she would raise her sons in the ways of the Kindred. She would be a much better mother than her own mother had been and she would love them unconditionally. They would know she was there for them always and they would grow up to be fine men and wonderful warriors.

Sylvan smiled at her.

"Truly, the Goddess is good."

"She certainly is." Lilli nodded. But inside, her mind moved from her own joy to the danger of the girl who was still stuck on Yonnie Six.

*Let her be safe, Goddess,* she prayed. *Protect her with your mighty power!*

After all, the Nightwalker Kindred had been framed for a gruesome murder—which they *knew* he had not committed. But what if whoever *had* killed his Mistress was still on the loose? And what if they targeted Councilor Imani because she was trying to help the male they'd tried to pin it on?

Lilli shivered at the thought. She would keep the other girl in her prayers, she decided.

Imani would need all the prayers she could get.

# THE END?

## OF COURSE NOT!

**Read on for a sneak peek at *Unleashed by the Defender*, Imani and the Nightwalker Kindred's book, coming soon!**

But first, if you've enjoyed this book, please consider leaving a short review. Good reviews are like gold for an author in this crazy-crowded book landscape. They let other readers know it's okay to take a chance on a new author or a new series. Plus they give me the warm fuzzies. : )

Thanks for being such an awesome reader!

Hugs,

Evangeline

EVANGELINE ANDERSON

# UNLEASHED
## BY THE
# DEFENDER

KINDRED TALES

# PROLOGUE

Pale green eyes, glowing in the darkness. Savage eyes…a beast's eyes.

Imani put a hand up to ward them off. They were coming for her —coming and there was nothing she could do to save herself— nowhere to run, no place she could hide. The eyes would find her and then…

She woke up with a start, her heart pounding, her palms sweating.

"Stop it," she told herself out loud, wincing at the sound of her own voice in the darkness. "Stop it, it's just a dream. Only a dream!"

But she couldn't seem to stop herself from searching the dark confines of her bedroom aboard the Kindred Mother Ship. Couldn't stop thinking that she saw those eyes watching her…waiting for her.

Waiting for what?

Imani didn't know but she was desperately afraid she was going to find out…

# ONE

"I'm sorry, but I just *can't* wear this—especially not to argue a case in court!"

Imani Williams looked down at the crazy outfit her new friend and advisor, Kat, had put her into with shock and dismay. It looked like something she might wear if she wanted to dance around a silver pole at a strip club—*not* a respectable ensemble she might put on to go to a courtroom.

The top half—because yes, it was actually a two-piece that showed her midriff—consisted of a thin band of mostly see-through pink lace that barely covered her nipples. This normally wouldn't have worked for Imani, since she was big up top and needed serious support for her double D cup breasts. But Kat had given her tiny little devices called "float dots" to use which, when applied to the bottom of each breast, right where they met her chest, caused her boobs to lift effortlessly and look positively perky.

The float dots were nice, Imani had to admit, but putting her breasts on display like this most certainly was *not*.

The bottom part of her new courtroom attire was a long, tight skirt, a darker shade of pink than the barely-there lace top. It would have been okay if not for the slit up the middle which went all the way to her navel. There was a lace panel which covered her panties—also made of lace—but it didn't do a very good job since it was mostly see-through and extremely short.

"I can't go into a courtroom on another planet looking like a prostitute!" Imani said, turning to Kat.

"You won't look like a prostitute, doll—you'll look like a high-powered female litigator—this is how they dress on Yonnie Six," Kat assured her. "And believe me, if you don't dress correctly, they won't give you the time of day. Those Yonnite women are *ruthless* when it comes to fashion."

"But how can it be a sign of female empowerment to show off my body this way?" Imani argued. She would rather crawl under a rock than appear in this get-up in public! "Showing your body means you're displaying yourself for a man or men and I thought Yonnie Six was ruled exclusively by *women.*"

"It is," Kat said patiently. "And on Yonnie Six, showing your body *is* a sign of empowerment. Essentially you're saying, 'look at me—I can show my body and not a single man here can touch me." She shrugged. "Because they're pretty much all slaves."

"Like my client." Imani frowned, her mind temporarily diverted from her current dress debacle. "He's been locked up in the Yonnite jail for *days* now and he's scheduled to be executed if I can't get him off."

"What are the details?" Kat asked curiously. "I've heard a little bit about this case from Sylvan, but I don't know the whole case."

"There aren't many," Imani admitted. "I'm supposed to get more detailed information once I reach Yonnie Six from a Kindred infor-mant. He's working undercover there and he's supposed to give me evidence to use in court. But essentially, my client has been accused of murdering his Mistress in cold blood."

"Wow!" Kat's lovely blue eyes widened. "That's a tall order, isn't it? Have you ever defended a murderer before?"

"I don't believe he *is* a murderer," Imani said, frowning. "Apparently there are some very fishy circumstances surrounding the crime. But the Yonnie Peace Keeper Squad didn't even *try* to find any other suspects—they just slapped my client in jail and charged him with murder. It's not unlike some cases I've seen on Earth, actually."

"So you *have* defended people in his position before, then," Kat said.

Imani nodded. "I haven't been an attorney for very long, but my specialty is defending people who have been wrongly accused and imprisoned. You'd be surprised and appalled at how many people have been locked away for crimes they didn't commit—just because those in authority wanted someone to blame and they were in the wrong place at the wrong time."

"You sound like it's personal for you," Kat remarked.

"It is." Imani sighed. "It happened to my older brother, Rashaad." Even now she couldn't think about her big brother without a lump forming in her throat. What had happened to him was so unneces-sary—so *wrong*. Every time she took a new case she thought of him— thought of the justice she would get for her client, which had been denied to her brother.

"What happened, if you don't mind me asking?" Kat asked quietly.

Imani shook her head. It hurt too much to talk about the inti-mate details of her brother's death. But she could give her new friend the quick and dirty version.

"A routine traffic stop which turned into a drug bust," she said tightly. "Only Rashaad didn't do drugs—he was a health freak, wouldn't even put caffeine in his body, let alone cocaine—which was what the cops claimed they found. And they claimed they had found enough of it to throw him in jail without bail because they said he was a flight risk."

"That's horrible!" Kat exclaimed. "Couldn't your family do anything about it?"

"We tried," Imani said. "My parents are well connected—my dad's a tax attorney and my mom is a doctor—a Pediatrician. They hired the best defense attorney they could find. But before the case could even get to court, my brother was…" She took a deep breath. "He was stabbed and killed. We only got word when my Mom and I went to visit him. My Mom was…" She shook her head, remembering the way her mother had broken down, sobbing, right there in the visitors' area. "She was devastated. We all were."

"Of course you were. How terrible!" Kat looked truly horrified. "And that's what made you want to go into law?"

Imani nodded.

"The next day I changed my major from pre-med to pre-law." She lifted her chin. "I wanted to fight for people like my brother—people who were unjustly accused and railroaded into prison."

"I think that's wonderful." Kat gave her an admiring look. "The fact that you're turning your personal tragedy into a crusade for justice."

Imani sighed.

"It's the best I can do, since there was nothing I could do for my brother. I'll do *anything* to help my clients." She looked down at herself and sighed. "Even, apparently, dress like a stripper."

"Believe me, doll, you *won't* be the only one there dressed like that," Kat assured her. "And don't worry, I'll be packing you more of the same, so if the hearing goes on multiple days, you'll have plenty of fashion choices."

"All of them obscene, I suppose?" Imani raised an eyebrow at her. "At least this color looks good with my complexion," she remarked. The dark pink did an excellent job of emphasizing her chocolaty brown skin tones—perhaps *too* good a job, she thought wryly, since so much skin was on display.

"They're all pretty skimpy," Kat admitted matter-of-factly. "But again, that's Yonnie Six for you. You have to dress the part or they won't have anything to do with you." She shrugged. "But at least you don't have to pretend to be one of them—if you were, we'd have to find a willing Kindred warrior to pretend to be your bodyslave."

"Bodyslave?" Imani asked, horrified.

"Sure." Kat nodded. "In Yonnite high society, you're nothing if you don't have a big hot guy trailing around on a leash and a pain collar after you. But since they already know you're coming from the Kindred, you don't have to pretend. Not that Sylvan won't send a guard to protect you, if you want one," she added.

Imani shook her head firmly.

"No thanks. I prefer to work alone. Besides, from what I'm reading about the Nightwalker Kindred, it's much better for me to come for him by myself than to present another male that he might see as a challenge. Nightwalkers are extremely territorial."

"Really?" Kat looked interested as she handed Imani a short, pink lace jacket that matched the band of lace covering her breasts. "Here, put this on—it might help you feel a *little* less naked."

A *very* little bit, Imani thought, as she tried the jacket on. It covered her arms all right but didn't meet in the middle, which meant her breasts were still exposed.

"Thanks," she said doubtfully.

"You look gorgeous if it's any consolation," Kat told her, smiling. "Better put on your regular clothes though, Sylvan wants us to come to a briefing before you go."

Imani was more than willing to take off the skimpy Yonnie Six court outfit and slip back into her normal workday clothes of a conservative button-down blouse and pencil skirt. She gave a sigh of relief as she stepped out from behind the folding screen Kat had set up in her office, which also included a clothing simulator—an amazing machine which could print out clothes from on-line images like a 3-D printer.

"Well, you look much more conservative now," Kat said, grinning as Imani emerged from behind the screen. "Ready for the briefing?"

"Ready." Imani nodded. She was eager to learn more details of the case she was about to try. She'd been taking a crash course in Yonnite Law from Lizabeth Paige to prepare for it. Lizabeth and her husband, Lone, headed up the Kindred's legal team but they had new twins to care for, so Imani had been chosen to go take care of this particular case.

Of course, the case *would* have fallen to her mentor, Allisandra Stone, but she had recently moved to an alternate universe to be with the Kindred husband who had Claimed her—which was mind-bogglingly weird as far as Imani was concerned. But everyone aboard the Mother Ship seemed to take it as a matter of course. Apparently strange things happened all the time when you associated with the Kindred.

Imani just hoped none of them happened to *her*.

# TWO

"Now, I understand you've been studying both Yonnite Law and the Nightwalker Kindred to prepare for this case." Commander Sylvan steepled his fingers as he leaned across his desk. He was the head of the Kindred High Council and also the one who had hired Imani in the first place—on the recommendation of her mentor.

"Yes." Imani nodded seriously. She sat across from Sylvan, and Kat was sitting right beside her.

The full-figured redhead was tasked with getting her ready to go to a whole different planet and she had done everything she could from making Imani a whole new Yonnie wardrobe to making sure she got a shot of translation bacteria so she wouldn't have to deal with a language barrier. Imani sort of wished she could take Kat all the way to Yonnie Six with her, for moral support, but Kat had her hands full with two husbands and three sons to take care of so Imani was on her own.

"I've got the law procedures down pretty well," Imani told Sylvan. "But the literature I could find on the Nightwalker Kindred was limited."

"Let me see if I can fill in the gaps." Sylvan sat back and his deep voice took on a lecturing tone. "Back when the Kindred first discovered Ulle Prime—the Nightwalker home world, a great catastrophe had just swept over the planet."

"Right—a disease that killed everyone with a Y chromosome." Imani nodded. "I read about that."

"Exactly," Sylvan said. "So when they came, the Kindred found only females. And since we are a race of mostly males, it made sense to make a genetic trade with them. Many Kindred males called Nightwalker brides."

"That sounds like an ideal situation," Kat remarked.

"It *seemed* so." Sylvan frowned. "Until the first children came along. You see, the original Nightwalker males were much different from their females who were kind and sweet-tempered. But as even-tempered as the females were, they still bore the traits in their DNA that made their sons into Nightwalker males."

"So, what was wrong with that?" Kat asked, frowning. "I thought Kindred genes usually mix well with the genes of other species?"

"In this case, they mixed *too* well." Sylvan's voice was grim. "You see, the original Nightwalker males were about twenty percent smaller than the females. But they were absolutely *savage*. Once the Kindred genes were added, that savagery was compounded by size, since the children all inherited the Kindred propensity to be extremely large and muscular."

Imani frowned.

"I read something about that, but I didn't really understand. Do you mean they're all crazy or what?"

"No, not *exactly.*" Sylvan shook his head. "The Nightwalker Kindred are a little like the Wulven Kindred."

"The ones who change into a beast at the full moon?" Kat's eyes widened.

"Yes, but the Nightwalkers don't change—well, their physical appearance doesn't change *much,* anyway." Sylvan leaned forward again. "You see, the Nightwalkers aren't separate from their beasts—

they *are* the beasts. That savage, wild temperament is always there, just below the surface. It's said they can go into Rage for any reason—not just to protect a female. And once they are in Rage, it's very difficult to get out of their feral state."

"Rage?" Imani frowned.

"It's a kind of berserker fury a Kindred warrior goes into if he thinks his woman is being threatened," Kat explained. She looked at Sylvan. "But you're saying the Nightwalker Kindred are in Rage *all the time?*"

"If provoked, they can go into a feral state where they are more animal than man," Sylvan said, nodding. He looked at Imani seriously. "It's *extremely* important that you don't allow your client to become provoked into that state."

"But what if he gets provoked and she can't help it?" Kat demanded. "Won't she be in danger if she has a huge, enraged feral warrior on her hands?"

"Actually, no," Sylvan said mildly. "Because, like almost all other Kindred, the Nightwalkers won't harm a female."

"Which is why we know the charges against my client *must* be false," Imani put in.

"You mean the charges that he murdered his Mistress?" Kat asked.

Imani nodded firmly.

"Exactly. Kindred are biologically incapable of harming a female, so the charges must be faked."

"Is that what you're going to argue in court?" Kat asked.

"Along with whatever evidence I'm presented with," Imani said.

"You'll get it the first night you're there," Sylvan promised. "We have an operative there who'll get you a file you can use during the pleading."

"How will I know him?" Imani asked.

"You'll know him," Sylvan said. "He'll approach you and say, 'Excuse me, Mistress—I think you dropped something.' Take the file he offers you and use it well. We believe that this Nightwalker

Kindred—savage and bestial though he may be—is completely innocent."

"And a Yonnite jail is no place for an innocent man," Kat remarked.

"That's certainly true." Sylvan sounded grim. "With the help of Councilor Lizabeth and her mate, Lone, we were recently able to see that their worst prison, BleakHall, was shut down. But as I understand it, none of their correctional facilities is exactly progressive."

"That's putting it mildly. When I think of some of the awful stories we heard about BleakHall…" Kat broke off with a shiver.

"True." Sylvan nodded. "We don't want to leave him in that place any longer than is absolutely necessary. Your job, Councilor Williams, is to gain his freedom and bring him back to his home world where he can hopefully live the rest of his days in peace."

"I'll do it," Imani promised. "I'll get him out, Commander Sylvan."

"Good." He nodded. "Then since Kat informs me that you're all packed, you can leave tonight. You'll be staying at The Luxx—the finest hotel in Opulex, which is the capital city of Yonnie Six."

"Oh, you didn't have to put me up in such an expensive place!" Imani protested.

"Oh, yes we did," Kat said dryly. "Believe me, status matters to the Yonnites. You have to appear as rich and powerful as they are to get anywhere with them."

"Kat is absolutely right," Sylvan remarked mildly. "Don't worry about the bill. The High Council can afford it and we want to be certain you have the best chance possible to free the Nightwalker."

"Does this guy have a name?" Kat asked, frowning. "We keep talking about him and referring to the kind of Kindred he is but what is he called?"

Imani had wondered the same thing—Kat had taken the question right out of her mouth.

Sylvan frowned.

"You know, I'm not certain of his name. We got this information from our informant in the first place—a secret transmission out of Yonnie Six that a Nightwalker was about to be executed and he had proof that the accused was innocent of the crime he was charged of." He shrugged, his broad shoulders rolling. "That's all we have for now. I'm sorry, Councilor Williams."

"That's all right," Imani said, lifting her chin. "I'm sure I'll find out the details from the court documents once I get there. You said they'll be waiting in my hotel?"

"Yes, just ask at the front desk of the Luxx and they'll give you a packet," Sylvan promised. "We're sending you early so you have time to prepare. The prisoner's hearing is set a week from now."

"Perfect." Imani nodded. "Then I'm ready to go."

"Excellent." Sylvan rose and offered her his hand. "Good luck on your quest for justice then, Councilor."

"Thank you." Imani smiled and shook hands with the big Kindred, who was her new boss—or would be if this case worked out and the High Council decided to hire her permanently. Soon she would be on her way.

She thought again about her big brother. How Rashaad had been stabbed by another inmate over a can of Coke. His promising young life had been snuffed out so early—so senselessly.

*I won't let that happen to my client,* she promised herself firmly. *It doesn't matter that I have to dress in crazy clothes and travel halfway across the galaxy. I'll see that he goes free no matter what I have to do in order to make it happen!*

She had no idea how far and to what extremes that particular vow would take her. If she had, she might not have made it. But by the time she stepped into the ship which was to take her to Yonnie Six, it was too late…

## GIVE A HOT KINDRED WARRIOR TO A FRIEND!

Do you love the Kindred? Do you want to talk about wishing you could go live on the Mother Ship without your friends thinking you're crazy? Well, now it's super easy to get them into the Kindred universe.

Just share this link, **https://bookhip.com/HLNPTP**, with them to download *Claimed*, the first book in my Brides of the Kindred series for FREE.

No strings attached—I don't even want to collect their email for my newsletter. I just want you to be able to share the Kindred world with your besties and have fun doing it.

Hugs and Happy Reading!

Evangeline

# SIGN UP FOR MY NEWSLETTER!

Sign up for my newsletter and you'll be the first to know when a new book comes out or I have some cool stuff to give away.

**www.evangelineanderson.com/newsletter**

Don't worry—I won't share your email with anyone else, I'll never spam you (way too busy writing books) and you can unsubscribe at any time.

As a thank-you gift you'll get a free copy of BONDING WITH THE BEAST delivered to your inbox right away. In the next days I'll also send you free copies of CLAIMED, book 1 in the Brides of Kindred series, and ABDUCTED, the first book in my Alien Mate Index series.

# DO YOU LOVE AUDIOBOOKS?

**You've read the book, now listen to the audiobook.**

My Kindred series is coming to audio one book at a time.
Sign up for my audiobook newsletter below.

**www.evangelineanderson.com/audio-newsletter**

Besides notifications about new audio releases you may also get an email if I'm running a contest with an audio-book prize. Otherwise I will leave you alone. : ).

# BECOME A VIP!

The Aliens & Alphas Bookstore offers you exclusive (pre-)releases, special box sets, and reissues of old favorites that you can't find anywhere else.

**www.shop.evangelineanderson.com**

Sign up for the Aliens & Alphas VIP list to never miss a release, get exclusive sneak peeks, discounts and so much more.

**www.shop.evangelineanderson.com/vip-list**

# ALSO BY EVANGELINE ANDERSON

Below you'll find a list of available and upcoming titles. But depending on when you read this list, new books will have come out by then that are not listed here. Make sure to check my website, www.evangelineanderson.com, for the latest releases and better yet, sign up for my newsletter (www.evangelineanderson.com/newsletter) to never miss a new book again.

———

**Brides of the Kindred series**

**(Sci-Fi / Action-Adventure Romance)**

CLAIMED*

HUNTED*

SOUGHT*

FOUND*

REVEALED*

PURSUED*

EXILED*

SHADOWED*

CHAINED*

DIVIDED*

DEVOURED*

ENHANCED*

CURSED*

ENSLAVED*

TARGETED*

FORGOTTEN*

SWITCHED*

UNCHARTED

UNBOUND

SURRENDERED

VANISHED

IMPRISONED

TWISTED

DECEIVED

BRIDES OF THE KINDRED VOLUME ONE

Contains *Claimed, Hunted, Sought* and *Found*

BRIDES OF THE KINDRED VOLUME TWO

Contains *Revealed, Pursued* and *Exiled*

BRIDES OF THE KINDRED VOLUME THREE

Contains *Shadowed, Chained* and *Divided*

BRIDES OF THE KINDRED VOLUME FOUR

Contains *Devoured, Enhanced* and *Cursed*

BRIDES OF THE KINDRED VOLUME FIVE

Contains *Enslaved, Targeted* and *Forgotten*

BRIDES OF THE KINDRED VOLUME SIX

Contains *Switched, Uncharted* and *Unbound*

BRIDES OF THE KINDRED VOLUME SEVEN

Contains *Surrendered, Vanished,* and *Imprisoned*

*Also Available in Audio*

*All Kindred novels are now available in PRINT.*

*Also, all Kindred novels are on their way to Audio, join my Audiobook*

*Newsletter (www.evangelineanderson.com/audio-newsletter) to be notified when they come out.*

---

**Kindred Tales**

*The Kindred Tales are side stories in the Brides of the Kindred series which stand alone outside the main story arc.*

**These can be read as STAND ALONE novels.**

MASTERING THE MISTRESS*

BONDING WITH THE BEAST*

SEEING WITH THE HEART*

FREEING THE PRISONER*

HEALING THE BROKEN* *(a Kindred Christmas novel)*

TAMING THE GIANT*

BRIDGING THE DISTANCE*

LOVING A STRANGER*

FINDING THE JEWEL*

BONDED BY ACCIDENT*

RELEASING THE DRAGON*

SHARING A MATE*

INSTRUCTING THE NOVICE*

AWAKENED BY THE GIANT*

HITTING THE TARGET*

HANDLING THE HYBRID*

TRAPPED IN TIME*

TIME TO HEAL*

PAIRING WITH THE PROTECTOR*

FALLING FOR KINDRED CLAUS

GUARDING THE GODDESS

STEALING HER HEART

TAMING TWO WARRIORS

THE KINDRED WARRIOR'S CAPTIVE BRIDE

DARK AND LIGHT

PROTECTING HIS MISTRESS

UNLEASHED BY THE DEFENDER

KINDRED TALES VOLUME 1

Contains *Mastering the Mistress, Bonding with the Beast* and *Seeing with the Heart*

KINDRED TALES VOLUME 2

Contains *Freeing the Prisoner, Healing the Broken* and *Taming the Giant*

KINDRED TALES VOLUME 3

Contains *Bridging the Distance, Loving a Stranger* and *Finding the Jewel*

KINDRED TALES VOLUME 4

Contains *Bonded by Accident, Releasing the Dragon,* and *Sharing a Mate*

KINDRED TALES VOLUME 5

Contains *Instructing the Novice, Awakened by the Giant,* and *Hitting the Target*

KINDRED TALES VOLUME 6

Contains *Handling the Hybrid, Trapped in Time,* and *Time to Heal*

*Also Available in Audio*

---

**Kindle Birthright series**

**(Sci-Fi / Action-Adventure Romance)**

The Children of the Kindred series

UNBONDABLE

---

**Born to Darkness series**

**(Paranormal / Action-Adventure Romance)**

CRIMSON DEBT*

SCARLET HEAT*

RUBY SHADOWS*

CARDINAL SINS (coming soon)

DESSERT (short novella following *Scarlet Heat*)

(Also Available in Audio)

BORN TO DARKNESS BOX SET

Contains *Crimson Debt*, *Scarlet Heat*, and *Ruby Shadows* all in one volume

*Also Available in Audio*

---

**Alien Mate Index series**

**(Sci-Fi / Action-Adventure Romance)**

ABDUCTED*

PROTECTED*

DESCENDED*

SEVERED*

ALIEN MATE INDEX VOLUME ONE

Contains *Abducted, Protected, Descended* and *Severed* all in one volume

*Also Available in Audio*

*All Alien Mate novels are now available in PRINT.*

---

**The Cougarville series**

**(Paranormal / Action-Adventure Romance)**

**(Older Woman / Younger Man**

BUCK NAKED*

COUGAR BAIT*

STONE COLD FOX*

BIG BAD WOLF (Coming Soon)

*Also Available in Audio*

---

**The CyBRG Files with Mina Carter**

**(Sci-Fi / Action-Adventure Romance)**

UNIT 77: BROKEN*

UNIT 78: RESCUED*

*Also Available in Audio*

---

**The Institute series**

**(Daddy-Dom / Age Play Romance)**

THE INSTITUTE: DADDY ISSUES*

THE INSTITUTE: MISHKA'S SPANKING

*Also Available in Audio*

---

The Swann Sister Chronicles

(Contemporary Fairy / Funny / Fantasy Romance)

WISHFUL THINKING*

BE CAREFUL WHAT YOU WISH FOR*

*Also Available in Audio

---

Nocturne Academy

(Young Adult Paranormal/Action-Adventure/Romance)

LOCK AND KEY*

FANG AND CLAW

STONE AND SECRET (Coming Soon)

---

Detectives Valenti and O'Brian

(1980s M/M Romance)

THE ASSIGNMENT

I'LL BE HOT FOR CHRISTMAS

FIREWORKS

THE ASSIGNMENT: HEART AND SOUL

---

Compendiums and Box Sets

ALIEN MATE INDEX VOLUME ONE

Contains *Abducted, Protected, Descended* and *Severed* all in one volume

BORN TO DARKNESS BOX SET

Contains *Crimson Debt, Scarlet Heat,* and *Ruby Shadows* all in one volume

BRIDES OF THE KINDRED VOLUME ONE

Contains *Claimed, Hunted, Sought* and *Found*

BRIDES OF THE KINDRED VOLUME TWO

Contains *Revealed, Pursued* and *Exiled*

BRIDES OF THE KINDRED VOLUME THREE

Contains *Shadowed, Chained* and *Divided*

BRIDES OF THE KINDRED VOLUME FOUR

Contains *Devoured, Enhanced* and *Cursed*

BRIDES OF THE KINDRED VOLUME FIVE

Contains *Enslaved, Targeted* and *Forgotten*

BRIDES OF THE KINDRED VOLUME SIX

Contains *Switched, Uncharted* and *Unbound*

HAVE YOURSELF A SEXY LITTLE CHRISTMAS

Contains *Kidnapped for Christmas, Cougar Christmas* and *Season's Spankings*

KINDRED TALES VOLUME 1

Contains *Mastering the Mistress, Bonding with the Beast* and *Seeing with the Heart*

KINDRED TALES VOLUME 2

Contains *Freeing the Prisoner, Healing the Broken* and *Taming the Giant*

KINDRED TALES VOLUME 3

Contains *Bridging the Distance, Loving a Stranger* and *Finding the Jewel*

KINDRED TALES VOLUME 4

Contains *Bonded by Accident, Releasing the Dragon,* and *Sharing a Mate*

KINDRED TALES VOLUME 5

Contains *Instructing the Novice, Awakened by the Giant,* and *Hitting the Target*

KINDRED TALES VOLUME 6

Contains *Handling the Hybrid, Trapped in Time,* and *Time to Heal*

NAUGHTY TALES: THE COLLECTION— Volume One

Contains *Putting on a Show, Willing Submission, The Institute: Daddy Issues, The Institute: Mishka's Spanking, Confessions of a Lingerie Model, Sin Eater, Speeding Ticket, Stress Relief* and *When Mr. Black Comes Home.*

ONE HOT HALLOWEEN

Contains *Red and the Wolf, Gypsy Moon* and *Taming the Beast*

ONE HOT HALLOWEEN Vol.2

Contains *The Covenant, Secret Thirst,* and *Kristen's Addiction* + BONUS: *Madeline's Mates*

---

**Stand Alone Titles**

**(Sci-Fi OR Paranormal Action-Adventure Romance)**

ANYONE U WANT

BEST KEPT SECRETS (Step-Brother romance)

BLIND DATE WITH A VAMPIRE

BLOOD KISS

CEREMONY OF THREE

DEAL WITH THE DEVIL*

DEFILED

EYES LIKE A WOLF (Foster Brother romance)

FOREVER BROKEN (M/M romance)

GYPSY MOON

HUNGER MOON RISING

MADELINE'S MATES

MARKED

OUTCAST

PLANET X*

PLEASURE PLANET

PLEDGE SLAVE (M/M romance)

PURITY*

RED AND THE WOLF

SECRET THIRST

SEX WITH STRANGERS

SHADOW DREAMS

SLAVE BOY (M/M romance)

STRESS RELIEF

SWEET DREAMS

TAMING THE BEAST

TANDEM UNIT

THE BARGAIN

THE COVENANT

THE LAST BITE (M/M romance)

THE LAST MAN ON EARTH

THE LOST BOOKS (M/M romance)

THE PLEASURE PALACE

THE SACRIFICE*

*Also Available in Audio

---

**Stand Alone Titles**

**(Contemporay Romance)**

A SPANKING FOR VALENTINE (BDSM)

BOUND AND DETERMINED, anthology with Lena Matthews, includes *The Punishment of Nicollett*

COUGAR CHRISTMAS (Older Woman / Younger Man)

DANGEROUS CRAVINGS (BDSM)

DIRTY GIRL

FULL EXPOSURE (with Lena Matthews)

KIDNAPPED FOR CHRISTMAS (BDSM)

MASKS, contains *The Man in the Leather Mask* and *Masks* (BDSM)

MORE THAN FRIENDS (BDSM)

PICTURE PERFECT (Step-Brother romance)

STR8TE BOYS (M/M romance)

---

**Naughty Tales**

**(Short Reads to Get You Hot and Bothered)**

CONFESSIONS OF A LINGERIE MODEL

PUTTING ON A SHOW (Step-Brother romance)

SIN EATER

SPEEDING TICKET

THE SWITCH (An erotic interlude with the characters of DANGEROUS CRAVINGS)

SEASON'S SPANKINGS

WHEN MR. BLACK COMES HOME

WILLING SUBMISSION

NAUGHTY TALES: THE COLLECTION— Volume One

Contains *Putting on a Show, Willing Submission, The Institute: Daddy Issues, The Institute: Mishka's Spanking, Confessions of a Lingerie Model, Sin Eater, Speeding Ticket, Stress Relief* and *When Mr. Black Comes Home.*

---

**YA Novels**

THE ACADEMY*

*Also Available in Audio

# ABOUT THE AUTHOR

Evangeline Anderson is the *New York Times* and *USA Today* bestselling author of the *Brides of the Kindred*, *Alien Mate Index*, *Cougarville*, and *Born to Darkness* series. She lives in Florida with a husband, a son, and the voices in her head. (Mostly characters who won't shut up.) She has been writing sci-fi and paranormal romance for years and she welcomes reader comments and suggestions at **www.evangelineanderson.com**.

Or, to be the first to find out about new books, join her newsletter: **www.evangelineanderson.com/newsletter**

For updates on Young Adult releases only sign up here instead: **www.evangelineanderson.com/young-adult-newsletter**

She's also got a mailing list for updates on audio books: **www.evangelineanderson.com/audio-newsletter**

facebook.com/evangelineandersonauthorpage

twitter.com/EvangelineA

instagram.com/evangeline_anderson_author

pinterest.com/vangiekitty

goodreads.com/evangelineanderson

bookbub.com/authors/evangeline-anderson